The Christmas Diary

Elyse Douglas

BROADBACK BOOKS USA

Love wakes men, once a lifetime each;
They lift their heavy lids, and look;
And, lo, what one sweet page can teach...

~Coventry Patmore 1823-1896

.

To our sister, Kathy, who loves all things Christmas.

The Christmas Diary

CHAPTER 1

There was a Christmas sale going on at Candlelight's Corner, a narrow, brick-faced gift shop on West 73rd Street in Manhattan. The store was festively decorated with white Christmas lights, snowy Victorian village scenes, and candles of all shapes and sizes. Thirty-one-year-old Alice Ferrell, the proprietor and lease holder, sat in her cramped backroom office, staring at the folded pages of the lease renewal, which was waiting for her signature. She desperately wanted to keep the shop, but she was nearly broke and the business was failing. How could she possibly sign it? What would she do with her life if she didn't sign it?

It was almost noon, just six days before Christmas. Suddenly, the store began to fill with customers. She stepped back into the shop and stood rigid. Worry and lack of sleep had made her edgy and tired. She glanced nervously around, eager for the hint of a sale—for any sign of pleasure or surprise in her customers' expressions, hoping for the final nod of approval or delight. But her customers seemed confused and hesitant, or just plain irritating, with their endless indecision. She could almost hear their thoughts.

"Good price, but will my mother like it?"

"That candle set is definitely not worth it, even at half price."

"What really is Feng Shui anyway?"

Alice studied a woman who tapped her cheek with a gloved hand. A tall, portly man nosed toward the gold unity candle set, removing his glasses and scrutinizing it, as if it were a laboratory specimen. His crumpled face held no conviction. She felt impatience flow into her stomach and dam up into a hot pool. "It's a half-price sale, for Pete's sake!" she screamed silently. "Just buy something!"

The smell of bayberry, cinnamon and vanilla filled the room. Coats were opened, scarves were unraveled. Alice narrowed her eyes, looking for shoplifters. The Arthur Fiedler Boston Pops Christmas CD was bouncing through *Sleigh Ride!* For some reason, people always bought more when it played. But today, even that wasn't working.

Alice felt an acid anxiety. She'd gone through all her savings and most of the money her Mom had left her when she died.

She sighed audibly, with concealed annoyance, then shut her eyes and folded her arms tightly about her while she took a couple of deep breaths. With a proud bearing, she paced and toed at the floor like a caged animal. The lunch crowd shoppers eased along the shelves, all arranged artistically with Feng Shui candle sets, taper candles, brightly colored pillar candles, friendship candles, scented jar candles, aromatherapy gift boxes, aromatherapy eye pillows, scented bath salts, massage body oil and body soap.

There were snowball candles, snowmen candles, Santa Claus and his reindeer candles, Victorian carolers candles, tree ornament candles, as well as a variety of other gifts: mother-of-pearl letter openers, women's and men's watches, earrings, Christmas cards and board games.

The arrangements were artistic and stylish, with bright red and green velvet ribbons, pine cones, candy canes and miniature Christmas trees. Alice and her assistant, Roland, had spent long hours on the store and window displays. They'd agonized over inventory, pricing, a low-priced catalog, the website and online marketing. To economize, Alice cleaned the shop, the bathroom and the windows herself. She'd attended retail seminars and webinars; had used Facebook and Twitter; had networked with friends and small business owners. Her last hope was Christmas. She prayed for robust sales that would pull her out of the red. But so far, it hadn't happened. She'd lost sleep, money, energy and faith.

Her sale totals each night were feeble. Depressingly meager.

Philip, her fiancé, would be arriving soon. She shrank a little at the thought, and glanced over at Roland, who was leaning beside the register with his usual boyish insouciance. He was in his early 30s, muscular and stylish. His silk red shirt, tight black jeans, golden hoop earring and bald shiny head gave him the look of a pirate. He'd been a modern dancer until an injury finished his career and sent him teaching dance part-time. He had worked with Alice for the two years the candle shop had been open and Alice trusted him implicitly. But today, he seemed dazed and spacey. She went to him.

"You're losing your focus, Roland," Alice said, trying to sound playful.

"Am I?" Roland said, his wet lips close to a snowman cookie covered with glittering red sprinkles. It waited, impatiently, between his two meaty fingers. He bit off the snowman's hat and chewed happily.

"And you're eating all the cookies!" Alice added.

"Hey, I brought them! Okay? I baked them, until one o'clock in the morning, okay?"

"And you gave them to the store. Okay?" she shot back.

"Well, aren't we possessive." he said, with an effeminate lilt.

Alice took another staggered breath. "I'm desperate, Roland," she said at a whisper. "Nobody's buying. They're all just looking."

"Well, I'm flattered that you think my cookies have the power to make people on the Upper West Side of Manhattan buy candles."

Alice ignored him and meandered back into the aisle. She asked several customers if she could help, but got the dismissive smile, the curt, "I'm just looking."

She glanced at her watch. Philip was probably on his way. She suspected she looked a mess, so she took the opportunity to steal off through the Employees Only door at the rear of the shop, descend the steep wrought-iron spiral staircase and move through the open brick hallway, slithering between stacked boxes of inventory, finally reaching the staff bathroom. The day had been a busy one despite the low sales. She hadn't eaten breakfast or made it to her morning yoga class. She felt low, dragging energy.

She switched on the light and studied her face. Her large brown eyes looked tired, her thick, long, auburn hair lifeless, and her diamond-shaped face tense and drawn. She looked every bit of her 31 years. How was it possible that she, Alice Ferrell, the girl everyone had always said never looked her age, now actually did look like a woman in her 30s? When did that happen? She worked out two times a week, weighed only 122 pounds and was proud of her 5'8" svelte figure, long legs and graceful neck. But there was no denying it: time, stress, and too many long work nights had caught up with her. She frowned and did the best she could with the makeup at hand.

She smoothed out her cream-colored silk blouse, stood on tiptoes to examine her oak- brown stretch pleated pants, then leaned over and brushed the lint off her suede boots.

Back upstairs, ten minutes later, she saw Roland ring up a sale, and she brightened. She arrived at the register just as the customer left.

"You look tired," Roland said.

"I am tired. I feel like I could sleep for a week."

"We sold a couple boxes of the votives," Roland said.

"The 50 in a box for ten dollars?" Alice asked.

"Yep."

Alice twisted up her mouth. "We didn't even break even."

"I also sold that giant Santa-Standing-on-the-Empire-State-Building candle. That was over fifty bucks."

She snapped a finger in irritation. "That was the last one, too! I tried to order more but they're out of stock."

"Maybe you should cut the prices some more."

"I can't! I'm losing money as it is."

Roland sniffed and tilted up his chin. "Well, then, Alice in Wonderland, we are going to need a Christmas miracle... like in the movies."

Alice sighed. "This isn't the movies, Roland. There'll be no miracles this Christmas."

"Especially if you marry Sir Philip in six days."

Alice looked at him despairingly. "Don't start that, okay?" she said, snatching a cookie: a Christmas tree with red sprinkles. She stared at it longingly, then stuck out her tongue and systemically licked off the sprinkles. "I love these things."

Roland grimaced. "That is so disgusting."

She shrank a little, glancing around. "Nobody's looking." She pushed the remaining cookie into her mouth and crunched down on it.

Roland glanced at her engagement ring. "And you're going to have a kid right away, so by next Christmas, you'll be living happily ever after."

"No, not kids! Not right away. Definitely not!"

"Oh, by the way, when you were downstairs, Philip called and said he's on his way over. He said he texted you. He also said he's leaving town earlier—via the corporate jet—in case the snowstorm hits."

Alice stared at him. "You had a lot of action in the ten minutes I was downstairs. Maybe I should go down there more often."

"Where's Sir Philip off to this time, taking *the* corporate jet?" Roland asked, with a mocking tone and an arched eyebrow.

"Denver. After his meeting, he's flying back to Pittsburgh, then driving up to the house in Holbrook. I should get there a couple hours before him."

"You did hear about the snowstorm?" Roland asked, with a flash of warning in his slate-gray eyes.

"Yes, but it's not supposed to start until later. I'll be in Holbrook before the worst of it hits."

"And if you're not and you get stuck in a major blizzard?"

"I'll find a motel. You always think the worst, Roland."

"Hey, it's my experience. I just go by my experience. Where exactly is Holbrook, Pennsylvania?"

"Western part of the state. I told you last week."

"It just seems so far away from New York. What does one possibly do there?"

"It's only four hours away, and it's a great little town."

"Why don't you fly to Pittsburgh like Philip?"

"No way. I never fly, if I can possibly avoid it. I hate the lines, the security and... well, everything else."

A customer waved for assistance. Alice scooted over to a stout woman in her mid-50s, dressed inexpensively, with wiry gray hair and eyes that radiated indecision and fear.

"I just think this aromatherapy basket is a little high... I don't think I can afford it."

Alice opened her mouth to speak but was cut off.

"... What if my daughter doesn't like aromatherapy things?"

"She can bring it back and exchange it for something comparable in price."

"Can't I get the money back?"

"Well, no, ma'am. The store's policy is exchange only."

The woman blinked in slow disappointment. "Well, I'll pass then."

Alice hated missing a sale, especially on a day like today. "Perhaps I could mark it down another five dollars..."

The woman's moon face opened into a radiant smile, reflecting back gratitude. "Aren't you nice! Yes, I'll take this, and can you gift wrap it, please?"

Alice lowered her eyes and smiled. "Of course."

Alice took the aromatherapy gift box over to a frowning Roland. She smiled much too broadly and twitched her eyebrows playfully. "Please gift wrap this, Roland."

"Yes, ma'am," he said, with cool, sinister eyes and a tight, dark smile that showed no teeth.

The woman came over and nestled up close to Alice. A little too close. "Something good is going to happen to you for your generosity," she said. "I just feel it."

"Well, I'm getting married on Christmas Day," Alice said, taking a step back. "That's certainly good."

Roland mumbled, folded and taped.

A moment later, Philip Bollinger entered, swinging a black leather brief case in one hand and gripping an overnight bag in the other. He was tall, with aristocratic angular features and raven black wavy hair. One immediately noticed his boyishly clear blue eyes and the determined jaw of a Kennedy. His black cashmere overcoat was unbuttoned, revealing a blue, 3-button Armani suit, white shirt and blue and gold tie. Philip was a magnetic extrovert who loved good conversation that leaned toward politics and finance. Often, when he smiled, there was a certain showbiz quality to it that suggested a tinge of insincerity. Not that Alice thought so, but Roland certainly did and had said so more than once.

Philip went to her and gave her a peck on the lips. He ignored Roland. "You look busy."

Alice stooped and whispered. "They're not buying."

Philip's forehead wrinkled. "So shut this place down, Alice. It's not working and it hasn't been working for months, and you can't afford the new lease."

"Let's not discuss it now."

"If not now, when? You're going to be thinking about this place 24 and 7, even when we're on our honeymoon. How do you think that makes me feel?"

Alice took his arm and led him back toward the door, away from the front counter and the customers. "Philip, I can't talk about this now. "

Philip interrupted. "... You never want to talk about it. Never. I'm getting really tired of this whole pretending thing." His eyes hardened. "Alice, it's over. Can't you admit that? You're going broke. It is over!"

She stiffened, averting his eyes. "I'm not ready to let it go. Not yet."

Philip lifted his hand in frustration and turned his irritated face from her. "Alice, look... All I know is you work all the time. Your brain never stops. Whenever we go out to dinner, a movie, a play, you're thinking, plotting, strategizing. You never stop and just, I don't know, look around and smell the smog or something. You're nearly bankrupt... and I just think you're sticking your head in the sand."

Alice shot back. "And you're busy and working all the time. You're always traveling or working until two or three in the morning."

"But when I'm with you... I'm *with* you," he said pointedly.

"That's not fair," Alice responded sharply.

Roland looked up from his red and green half-wrapped package. His eyes bulged, his lips made a silent "shh."

She whispered. "That's not fair. I've had more to do. Besides running this business, I've also been planning our wedding. Thirty people doesn't sound like many, but there are a lot of details."

"We could have hired someone, but you wouldn't listen to me."

"I wanted to do it for us. I wanted it to be personal. I thought it would be fun."

Philip pinched the bridge of his nose. "Okay, okay. Look, why don't you do us both a favor and fly to Pittsburg tonight? You can rest. Sleep."

Alice softened, aware that nerves were making her come on too strong. She touched his arm and gently squeezed it. "You know how I hate to fly. Driving relaxes me."

Philip jerked his arm away. "Dammit, Alice, you're driving me crazy!"

His violent action startled her. She took a step back.

They stood staring at each other, Alice wounded, Philip seething with frustration.

Alice's mouth trembled a little. "Okay... all right..."

Alice turned to walk away. Philip seized her arm, holding it firmly. "Alice, face reality. That's all I'm asking. You know this place is dead. Just face it. Please."

Alice licked her lips, lowering her voice. "Let's not do this... We argue all the time, Philip. We didn't use to."

"Then don't sign that lease." he countered. "Walk away so we can make a new life and finally be finished with this... this..." he lifted his hand, struggling for the word. "... this silly, stupid shop."

They stood in an awkward silence, as the room now bulged with browsing customers. Alice was conflicted, on the verge of tears.

Philip shook his head. "Just do what you need to do, okay? If you want to drive, drive. Just... leave early. Before the snowstorm."

She avoided his eyes. "They said the worst won't come until late. After 9 tonight. I'll be in Holbrook by then."

Philip forced a light tone, but it fell flat. "I'll be waiting, sipping wine and looking out on a winter wonderland." He turned his attention to the room and heaved out a breath. "... And in a week, we'll laugh about all this when we're honeymooning in St. Martin."

Alice remained still, eyes focused on the shop.

Philip's cell phone rang. He reached into his inside coat pocket, seizing it with electrifying efficiency. "Philip here."

Alice watched him immediately, almost chillingly, disconnect from her and turn away. He dropped his bags near the counter, pushed the front door open and stepped outside into the flat gray afternoon light.

The moon-faced woman came to the door, holding her festively wrapped and bagged package. "I hope you have the merriest of Christmases," she said, warmly.

Alice smiled. "Thank you. I hope your daughter loves the gift."

After the woman left, Alice passed the minutes watching Philip through the glass. He paced around the bustling crowd, arguing into the phone. He was clearly agitated, perhaps a little frightened, occasionally jabbing a finger into the air, his face flushed, from anger or cold, she couldn't tell. She'd never seen him in such a state. Not in two years.

She turned away and went back to Roland.

"Another happy customer," Roland said, dryly, slapping a red bow onto his forehead.

Alice swept the shop with her eyes, preoccupied. "Yes..."

"That's more than I can say for Philip," he continued, gazing outside, through the Christmas window display, watching Philip fume into the phone.

It was nearly two years to the day, December 21st, that Alice and Philip had met. They were both stranded at LaGuardia Airport because of a snowstorm. They were on their way home for the holidays, he to Pittsburgh and she to Cincinnati. She was in an airport bookstore, leafing through magazines, when she turned sharply and tripped over Philip's carry-on that he had absently placed behind her while he examined a paperback. He had apologized profusely and insisted that he buy her dinner at a restaurant down the concourse. She didn't refuse. She learned he was a corporate attorney and came from a wealthy family in Pittsburgh, although she had to pry it out of him slowly. Philip was proud, but not boastful. She'd always found that attractive.

Once the storm had passed and the flights resumed, they'd agreed to meet after the holidays for dinner and a movie. Their relationship took off after that, even though he spent much of his time traveling and she worked long hours. They moved in together five months later, to a beautiful two-bedroom apartment that overlooked Central Park West, and within two months, she had met Philip's parents in Pittsburgh. That same weekend, he'd asked her to marry him.

She was surprised that she'd agreed. She hadn't really intended to, since there was a secrecy about Philip that she wasn't all that comfortable with. It was as if he held a part of himself in reserve, refusing to discuss certain issues, such as his past, or having children, or moving out of Manhattan to a house in the suburbs.

"Let's not talk about that now, Alice," he'd say. Or he would deflect the conversation altogether. He always refused to talk about his parents or his childhood.

"Old business," he'd say. "I like to live in the present."

Alice found his mother inaccessible, with a cold graciousness and a fondness for scotch and water. She had none of her husband's easy manner or her son's charisma. Alice felt sorry for her because she always seemed alone, even in a crowd of people. In contrast, his father was smooth, intelligent and practiced in the calculated arts of the professional businessman.

In the end, she realized that she and Philip had a lot in common: good books (mostly mysteries), good wine, good food and a great love for baseball: him for the Yankees and her for the Cincinnati Reds. He was also a good conversationalist, generous, curious and well-read. And he knew a lot of interesting people: legal, political and artistic. He had a fantastic job with a leading law firm, and she was sure he would run for political office in the next few years. She loved his ambition.

Before meeting Philip, Alice had had only one serious relationship, with a jock type, who was becoming a tennis star. But when she discovered that he was cheating on her, she moved out and never saw him again. She had little time for dating after college. Her career was the most important aspect of her life.

When Philip returned, he saw Alice and, instantly, his face shifted from brooding conflict to forced merriment. "Always something," he said.

"Everything all right?"

He went for his bags. "Yeah. The usual."

"That didn't look usual. You looked mad and scared."

He dropped down and gave her another peck on the lips. "Never trust a lawyer..." he stopped and smiled wryly. "Well, some you can trust, as for the others, you'd better get a good lawyer." He laughed at his own joke. "See you tonight. Safe trip. I'll call you."

After he left, Alice ate three more cookies and managed the register while Roland went for a late lunch. She checked her laptop for the updated weather report. The snowstorm was approaching rapidly. Travel warnings were issued.

The fingers of her right hand tapped the counter. Her left hand supported her chin.

She suddenly felt the swell of anxiety and an inexplicable feeling of loneliness. Through the window, she saw lazy flurries. She decided she'd better leave an hour earlier, at 4 o'clock. The last thing she wanted was to get stuck in a snowstorm.

CHAPTER 2

Alice finally left the shop at 5:10, much later than she'd intended, and drove down Broadway toward 9th Avenue. As Friday night descended, a light snow continued to fall—little specks, harassed by a quick wind, crashed into the windshield, making the night seem slightly hectic and out of focus. She was distracted by thoughts of Philip and the wedding. Philip's parents and brother would be there, as well as her father and sister and some twenty or so of their closest friends—mostly Philip's. She didn't have many close friends in the area, and some of those who could have attended the wedding preferred to spend Christmas at home with their families, which was certainly understandable.

She was happy her father, John, was coming in from Cincinnati and her sister, Jacinta, from Maine. Jacinta was coming alone, without her husband, Chris, or their three kids, because Chris' parents would be in Maine for the holidays. Jacinta planned to fly back home late on Christmas Day, after Alice's wedding. Over the past month, she had spent most of her free time (which wasn't much) helping Alice plan the wedding, and offering tips on everything from wedding dresses to food. She had always been a generous sister and Alice loved her deeply.

"I just wish Mom could be here too," Jacinta had said. Their mother, Elizabeth Ferrell, had died of cancer six years before.

Unfortunately, after she'd married Chris, and after Alice had opened the shop, they'd had little time for trips to Maine or New York. Alice missed her and was looking forward to their spending time together, no matter how harried it would be.

Traffic crawled, horns blared and cars bounced forward, seeking any opportunity to break away from the pack, as if that were even remotely possible in Manhattan at that hour. Alice could already feel her thin patience slipping away into irritation.

Snow covered the roofs of parked cars and wrought iron fire escapes, but melted on the streets and sidewalks. The promise of snow had brought even more tourists into the city from New Jersey, Long Island and Northern New York, bloating the sidewalks, filling the restaurants and department stores and lending a party-like atmosphere. Alice wished she felt more of the Christmas spirit, but, at this point, she was grateful to be getting away from it all, even if the thought of the thousands of little details and tasks that lay before her seemed exhausting and overwhelming.

By the time she reached the New Jersey Turnpike, the snow had thickened, blowing across her headlights like a mass of insects, blanketing the road and distant landscape. It never ceased to amaze her that, even in the most inclement weather, be it snow, sleet or heavy rain, many drivers simply ignored the potential hazardous conditions and shot by her as if they were fleeing some catastrophic event, totally unaware that their irresponsible driving could cause one.

She drifted over into the right-hand lane and reduced her speed, as the windshield wipers slapped away the snow. She switched on the radio and got the latest weather report. The snow had definitely moved in faster than the weather models first projected. New York City was to get five to seven inches, the bulk of it falling in the early morning hours. Pennsylvania could easily get 12 to 14 inches, and, depending on the track of the storm, they could receive more. In Western Pennsylvania, an inch had already accumulated.

Swallowing away apprehension, Alice found a light jazz station where a lively sax belched out *Santa Claus is Coming to Town*. She settled back in her seat and tried to breathe easily. This was going to be anything but a relaxing drive, she thought. Still, she was confident that she'd be able to make it to Holbrook before the heaviest snow. She was driving an all-wheel drive silver-gray Audi, Philip's suggestion to buy, and she had good tires. She was a careful driver. If worse came to worst, she could always stop at a motel for the night.

Philip would probably call in the next hour, so she made sure her cell phone was lying next to her on the seat. When she glanced at it, she felt an unexpected sorrow. She stared at the phone for an uneasy moment, puzzling over the feeling, then quickly swung her eyes back to the road, watching cars pass—watching the glint of their red taillights slowly fade into the darkness.

About 20 minutes later, the leather-trimmed seat felt uncomfortable, and she readjusted it several times before giving up, finally massaging the back of her neck with her left hand, while humming absently to the music on the radio. What was the tune? Oh yes, *Let it Snow, Let it Snow, Let it Snow.*

A dark green sedan raced past, spewing wet snow from its tires, like an obstinate child, determined to test the limits of an angry parent. Alice struggled to conquer her nerves. She switched off the radio and listened to the rhythm of the wipers, aware that her pulse had quickened and beads of sweat had popped out on her forehead.

She was still not ready to admit that driving had been a bad idea, despite the feeling that everything suddenly seemed to be closing in on her—the weather, the wedding, her failing candle shop. Especially that. She had pushed the anger and irritation away for weeks, nearly working around the clock on four hours' sleep a night, trying to make the thing stay afloat: changing displays, repackaging, lowering prices, advertising on local cable, handing out flyers. Nothing had worked. But, during that time, she hadn't allowed herself to think about failure. She had just worked. She believed that if she worked hard enough—believed hard enough, focused every bit of energy on the task—everything would work out.

Now, alone, driving in a blowing snowstorm, anger rose, unchecked. She was angry at herself for taking the risk, when so many people had told her how chancy it was. She was angry at the economy, at fate, at everything. She also felt foolish—foolish because she had been so positive she could make it work. The numbers had checked out, the advertising was targeted, the location was fantastic: 73rd Street and Columbus! She had done everything by the book. She had even prayed—prayed her heart out—begged!

She'd have to face it all at the wedding, because Philip, of course, knew everything about the business, so she wouldn't be able to lie to family or friends or pretend things were improving. God, how she dreaded that. Lines of dialogue quickly ran through her head—little phrases she could say to deflect the sympathetic expressions, sorrowful eyes and pitiful stares she would undoubtedly have to endure.

"I'm not finished yet!" she could say, enthusiastically. But that sounded forced. "Well, if it does fail, with every ending comes a new beginning," she would say. "Got to stay optimistic!" She immediately shook her head and made an ugly face. "These kinds of things happen to a lot of people and it's not the end of the world," she might say. Alice felt some of the energy drain from her body. She was bitterly disappointed and sick at heart.

"Well, obviously it's time to move on to other things," she could say. "No big deal. I took a risk. There's nothing wrong with taking a risk."

She hated the sound of that, too! It sounded like failure and she was raised by parents who had taught her that if you're smart, hard-working and well-prepared, you should never fail. She had fulfilled all of those requirements, but...

The shop had done fairly well in the beginning, until the economy sank and so many people lost their jobs. Then it tanked. The worst part was that she'd invested all the money her mother had left her, first to set up the shop and then to keep herself afloat for over a year. She'd lost most of the small business loan as well. Her father would grill her about it at the wedding, because he'd been against her leaving a solid, well-paying accounting job to open a shop "selling those smelly candles and whatnots." But she wanted something of her own. She wanted to be her own boss! Well, she'd pay a big price for it. Literally and figuratively. Emotionally and physically, she was exhausted. She hadn't had a good night's sleep in over three months.

There was a small part of her that still believed she could make the shop work, if she just had more money. She had some investments, but she'd secretly used up most of them on the shop without telling Philip. Philip had offered money, but she'd declined. If she failed, if the numbers fell deeper into the red and she lost the shop, she was certain she'd lose Philip's respect and her own self-esteem. It would strain the marriage just as it was getting started and, anyway, she'd seen Philip's evasive eyes when he'd offered her money. She'd heard the hesitancy in his voice. He was secretly hoping she'd turn him down. And who could blame him?

Suddenly, Alice felt a punch of wind shake the car. Her back tires slid away. The car drifted right toward the shoulder. She yanked her foot off the accelerator; nudged the steering wheel, gently, until the tires regained traction. She released the trapped air in her lungs, just as a red SUV shot past, undaunted, fishtailing wildly. She wanted to roll down her window and scream at it, but it moved away, clumsily, like a thrill-ride at an amusement park.

She rolled her window down anyway, and out went her head. "You idiot!" she shouted. "Slow down!"

About forty minutes later, the storm turned ferocious. It raged and swirled as if some giant had picked up the snow globe world and was frantically shaking it. The roads had turned vicious. When her cell phone rang, Alice jumped, as if she'd been touched by a live wire. She snatched for the phone.

"Hello... Who is it!"

"Alice, it's Philip. You okay? You sound funny."

"Yeah, fine," she said, agitated. "Where are you?"

His deep voice, usually calm, sounded irritated and strained. "I'm still in Denver. My flight's been canceled. I'm not going to be able to get into Pittsburgh tonight. They've shut down the airports for hundreds of miles around. Where are you?"

"Somewhere on I-78. I don't know if I'm going to make it either. It's really getting wild out there. The storm's moved in much faster than they said it would. There must be at least three or four inches on the ground already."

"You'd better pull off and find some place to stay for the night," Philip said. "It's only going to get worse the further west you go, and the longer you wait, the more the motels are going to fill up."

Alice wished he hadn't said that, even though she knew he was right. The muscles in her shoulders knotted up. Her eyes burned. "Yeah... I've already started looking. The visibility is so bad I can barely see the signs in front of me, and most of them are already caked with snow. What a way to start the wedding," Alice added.

Philip forced a laugh. "Maybe it's testing our conviction."

"That's not funny."

"Lighten up, Alice, it's just a snow storm. At least it'll be a white Christmas."

"But we have so much to do."

"We've got six days before the wedding. That's plenty of time."

"That's not plenty of time!"

"Alice... you sound tired and stressed. Find a motel and get some sleep. Call or text me when you get there. How did you leave the shop?"

"Roland is going to stay through Christmas. Until I can make some decisions."

"Okay, well, what else can I say?" She heard the disappointment in his voice.

"Roland needs the money and... well, I can trust him to take care of things until after we get back from our honeymoon. I still have two weeks to sign the lease renewal. Another couple of weeks isn't going to matter that much at this point."

Silence.

"Are you there?" Alice asked.

"Yes, yes," Philip said, forcing an optimistic tone. "Hey, this time next week we'll be on a gorgeous beach. We'll have a good laugh about all of this."

Alice relaxed her shoulders. "Yeah... I'm sure we will."

"Find a motel, Alice, and sleep."

For ten minutes, Alice searched for a road sign or motel. She couldn't see anything and she was beginning to despair. Traffic slowed to a crawl.

At first, it was only a suggestion of trouble: a cluster of distant blinking taillights; little or no on-coming traffic. Then, as she approached the exit, she saw it: a chaotic tangle of cars ahead and the urgent rush of hooded people waving at her to stop, while others scrambled to help. A red flare blazed in the center of the road; the distant scream of sirens cut into the eerie howl of the storm.

Fear surged. She tapped her brakes and slowed to a crawl. As she approached the pile-up, she saw the devastation: an ugly mass of cars knotted and melted together. Some were twisted sideways, car parts strewn along the road, others were beaten and punched, windows shattered; a brown SUV had flipped over entirely and was lying off the shoulder of the road on its top. Men were frantically trying to open the jammed doors.

A heavy man wearing a dark blue coat and red ski cap waved at her to stop, then hurried over with the look of desperation on his face. She rolled down her window and he shouted at her, as fat snowflakes blew in.

"You have to turn off. You can't get through here."

"Is anyone hurt?" Alice asked.

"Yes, Yes. It's terrible. Get off the road!" He pointed to his left. "Over there. There's a road. Take it."

"Is there any place to stay around here?"

"I don't know! Get off the road, Now! Clear the road for the ambulances!"

Alice rolled up her window and carefully angled toward the exit, aware that her hands were sweaty and shaky, her legs twitching. Through her rearview mirror, she watched ambulances arrive at the scene and saw the wide sweep of their red domes stabbing into the night. She was profoundly sad, deeply sorry for the people injured in the accident.

The road before her was narrow and dark. There were no streetlights, no signs and no cars in front or in back of her. It eventually led to a lonely two-lane highway, where snow, driven by a stiff wind, was gathering in tall drifts, piling up against tall pines and white birch trees. In the distance, her headlights revealed the silhouette of a solitary leaning barn that would be lucky to survive the night. Everywhere she looked were ominous smudges of moving shadows.

Not knowing which direction to go and feeling trapped by nature, Alice took a chance and turned left. Within minutes, she was completely isolated. She turned on the radio to comfort and cheer her, but no matter which station she selected, she got white noise. She turned it off, wiped her damp forehead and reached for her cell phone. This was an emergency and in an emergency she could call the local police and ask for help. They could at least tell her where the nearest motel was.

She couldn't get a signal. She kept trying, but the phone wouldn't connect. "Think of your options, Alice," she said aloud. She had an emergency kit in the trunk—some candles, a bottle of water and some matches. She also had a flashlight in the glove compartment. "If worse comes to worst, you can stay in the car—wait until morning, when you can see," she said aloud, trying to comfort herself with the sound of her own voice.

But what if the storm didn't subside? And from the looks of it, it was just getting started. She glanced at her gas gauge: over half a tank. That was good. No problem. That would be enough. Surely she would eventually find a house or someplace where she could stop and spend the night. But the further she drove, the more desolate the landscape became; the more she felt she was being swallowed up by darkness.

Fifteen minutes later, her heart was thumping in her ears. She was edgy and tired. She was completely alone. She had not passed a single car and none had approached her from the other direction. How could that be? How was it possible not to pass a house, not to see another car, a truck, something?

She reached for the phone and tried again. Nothing. No signal. She cursed and tossed the phone. It bounced off the seat to the floor. The further she traveled, the deeper the snow and the more difficult it became for the tires to find traction. Her hands gripped the steering wheel so tightly that they hurt.

When the man darted out in front of her, she slammed on her brakes. The wheels locked and the car slid right, out of control. She screamed. The car spun in a crazy circle, finally coming to rest on the opposite side of the road, facing the opposite direction.

When it stopped, Alice was still gripping the steering wheel, puffing air, stunned and confused. She suddenly remembered the man and quickly recovered, fumbling to release the seat belt, shoving the door open and stepping out, coatless. She'd changed into comfortable travel clothes before leaving the shop, but as snow swirled and the wind gusted, she was instantly aware that the red woolen sweater and blue jeans were not going to keep her warm. She shielded her eyes from the attacking flakes, as her brown loafers sunk into deep snow and her face registered the shock of frigid impact. Where was the man?! For warmth, she wrapped her arms tightly around her body.

Then she saw him, a large man in his 70s, hatless, with a cinderblock head, broad chest, angry-looking black spectacles and a ferocious, hawk-like gaze. He walked toward the glare of the headlights. He had a grandfatherly menace about him, and a stiff awkward gait. His dark overcoat flapped in the cruel wind; his thin gray hair was whipped up and wild. He stopped about 10 feet away, shoved his hands deep into his pockets and hunched his shoulders forward. Alice stepped back, noticing his iceberg eyes and pallid skin. A little scar above his right eyebrow added a sinister quality.

Alice finally found a small voice. "Are you all right?"

"Yeah... no thanks to you," he said loudly, in a scratchy voice. "You almost hit me! You were driving too damned fast!"

Alice shivered in the wind. "I was barely going thirty miles an hour. You ran out right in front of me."

"You're supposed to reduce your speed in bad weather."

"I did. I did reduce my speed. I always reduce my speed in bad weather," she said, defensively.

He pointed to her car. "Then why is your car out in the middle of the road pointing in the wrong direction?"

"Because you ran out in front of me!"

"A man can't feel safe taking a leisurely walk, without some out-of-towner trying to run him down. I ought to call the cops on you!"

Sudden anger gave her new strength. "Good! You do that. Call the cops. I am completely lost and haven't seen a house or a car in miles."

The old man shook his head and barked out a laugh. "Unbelievable. You don't even know where the hell you are."

"Look, I'm not going to stand out here arguing with you in the middle of a blizzard. I'm lost, I'm freezing and I'm scared. I need to find somewhere to stay for the night."

"Why didn't you say so in the first place, instead of babbling on like some silly goose?"

"Because you didn't give me the chance."

He scratched his head. "I know where you can stay," he said, and then started toward her car. Alice backed away and watched as he tramped to the passenger side, yanked the door open and slid in, slamming it behind him. Alice stared in disbelief. She turned in a circle, her toes feeling like little popsicles. She didn't have a good feeling about this. Who would be out walking in the middle of a blizzard?

She was chilled to the bone. Her teeth began to chatter. She couldn't very well ask him to get out in this weather, could she? She sighed, resigned but shaky.

She eased in behind the wheel, not closing the door behind her. The man narrowed his eyes at her.

"You going to drive with the door open?"

Still reluctant, Alice closed it, avoiding the man's eyes. The engine purred. The heat felt good on her wet feet and cold face.

Alice tried for an easy, non-fearful tone. "So... you're from around here?"

"Not really."

Alice slowly put the car in gear. "You said you knew a place where I could spend the night?"

"Yep," he said, not offering more.

"Is it close by?" Alice asked.

"Yep," he said closing his thin mouth tightly.

Alice placed her hands on the steering wheel. "Which way?"

"The way you were going before you tried to hit me."

Alice looked away and rolled her eyes. Applying the gas, she made a slow, careful U-turn and urged the car back into the right lane. She started off into the uncertain night, stealing occasional glances toward her passenger. He gave her the impression that he had no particular destination in mind and was in no hurry to get anywhere.

CHAPTER 3

Alice felt the saliva thickening in her throat; felt a
mounting panic, almost certain now that she had
put herself in a very dangerous situation. Her clothes
were still damp and sticky and that added to her distress.
She examined her worried face in the rearview mirror,
and then turned her attention to the windows, searching
with hopeful eyes for any signs of life. She'd already decided that at the first house, she'd burst from the car and
run for help. But there was no house. They had passed
nothing—for miles! She'd seen no one! The wind
moaned like a wounded animal; tree branches shook and
reached in frantic gestures. Alice had never felt so scared,
lost and alone. It was almost as if she and this crazy old
man were the only two people alive in this raging, chaotic
storm. There had to be a town, a person, an animal
somewhere.

The man beside her remained perfectly still—his
hands folded tightly and resting in his lap. There was a
haggard sorrow about him that was disconcerting. If he
weren't so frightening, Alice would feel pity for him. She
whispered a silent prayer, asking for help.

To deflect the tension, she decided to talk.

"How much further?" she asked, softly.

"We're close now," he said, with an edge.

"Close to what? A town?"

"Hattie's Bed and Breakfast."

"Do you think she'll have room?"

"Of course she'll have a room! Why would I take you to a place that didn't have a room? I may be old but I'm not stupid!"

Alice ignored his toxic tone. "What's the name of the town?"

"Eden Grove."

"What do you do there?"

"I don't do anything. Why the hell should I do anything?"

"Okay, okay. I was just asking," Alice said, shaking her head. "Forget it."

There was an icy silence.

"I'm a doctor," the man said.

Alice looked at him doubtfully. "Really...?"

He faced her, eyes flashing anger. "You don't believe me?" he asked, raising his voice in a challenge. "Do you think I'm a liar?"

"Sure I believe you. Why shouldn't I?" Of course she didn't believe him. "What were you doing walking way out here in the middle of a snowstorm?"

He looked away. "A sort of house call. Or a car call?" he said, and then he snickered mirthlessly at his own personal joke.

"What house? I haven't seen a house or car in miles."

He ignored her. "Hattie will probably put you in the Rose Room." He suddenly turned to her. His expression was earnest, dark eyes focused. "Listen to me. Listen carefully. You'll find a bookshelf in the corner of the room with some old paperbacks and maybe a hardback or two stuffed in the shelves. Guests often bring their books in and trade them. Browse the shelves. Take a real good look, even at things behind the books... in the very back of the shelves." He narrowed his eyes. "Especially look for things behind the books."

She glanced at him. His eye sockets revealed weary black holes. His face was a road map of misery. This man gave her the creeps.

Suddenly, he pointed to the right. "Over there. That's Hattie's."

When Alice saw the dim lights of a house, she wanted to scream out with joy. She craned her neck, searching. Christmas lights were strewn from the eaves and in the neighboring pines. In the haze of falling snow, it appeared warm and inviting. Her mood instantly brightened.

"The driveway is about a quarter mile up the road," the man said. "Slow down. Slow down!"

"I'm only going 25 miles an hour."

"That's too fast."

Alice blew out an irritated sigh and slowed down.

"You won't be able to see much of it tonight, but it's an old stone farmhouse. Twelve acres of gorgeous land. It was built in the 1870s, by a guy named Wheeler."

Alice eventually found the driveway and eagerly turned right, guiding the car along the narrow driveway past towering trees, heavy with snow. Finally, she arrived at the front of the house. She stopped the car, feeling an exhausted sense of relief.

The man looked at her with a sullen remoteness. "You go and register. I'll wait."

Alice hesitated. "Are you going to stay here tonight?"

He dismissed her with a flick of his hand. "Don't worry about me. I'll be all right."

"Where are you going to stay?"

He gave her a roguish grin. "Don't worry about me, Alice. You're the one you should be worrying about."

Cold goose bumps crawled up her spine, neck and arms. She spoke in a low, hesitant voice. "How do you know my name?"

"Just a guess," he said offhandedly. "Just a damn good guess."

She reached for the door handle, jittery. Her eyes widened on him. "Who are you?"

"I told you. A doctor. Now go on. Register before somebody else comes along while you're jabbering and takes the room from you!"

Suddenly, Alice just had to get away from him. She shut off the engine, snatched the keys and got out, slamming the door hard, as if to end the whole terrifying and distasteful episode. Carefully, but purposefully, she stepped across the freshly shoveled and salted surface, hurried up the four stairs onto the porch, and drew a shallow breath. She didn't look back.

The lobby of the B&B was gorgeous, with high ceilings, walnut paneling and deep blue carpeting. A thin woman appeared from an adjoining room. Her wire-rimmed glasses made her look professorial, as if she had just finished giving a lecture on economics. She wore a green sweatshirt that said "Home for the Holidays" printed on the front. Her hair was short and gray, her eyes friendly, her mouth thin and tight. Alice figured her to be in her late 50s.

"Are you Hattie?" Alice asked, grateful for safety and for another normal-looking person.

"Yes…"

"I'm praying you have a free room for the night."

31

Hattie saw the fatigue in her face. "Have you been traveling long?"

"Forever. From New York. Do you have a room?"

Hattie folded her hands. "Fortunately, the Johnsons just called, not more than five minutes ago. They're from Philadelphia. For the last three years they've reserved a room at this time of year, but because of the weather, they had to cancel the trip. So, yes I have a room. The Rose Room. And I'm so happy I don't have to turn you away on a night like tonight."

Alice released her tight shoulders and raked her fingers through her hair, remembering the man. She turned haltingly toward the front door. "There is someone else out in the car..."

"Oh? Will they be staying with you?" Hattie asked.

Alice twisted her hands. "Well... actually, he said he's a doctor. I presume that maybe he's the town doctor. He ran right out in front of me a few miles back. Maybe you know someone, a family member, who could come and get him."

Alice was not going to drive him home. She didn't like or trust him, and she was bone tired.

Hattie blinked rapidly. "The town doctor? You mean Dr. Ainsley?"

"He didn't actually tell me his name."

"Well, I don't know why Dr. Ainsley would be out in this kind of weather…"

"He said he was making a house call."

Hattie looked perplexed. "Why didn't he come in with you?"

Alice shrugged.

"Well, why don't we go out and get your suitcase and I'll ask Dr. Ainsley, or whomever, to come in."

Alice waited while Hattie swung into a dark green
down coat and a black cap with hanging earflaps, then
Alice followed her out of the house, down the stairs and
over to the car. Under the warm glowing lights, Alice
immediately saw that the car was empty. Hattie noticed
too and looked to Alice for answers.

Alice moved to the passenger side and opened the
door. The doctor was gone.

"He was here. That's strange."

Alice picked her cell phone off the floor and pocketed
it. Both women scanned the immediate area, searching
for any signs of life or for footprints leading away from
the car. There were none.

Hattie pushed her hands into her coat pockets.
"You'd better put a coat on. You're trembling." Hattie
walked around to the trunk. "I'll help you with your suitcase."

Alice stood stiffly, massaging her eyes. "He was here.
I'm not making it up. He could freeze to death in this
weather."

"I'll call Sarah Ainsley, his wife, as soon as we get your
bags inside."

Inside, Alice sat at an antique rollaway desk, filling out
the registration form. Hattie was in the office next to the
front entrance, dialing the Ainsleys. Alice cocked an ear
toward the open office door.

"Sarah? It's Hattie Edwards. Yes... fine... oh, my yes,
what a storm. Listen, the reason I'm calling, is Dr. Ainsley out on a house call? ... I see... yes... No, everything is
fine. No... one of my guests thought she saw him, that's
all. Well... I'm glad to hear it and please send my regards.
Yes, we're all prepared for the storm. Okay, Sarah, I'll
talk to you later."

Alice quickly completed the form and was on her feet when Hattie returned to her.

"Well, I don't know who it was you gave a ride to, but it wasn't Dr. Ainsley," Hattie said. "He's been at home all evening. He left the office early and hasn't made any house calls."

Alice remained silent for a moment. She handed Hattie her registration form. "I am concerned, Mrs. Edwards, that whoever it was, he's out there somewhere and could freeze to death."

"I'll call the sheriff and let him know," Hattie said. "What does he look like?"

"Big man, white hair. Probably early 70s."

"Well that's definitely not Dr. Ainsley. Dr. Ainsley is in his late 30s and is short and thin," Hattie said.

"I didn't believe he was a doctor, but that's what he told me. He's probably homeless. You really should call the sheriff."

"I will... and I'll give him your description. Are you hungry? Would you like something to eat?"

Alice shook her head. "No, thanks, I'm really tired. I think I'll just go to my room and get some sleep."

"That sounds like a great idea. Hopefully by tomorrow, the storm will have passed and you'll be rested."

Alice nodded. "You have a beautiful place here. It's so peaceful and wonderfully decorated."

She viewed the room, filled with red poinsettias and furnished with colonial antiques. She faced the impressive two-story chestnut winding staircase, walked over to it, and touched its smooth broad banister. The seven foot tall balsam Christmas tree, garlanded with burgundy ribbon and Victorian Christmas ornaments, twinkled with colored lights. In the reading room, the fire from a generous stone fireplace bathed the room in a quiet glow.

The place had an aura of hushed enchantment, as if years of good wishes and happy memories lingered in the air.

Hattie smiled, pleased. "I'm glad you like it. I hope you sleep well."

"I'm sure I will," Alice said. She took to the stairs with a slight hesitation. "You'll call the sheriff, won't you?"

Hattie blinked rapidly again. "I'll call him right now. Don't worry."

Upstairs, Alice opened the door to the Rose Room and switched on the light. The walls were mauve, the ceiling a creamy white. On the left, the queen-sized iron bed was topped with a homemade flower quilt and a variety of colorful thick pillows. She parked her suitcase beside it and dropped her garment bag, taking in the rest of the room. An inviting, velvet burgundy Victorian love seat sat in the corner, on the other side of the bed. Facing the bed was a fireplace with logs stacked on the hearth; on its right was a five-foot mahogany bookshelf built into the wall near the window seat. Alice allowed her eyes to linger on the paper back and hardback books, all neatly stacked. Why had that crazy man mentioned the bookshelf? What had he said? "Take a real good look, even at things behind the books… in the very back of the shelves."

She shook off the cold and drifted into the bathroom, viewing the "his" and "hers" gilt wood Victorian mirrors with gold leafing. She ran her hand along the marble countertop of the generous sink, with its scented soaps— rose of course—and felt the red fluffy towels. A real classy place. How lucky she'd been to have found it! That thought stopped her. *He* had found it. That crazy old man had guided her here.

When she spotted the deep, inviting, claw-foot tub, she realized that a hot bath would be heaven. She turned on the water and watched the steam rise, letting her face drift over it. The warmth felt wonderful. She found some bubble bath packets lying on the sink in a gold and rose porcelain soap dish and sprinkled half a package of the, what else, rose, into the full stream of water. It bubbled up in the churning water; the sight and smell cheered her.

Ten minutes later she was inside the tub, warm, contented, engulfed in bubbles, eyes closed. At one point she thought she should call Philip and let him know she was okay, but the water felt so luxurious and relaxing that it was lulling her into a peaceful trance. She wanted to make the most of it. She decided to wait until after she got in bed. She sank further into the tub and nearly fell asleep.

A half hour later, fully relaxed, she climbed out, dried herself on one of those giant luxurious red towels and slipped into a blue terrycloth robe.

She considered lighting a fire but decided against it, since she had little experience with fireplaces and didn't want to burn the place down. The digital clock on the night table near the bed said 10:12. She was sleepy, but oddly restless, so she drifted to the bookshelf and perused some titles on four separate shelves. There were mysteries—she loved mysteries—but she'd read most of them; there were several biographies; some horror novels; a few "women in jeopardy" stories; and a number of self-help books. Suddenly uneasy, she backed away and stared out the window, watching the snow fall into drifts on the window sill. She wondered if the old man was still out there, wandering around in the storm.

It was a strange moment: her eyes felt heavy and she longed for sleep, but instead of going to bed, she felt absolutely compelled to go to the bookshelf and examine each shelf again. She nosed forward, sampling the occasional book, reading a paragraph or two, then replacing it and reaching for another. Eventually, she came to the bottom shelf. She leaned over and selected a hardback, being caught by the title, *Christmas Hideaways*. She tried to remove it but the books were packed so tightly that she had to grip the spine and wriggle it a couple of times before it slithered free. As she did so, she caught a glimpse of a book wedged sideways behind it. She took a closer look. It was a slender book.

Perhaps it was the sudden excitement and curiosity of retrieving an old book that sent her to her knees. After all, if it's hidden, maybe it tells an unusual old story or holds forbidden secrets.

Alice snaked her hand into the narrow space between the remaining books, curving her hand around a hardback copy of John Grisham's *The Summons* until she felt a smooth leathery texture. She tried to grasp and pull, but it was trapped behind other stubborn books. She retracted her hand and quickly removed the books obstructing her way, raking them into a careless pile beside her. She lay on her stomach, gazed in, focused, and saw it. She felt a rush of exhilaration as she reached in and gently wrestled it free. "I've got it!" she whispered, holding it up. Success. She sat back in a cross-legged posture, staring at the book in wonder.

It was 5 x 7 inches, with a soft brown leather cover and a burgundy silk ribbon bookmark. Alice turned it over. The back was covered by a thin layer of dust and was slightly soiled with water spots and dark stains. She grabbed a tissue from the box near the bed and began wiping away the dust, sneezing twice before it was clean.

Intrigued now, Alice sat down at the foot of the bed, holding the book in her right hand, nibbling on her lower lip. It was undoubtedly a diary of some kind. She glanced around for any invisible eyes, excited at the thought that it could be filled with secrets and stories. Surely, she rationalized, Hattie must know that the diary exists; maybe she keeps it in the bookshelf to entertain her guests on cold winter nights.

She looked again at the bookcase, thinking it was possible the diary had been hidden behind the rack of books and hadn't been seen for years. She brushed the soft cool cover once more with the flat of her hand before opening it. She turned to the first page. It was lineless, slightly yellowed with age. A dedication, in black ink, had been written in a flowing, dramatic script.

To Jack, who walks the Earth so lightly; who loves so easily; who takes comfort in the simplest of things. May I learn your magic. I challenge you to fill these pages and discover who you really are. You might be astounded!

Merry Christmas!

Love, Darla

Alice turned to the next page. Jack's handwriting was small. The letters clear and carefully made. Ruler straight lines.

Alice wasn't prepared for what she read.

Darla, you gave me this diary for Christmas. I'm not a writer. I barely passed English in high school. I still have trouble spelling. I'm more comfortable working with my hands. But you said it would be good for me to write things down now and then. You said a diary reveals things about yourself, often the hidden parts, and helps you grow (you put it better than that).

Okay, I will write, but only because you gave this to me and told me that part of the Christmas gift was for me to fill up these empty white pages with words. But you, Darla, are the writer. You want to write books and that's fine with me. Whatever you do is fine with me. Just be happy. I just want to always be a part of your life. I want us to grow old together.

I'm not sure how I fell in love with you, but I remember the instant it happened. You were on your bicycle riding through the center of town. Your long blond hair was so shiny in the sun. A beautiful spring day. Golden sun. Your golden hair. I just stepped out of the barber shop, saw you and fell in love. Hey, I thought I looked pretty good with my new haircut! Just as you passed, I called out to you. Don't ask me why. I never did that to any other girl before. I hated guys that did that kind of thing. My mother would have slapped me across the face. But, hey, what could I do. I knew you were the girl for me: the new girl in town, whose family had come from Chicago. The "stuck up girl" that everybody—at least all the girls who were jealous—called you. I knew then that I was going to marry you, so it just sort of came out. And you turned around and smiled. I was stunned! Shocked! Stupid! I melted right there, like ice cream in the hot sun.

On our first date you were quiet for a long time. I thought you didn't like me, but then after the movie, over a pizza, you looked at me and smiled that same smile

39

that still makes me dizzy. I felt like I had drunk three or four beers.

When I walked you to your door, you turned to me. You kissed me, before I had a chance to say anything. "Jack...," you said. "I like your eyes. They're honest. I bet you've never told a lie in your entire life."

I didn't know what to say. It wasn't what I'd expected. Then I kissed you and you touched my face, turned and went inside. I went back to the car, got in and just sat there for a long time. I ached, like I never ached before. Ached like death was coming on.

Our dates after that always wound up in quiet places, away from my baseball friends. Near a quiet lake, hiking in the woods, in the deserted baseball diamond where you danced in the moonlight and told me you were going to be a writer. Every kiss took me by surprise and when I held you, I felt the power of us. As Coach Dickson said about our baseball team, "We were a power to be reckoned with."

Six months after high school, we got married. That will always be my best reason for being alive. You were so beautiful... so angelic.

So, this is our first Christmas together and you've given me this diary. Darla, I will love you until the day I die. There's nothing hidden about that—nothing about my love for you that needs to be hidden. I don't even know if my love for you can grow past what it already is. I think I would explode. But I'll keep writing things.

So, Darla, I'm just a dumb lucky guy. Lucky, that the new girl in town, so smart and so pretty, saw some-

thing in me that I never knew was there and said, "Yes, Jack, I'll marry you."

Merry Christmas, Darla.

Alice's eyes had unexpectedly filled with tears as she read his loving words. "I must be tired," she thought, sniffling. She gently wiped her eyes and looked at the date at the bottom. It had been written 15 years ago. Without hesitating, she turned the page.

CHAPTER 4

Alice read deep into the night, unable to pull herself away from it. She had never known a man capable of such intimacy.

> *When you told me you were pregnant, you were quiet. I've never been able to read your eyes the same way that you say you can read mine. But I kissed you and then went outside and looked up at the stars, grateful for life. A crescent moon was in the sky and I almost felt like I could reach out and touch it, because I felt close to things that night; a part of, and connected to all things, close and far. Just knowing that you were carrying our child made me think these thoughts—feel strange and wonderful things. Our love has somehow made all of my life seem good and worthy, even the bad things, and I can't say I understand that. But then, when you gave me this diary, you said writing in it would reveal hidden things about myself. You were right, Darla, my love.*

What did Jack look like? Alice wondered. Was he tall? Short? Blond? Dark-haired? Did he speak the way he wrote, with such heartfelt simplicity? Suddenly weary, she leaned back, held the diary on her chest and drifted off to sleep.

She awoke at five in the morning, disoriented. The light was still on. The diary had fallen beside her on the bed. She reached for it, as if there were an urgency; propped herself up against the headboard with two thick pillows, wiped her sleepy eyes and once again began to read.

Darla asked me if I ever thought about going to college. I know what she's really saying, because she knows that I love what I do. I love fixing things, building things—especially out of wood. I love being a carpenter. I went to a special school for it. Took it in high school. I love repairing things around the house, and it gives me a great sense of satisfaction when people in town call me to fix something in their house or office, after another contractor has totally messed the job up, or they just hadn't bothered to show up. I love the challenge of figuring out the problems, like putting in an entrance way in someone's weirdly designed house or building shelving units on a crooked wall or putting up a gazebo in someone's backyard.

Most people don't realize how much math goes into being a carpenter—how the wood almost seems to talk to you sometimes if you're really in the zone—how it reveals things to you, like that time I had to set up bookcases in the kindergarten, so that there was no chance of them falling over on the kids. The wood kind of spoke to me on that job. Sometimes it's just the smell of the wood, or the patterns or the way a piece fits together that just makes you feel good inside. Like you've done something good for the world.

But I think Darla asked me about college because she wants to go to college. It's okay with me, but then she doesn't make a move on it. She's been writing, but she won't show me any of her work. She won't even talk about it.

Alice skimmed the next few pages, when Jack wrote about his work and mentioned that Darla was spending a lot of time alone outside in the woods or in her room writing.

Kristie's almost two years old now and Darla is pregnant again and about to deliver. This is a difficult pregnancy for her and sometimes she won't talk to me. She's still writing, though, but still won't talk about it or show me any of it. Sometimes she wants to sleep alone now.

I put little Kristie in the garden in the mornings and she looks for bugs and worms and throws dirt at me. I've been teaching her how to plant seeds but she hates it. I think she's more like her mother: Smart and interested in those little plastic books and clapping her hands to music. But she's a beauty, blond like her Momma, and she's the love of my life. She hurts me with the love of her just like her Momma does. Sure didn't get all that beauty from me.

Darla says the house is too small—that she needs more space—especially with another baby coming. I've been looking at places and thinking that maybe we could buy a place and turn it into a bed and breakfast. I looked at a place in Eden Grove that's a little steep in price, but if I can negotiate it down, I think it would be perfect. It was built in the 1870s. The seller seems des-

perate to sell. It needs some work, but that would be fun. It's an old stone farmhouse, with plenty of cozy rooms and a cottage out back. The stone fireplace is real nice. Can walk around in there. The plumbing's only 5 years old and the roof's 6. Not bad. Foundation is good for the age. There's some beautiful woodwork in the chestnut staircase. Dining room has oak paneling. Parquet floors lead to a little library. Twelve acres of beautiful land, with Red and Norway maple, yellow and sweet birch, some Colorado blue spruce, some pine, elm and oak. I'll take Darla to see it in the next day or so. If she likes it, I'm going to put a bid on it.

Alice noticed that Jack's next entry was nearly a year later. The handwriting was a little more careless and hurried, the lines not as straight.

Have been so busy... bought the house... a lot of work. Andrew was born almost a year ago, and he is as wild as a little bear. I just want to grab him and wrestle... and I do. He has my energy, though, and my thick black hair and dark eyes. He cries a lot at night and none of us are sleeping much because of that. Both Darla and I fly-off at each other, just because we're so tired and stressed about the new place. I have Kristie doing the mid-summer weeding, (start them early) but she's doing more harm than good. I have to watch her or she pulls up flowers too. She's an enthusiastic worker and likes everything neat and straight (not like her Momma) but she also loves to destroy things.

I have been teaching her to add vegetable cuttings to the compost bin. We often dig deep into it to get some of the rich black compost to top off the garden. Kristie hates the worms and the half decomposed egg shells. I love the earthy smell and watching her bark at the robins as they bounce by.

Darla has been busy booking guests, cleaning and cooking. Most of the guests are real nice. Some are frankly a pain in the ass. I had to ask one man to leave because he was drunk and he made a pass at Darla. I almost punched him in the face, but didn't because Andrew was close by and I didn't want him to see it. Kids never forget things like that, like I never forgot some things my father did when he was drunk and yelling and beating me and my mother. No way Andrew's ever going to see me mad and violent. I made a vow to God that I would never be like my father. Never ever hurt my wife and my beautiful kids. I'll always protect them! With my dying breath!

Most of the time Darla seems happy, although she hasn't had the time to write. I feel bad about that and when I ask her about it, she just shakes her head and says she was no good anyway. It upsets me when she says that, because I know and believe deep down that she's a great writer. She feels things deep and is so smart and observant about people and things and she uses language real well. I just wish she'd keep at it. Maybe if she hadn't married me, she could have gone to college and become a writer.

Sometimes late at night I watch her when she's sleeping and I get scared. We've been married over four years and sometimes I feel like I don't know her at all. This woman who I love more than my own life is becoming more of a mystery to me. I hope she's not pulling away from me. I try not to think too much about it, because if I lost Darla, I might as well just stop breathing.

Alice closed the diary and looked out the window. The pearly light of dawn revealed a steady shower of heavy snow. It hadn't let up at all. A little snow mountain had formed outside the window sill, and the trees in the distance were covered with white.

She wouldn't be able to drive to Holbrook as long as the storm continued. Anyway, it was much more appealing to stay where she was, marooned in this lovely B&B, relaxed for the first time in weeks, and caught by the beauty of this diary. Why would she want to battle the storm and the floating unease of what lay before her? She opened the diary and read further.

I love the house and the seasons that surround it. I love the summer picnics by the pond, with the homemade quilts spread out on the newly cut grass, watching the kids scream and play under a great blue sky and chase the dragonflies and butterflies. Darla always seems more relaxed and happy in the summer. I love kissing her after she's had a sip or two of white wine. That always turns me on. I love the smell of her in summer and the way her hair blows in the wind and covers her face—how she rakes it away with long slender fingers. How she reaches for me when the kids aren't looking. Who needs to go to heaven—who wants to go to paradise when you're already there? Do I sound in love or what? Yes... these are good days. Warm summer days when everything is perfect. I hope none of my friends ever find this diary. I'll have to leave town.

$$* \qquad * \qquad *$$

We went over to the putt-putt golf course tonight. A big mistake. The kids are too young for it. A cool September night. Andrew didn't really understand the game, so he slapped Kristie. She cried and Darla slapped Andrew, knocking him down. He screamed and Darla slapped him again. Then he really cried. I asked Darla not to hit him so hard and she told me to shut up. Then I told her never to tell me to shut up. She said I was too easy on the kids and that she would never shut up. I said I would never shut up either and so neither one of us shut up. We just kept arguing about the fact that neither one of us was ever going to shut up. Kristie and Andrew kept crying and Darla and I argued all the way home. So much for a fun family outing.

*   *   *

It's winter and Darla is depressed. She won't come out of her room. I don't know what to do. There are eight inches of snow on the ground. That's a lot of snow to shovel, even with the plow, not to mention the water heater that's not working right, the roof that's leaking in the Rose Room and Kristie has strep throat. Thank God Andrew's in day-care.

Darla's been drinking. Not a lot. Just here and there. But sometimes I think it makes things worse. It always did with my father. She doesn't drink around the kids. I went in and talked to her the other morning when she wouldn't get out of bed. She kept saying over and over that she couldn't take it anymore. I kept asking her what she meant, but she turned away and said it wasn't me. It was her. I said that she should start writing again, but she got angry and told me to get out.

I've got so much to do today. I shouldn't be writing in this diary. What's the use anyway? But I'll keep writing because I told her I would. She told me to fill up all the pages and I still have a ways to go. So, I'll write.

Alice lay quietly in bed, watching the rise and fall of her chest. The diary was having a subtle but profound impact on her. It was so tenderly private and honest—so compelling in its simple style—and it moved her in unfamiliar ways. Had she ever loved anyone like that? Or been loved in that way? She'd seen movies about this kind of love, but never believed it could exist in reality.

She eased herself out of bed and returned to the window. The distant hills looked creamy, soft and nebulous; a kind of Never-Never Land. She closed her eyes, drew a deep breath and held it, a relaxation technique she'd learned in yoga class. Suddenly she heard the approach of ringing bells. She opened her eyes, exhaling quickly. Below her was a beautiful chestnut horse drawing a silver sleigh! She had never seen anything like it! A hunched man held the reins, dressed in brown and green, with a broad-brimmed hat pulled tightly over his head. The sleigh carried chopped wood, stacked neatly in rows, frosted with snow. Delighted by the sight, Alice watched the sleigh drift by, meander through a bank of trees and then slowly drop from sight beyond a sloping hill. It was a lovely sight, one she'd never seen before.

Alice stood in the silence, just staring. Not thinking. Not anticipating. Not wanting. And then, from deep within her gut, she felt a strange regret. What was this sadness? It took her a few minutes to identify the source. Finally, it came. It was the feeling that she'd missed out. Somehow, her life had slipped by her, in all her hectic, harried and hollow days. She shut her eyes, seeing herself in New York, dashing from activity to activity, never stopping to explore what was really going on inside her. The unhurried sleigh seemed to be saying, "Slow down, Alice. Slow down a little bit." Her shoulders dropped. She realized she was wound as tight as a spring.

She wandered aimlessly back to the bed and stood for a time looking down at the diary, as if it held some secret truth. Finally, drawn by its humble force, she sat on the edge of the bed and reached for it again, opening to the page where she'd left off; but this time, she merely stared at it in a kind of hypnotic standstill.

She allowed herself to imagine what it would be like to have someone like Jack in her life, someone she could really talk to, someone who might help her uncover her deepest feelings. Her chest warmed and ached at the thought of it. Jack was so naturally honest, so thoughtful and passionate. Of course, with Philip there was passion, but when they made love, it seemed as if they were both playing a role. If their eyes happened to meet, they looked away quickly, in embarrassment.

She stood up and went to the mirror, lowering her robe below her shoulders. She studied her neck and her chin, turning from side to side in the early morning light. Her skin was still smooth and clear; her shoulders were elegant. She knew she was still attractive. Just the other day, she'd heard Philip boast to a colleague that his fiancée had "a sophisticated beauty about her", and that men often looked her over when they went into the shop. In fact, sometimes Alice was actually surprised by the look of approval younger men gave her, making her feel girlish and "in the game," even though she really thought of herself as *out* of the game. After all, she was engaged to be married, and she knew Philip loved her. They would have a good life together.

She glanced at the clock. It was 7:15, time to get going. She pulled on jeans, a white turtleneck and a blue cashmere sweater, then tied her hair into a ponytail with a white silk scarf and applied a little makeup. As she sat on the bed, pulling on her socks and boots, she looked furtively toward the diary. She almost reached for it, but stopped. Her stomach was growling. Breakfast was served from 6 to 9, and so she headed downstairs.

The house was quiet. She entered the living room, stepped briskly across the chocolate brown carpet and passed a heavy wooden rocker near the cheery stone fireplace. A comfortable fire blazed; logs shifted and popped. Alice watched it briefly, with pleasure, and then walked into the adjoining dining room.

Hattie was alone at an antique oak table, sitting in a solid cherry ladder back armchair, sipping coffee from a broad-lipped mug and looking out the two windows. She had on the exact same outfit she'd worn the night before: the same glasses and the same pensive expression. The smell of coffee permeated the air and increased Alice's hunger.

"Good morning," Hattie said, smiling drowsily. "You're up early. Did you sleep well?"

"Yes..."

Alice followed Hattie's eyes toward the falling snow and the distant wooded hills and pond. "We already have 14 inches," Hattie said. "But they're saying the storm has about run its course."

Alice scratched her forehead. "Really... but I still don't want to travel in it. I hope I can stay another night."

"Your room is open. I've had two more cancelations. A little snow is great for business, but a storm... well..." Hattie lifted her thin hand and then dropped it on the table. "Take a seat. I hope you don't mind that we're informal here."

Alice sat opposite her in a duplicate ladder-back chair, noticing the rich cherry wood cupboard in the corner that held china and glasses. "No, of course not. It's very relaxing."

Hattie stood, went to the side table to retrieve a laminated menu, and handed it to Alice. "The blueberry muffins are homemade—by me—also the pancakes."

Alice glanced at the menu. "And the Amish granola is made by the Amish?"

Hattie nodded. "Yes, and it's the best I've ever tasted."

Alice ordered the pancakes, sausage and coffee. Hattie retreated to the kitchen, soon returning with a fresh mug of steaming coffee.

"I really love my room," Alice said.

"It's nearly everyone's favorite," Hattie said.

"Were you able to call the police about my passenger?" Alice asked.

"Yes I did. They said they'd send out a patrol car. I guess they didn't find anything because they said they'd call if they did."

"Maybe he lives close by," Alice said.

Hattie tilted her head slightly to the left. "Maybe. Were you warm enough last night?"

"Oh, yes. Very cozy. There are some good books up there."

Hattie stopped before returning to the kitchen. "People mostly bring them and exchange their old ones for new ones and vice versa. Now with all the electronic gadgets, people don't bring so many books anymore."

Alice took a quick sip of the coffee, feeling the warmth of it on her throat and in her chest. She wrapped her hands around the mug. "Have you read all the books up there?" she asked, staring into her coffee.

52

"No. I read mostly biographies," Hattie said. "I love history, mostly American history. Don't read much fiction."

Hattie opened the kitchen door. "I'll be back with your pancakes and sausage in a few minutes. You just relax and watch the snow and enjoy the scenery."

Alice could hear the radio in the kitchen. Bing Crosby was singing *White Christmas*. The smell of the frying sausage reached Alice's nose and she smiled, feeling relaxed and at peace for the first time in weeks. She looked around and tried to imagine Jack and his family in the house: the springs, summers, winters and Christmases. The birthdays, illnesses and all the rhythms and seasons of their lives. Why and when did they leave? He seemed to love it so much. What had happened? Alice shifted in the chair, feeling guilty that she had read the diary and intended to keep reading it. It was so very private. Jack would surely be horrified if he knew she was reading his deepest, heartfelt secrets. If the situation were reversed, she would be livid and humiliated if anyone had read anything of hers that was so personal. But then he'd never know, would he? So what was the harm of it? And why had he left the diary anyway? Maybe he didn't care at all. Had anyone else seen it or read it? Had it been imprisoned in that bookcase for years without anyone else seeing it? Surely not.

She considered mentioning it to Hattie, just to have someone else "in on it", but she was afraid Hattie would take it from her. And, anyway, she didn't want to admit that she was reading it and was so captivated by it that she didn't have the willpower to stop. There was absolutely no way she was going to leave without finishing it. That was impossible. She had to know what happened to Jack and his family. She might even take it with her.

Hattie entered, carrying a coffee pot in one hand and a heavy yellow plate laden with fluffy pancakes and sausage in the other. She sat them down in front of Alice, beaming. Alice leaned forward and took a whiff. "It all smells fantastic."

"Believe it or not, the pancakes are my husband's recipe," Hattie said, returning to her chair and reaching for the coffee pot. She filled her mug, while Alice drizzled maple syrup over her pancakes and watched it stream down the sides and form little pools.

"Is your husband around?" Alice asked.

"He had to go out of town on family business. He'll be back in a couple of days."

Alice took a bite and savored it. "Delicious," she said, with her mouth full. After she swallowed, she cut into the sausage. "Have you and your husband been here long?"

"Just over three years."

"Three years... who had the place before you?"

"A very nice couple from California. I don't exactly remember how they wound up here, but they owned the place for about seven years and then decided it was time to go back. I believe they'd made a lot of money in computers or something and decided they wanted to do something completely different. I think they just got tired of it."

Alice chewed her sausage. "Do you know who owned it before that?"

Hattie dropped two teaspoons of sugar into her coffee and stirred. "No. I have no idea. I just heard that it was run by a family."

"You ever hear what happened to them?"

"No."

"Is there anyone around town who might know what happened to them?"

Hattie looked at her curiously. "Why so interested?"

"Oh, no special reason. I'm just, you know, curious. Is anyone else staying in the house?"

"Another couple is staying out at the cottage. They keep pretty much to themselves. A family of three is scheduled to come in this afternoon. I hope they make it."

After breakfast, Alice returned to her room, anxious to finish the diary. She closed the door and leaned back against it, looking toward the bed with a nervous excitement. There was the diary, waiting. It was a different and very intriguing kind of mystery.

A moment later, she was stretched out on the bed, reading. The handwriting was barely legible now. It was small and awkward, some of the letters skewed. There was little punctuation.

I'm in the Rose Room reading a letter from Darla. I'm going to copy it into the diary, word for word. It should be here. It's only right that I copy it in here.

She left it on the kitchen table this morning, December 10th. It's snowing, lightly. No accumulation yet. The kids are still asleep. I don't know what time it is. The clouds are low and I see a deer out near the pond. The pond Darla and I ice-skated on last winter when it was so bitterly cold. We had such a good time that day. We brought a thermos of hot chocolate, skated and talked about all the things we were going to do with the house. We'd even discussed having another baby.

We were alone. The neighbors took the kids sledding with theirs. What a lovely peace it was to have them out of the house for a while and to have some time with Darla. Darla... It seems like a hundred damn years ago. I just keep staring at the envelope. It just says "Jack" on it; written with the blue felt-tip pen we keep at the table for the grocery list. I knew Darla had left the bed at some point during the night, because I reached for her. But I thought she had moved to the Autumn Room, like she often did when she couldn't sleep.

I've read the letter four times, slowly. She said she was leaving and she wouldn't be coming back. It wasn't me, she said. It's not the kids. I didn't understand. I don't understand. But this is what she said:

"I feel like I'm dying. I've got to go, Jack, or I'll die. You know I have to leave and you know why. Don't try to find me. You won't be able to. I'm going to start a brand-new life. I know you'll be hurt and will probably never forgive me, but I'll just have to live with that. I'll also have to live with the guilt of leaving Andrew and Kristie. I hope I can. But you're the greatest father in the world and the kids love you so much. I won't worry.

I hope I can start another life. I hope I make it. Forgive me, Jack. Forgive me for failing you—for failing as a wife and mother. I thought I could do it, but I can't. I'm lost and I've got to try to find myself, Jack. I've never been able to before. But I've got to try, don't you see?

Goodbye, Jack. Kiss the children and tell them that I'll always love them.

Darla... Darla... There's no more to write.

56

Alice didn't move. She slowly leafed through the remaining pages, disappointed to see that they were all blank. At least 20 pages, yellow and empty. She felt such sadness that tears sprang to her eyes. She closed them and gently set the diary aside. A moment later, she pulled a tissue and blotted her nose.

How could Darla have left them like that? How was it possible? What kind of pain or emptiness had driven her to do it?

According to the last entry of the diary, it had been written ten years ago. Almost ten years to the day when Jack had read the letter from Darla. Had she never returned? Surely so. How could she have stayed away for all of these years? Andrew would be about 12 or 13. Kristie, 15. Jack, in his early or mid-30s. What had happened to them? What had happened to Jack?

Alice paced the room, working on a prickly thought. How hard would it be to find out what had happened to them? If she knew his last name, she could Google him. Surely someone in town would remember them—would remember Jack—maybe even kept in touch with him. After all, he probably repaired floors, hung ceiling fans, put up tool sheds or gazebos for many of his neighbors. There was no harm in driving into town and asking around, while she looked at the shops and restaurants. No harm at all.

She glanced at the phone as she grabbed her winter coat. Should she text Philip? Call him? It was only about 6 a.m. in Denver. She'd wait until she got back. It wouldn't take long.

CHAPTER 5

It took Alice fifteen minutes to clean the layers of snow off her car. As she worked, she saw two deer nearby gazing back at her. They weren't frightened, but seemed bored. Finally, they leapt away toward the pond and disappeared into the cover of trees.

The sky was dull blue and white when Alice drove out of Hattie's salted driveway and turned onto the two-lane highway that would eventually lead to Eden Grove. Snow flurries sailed on currents of a wet, gusty wind, and were scattered across snow-covered fields, rambling forests and small hills. Some of the drifts had buried fence posts, mailboxes, and fieldstone walls.

The world was expanded out here, Alice thought— away from the obstructions and clutter of the city. She felt a remarkable peace and a welcomed serenity. The main highway had been plowed during the night, but another two inches had fallen since then; Alice reduced her speed and kept a sharp eye for icy patches.

Cars approached with skis and snowboards strapped to the roof, obviously en route to a ski resort nearby, and not a few SUVs were out, rolling past her like Great Danes chasing squirrels. She thought of last night's interstate pileup, hoping the injuries weren't serious, that the people in the overturned SUV were okay.

But what had happened to that strange old man—the doctor? She would ask about him in town, too, in case anyone could identify him. Not only had he led her to Hattie's and knew her first name, but he had also encouraged her to look through the bookshelf where she found the diary. Even in the light of day, with the car heater on high blowing warm air, she turned cold at the thought of him.

She glanced down guiltily at the seat beside her, where her cell phone sat. She shouldn't talk and drive, she thought. Philip was probably sleeping in anyway. He often slept late when he got the chance, since he was usually sleep deprived. The trip to Denver was one he had dreaded. As he'd put it, "they were going to be playing hardball out there," although he never really explained what that meant. She wondered sometimes if Philip really liked being an attorney. He'd once said, in one of his rare candid moments about his past, that getting a law degree from Columbia University had been expected of him and his brother since they were born. That's what his father and grandfather had done. Philip's brother didn't make it—didn't have the aptitude, as Philip put it. He'd become an embarrassment to the family. He worked as a yoga instructor in a Pittsburgh health club and managed a health food store nearby.

A black and white sign announced that Eden Grove was two miles ahead. She adjusted her rearview mirror, checked her lipstick, and turned on the radio. She found a station that was playing a piano piece by Beethoven, *Für Elise*; she recognized it because she'd practiced it a million times during her freshman year in college, when she was thinking of being a music major. During her sophomore year, she'd changed her major to accounting, afraid it would be difficult to find a well-paying job after graduation if she studied music.

She drummed her fingers into the steering wheel, pretending to play along, and nodded her head to the rhythm. When her cell phone rang, she snatched it up; from the LCD display, she saw it was Philip.

"Good morning," she said pleasantly.

His voice sounded scratchy and asleep. "You sound awake, for 8:30, or something close to that, in the morning."

"Life begins early on the farm," Alice said.

"It sounds like you didn't have any problems finding a place to stay for the night. You didn't call me."

"Sorry. I was reading something and fell sound asleep."

"So, obviously, you did find a place?"

"Yes. It's a wild story. I'll tell you all about it when I see you. How was the meeting?"

"Same old, same old. You sound like you're in a good mood. How is that possible? We're not together. We're supposed to be. We're supposed to be in that king-sized bed in my beautiful Swiss chalet overlooking forests, lakes and mountains."

"*My?*"

"My what?"

"You said, *my* beautiful Swiss chalet."

"You know what I mean."

"Do I?"

"Okay, *our* beautiful Swiss chalet."

"But you're right."

"About what?"

"About it being yours. Legally, it is yours and not ours, and you should know that being an attorney. We're not married yet."

"Whatever.... Where are you?"

"About a mile out of Eden Grove, Pennsylvania."

"You're on the road? Has the storm passed?"

"It's moving off. Just a few flurries. The roads aren't too bad. Will you be able to get a flight out today?"

"Not on the corporate jet. It left early. I'll have to do commercial. I'm sure I'll get one eventually. How long do you think it will take you to get to Holbrook?"

Alice waited.

"Alice? Are you there?"

"I'm going to stay on another night, Philip. I don't really feel safe driving in this. We got over 14 inches of snow."

"Why are you driving into town then?"

Alice started to speak, but he cut her off.

"Don't tell me. Shopping."

"Well... yes... and just to look around. It's beautiful out here."

"Yes, Pennsylvania is fantastic. That's why I built a house there. Okay, I'll see if I can get a flight out this morning and get up to the house at least by this evening. If you leave in the morning, you shouldn't have any trouble making it to the house by early afternoon. I'll call you a little later today and let you know what's going on."

By the time they'd finished their conversation, Alice was driving along Main Street in Eden Grove, passing 19th-century buildings, with high roofs, steep slopes and prominent gables. These were mostly locally owned stores and shops. No fast-food restaurants. The streets were quiet; only a handful of parked cars and pickups. A young couple was window shopping at the hardware store, and a chunky man, with a brown-and-white base-ball cap pulled snugly over his head, tramped through the snow to a nearby restaurant.

She passed an old movie theater whose double feature was *Polar Express* and *Jingle All the Way*. The courthouse had enormous windows and a red brick clock tower that reminded her of the courthouse in the movie *Back to the Future*. She looked left to see the red brick fire station and a squat, fat Christmas tree, blinking red and green lights. The antique streetlights were draped with red and green tensile and little silver snowmen were turning in the wind.

Alice decided to start her investigation at the restaurant. The neon green and red sign said *Red's Hometown Restaurant*. She found a parking place, but approached the space carefully and parked awkwardly, hearing the tires crunch the fresh snow, worried that she'd trapped herself and might need a push when she was ready to leave.

She climbed out, examined her parking job, and decided it was all right. The wind was sharp and quick so she pulled up the collar of her full-length black cashmere coat and wrapped a pink wool scarf around her neck. Weak sunlight struggled to break through a white quilted sky, and Alice looked up just in time to see a flock of geese beating west in a V formation. It seemed an innocent morning, and as she started for the restaurant across the sparkling empty sidewalks, a distant church bell chimed. She smiled, comforted by the sound. Fortunately, she'd worn her black boots with low heels and good traction, so she felt safe on the snowy and icy sidewalk.

When she tugged open the double glass doors of the restaurant, she felt the warm breath of heat. It was a long, narrow place with a diner feel. There were eight red-topped swivel stools at the counter, and ten generous, red plastic booths on the other side, with green circular lights hanging above them. It was a place built for Christmas, and it looked like Christmas. A six-foot Douglas fir Christmas tree, decorated with green and red ornaments, stood near the cash register, giving off the fresh smell of pine. Dean Martin sang *Silver Bells* from a red and silver metallic corner jukebox, in his sliding, easy manner, as if he had recorded it while sitting in a recliner, sipping eggnog and staring lazily at his own Christmas stocking.

The place probably sat 60, but there were only 15 patrons now, sipping coffee, eating eggs, and mumbling conversations. They all stopped when she walked in, turning to stare at Alice. Their eyes held a low-key curiosity that fit the music perfectly. The faces were friendly but private. Alice lowered her head, slightly, went to the counter and eased down on one of the stools, near the man with the brown-and-white baseball cap and a thin woman who was eating quick bites of home fries and eggs.

A roundish man, with short red hair, a generous stomach and a ruddy face stood behind the counter. He approached Alice, carrying a coffee pot and a red mug.

"Morning..."

"Good morning," Alice said.

"Coffee?" he asked.

"Yes... Thanks."

"You get stuck in the storm last night?" he asked, pouring the coffee.

Alice smiled. "Yes, I did. I stayed at Hattie's Bed and Breakfast."

He lifted a red bushy eyebrow. "Great spot. She keeps a real good place. My name's Red. I'm the owner and the best waiter in the place. What can I get you?"

"Just a muffin. Banana or cranberry."

"I can do banana," he said, and he took three steps backward, lifted a clear plastic domed lid covering a little mountain of muffins, snatched one, spun right, grabbed a green plate and had the muffin on the plate and in front of her in seconds. He placed his right hand on his hip and stood a little taller, obviously proud of his efficiency. "Like I said, I'm the best waiter in the place."

Alice smiled. "Yes you are!" He was friendly, so she decided to seize the moment. "How long has Hattie had the bed and breakfast?"

"Hattie?" he asked, considering her question. "... Oh, about three years I'd say." He looked left at the thin woman for corroboration. "What do you say, Gladys?"

Gladys was finishing her last bite of home fries. Her light gray hair was pulled severely back off her forehead, and she sat on the stool in a gnarly knot of defiance. When she looked up, her blueberry eyes were small and probing. She jerked a nod of agreement.

Perhaps Gladys was the local authority. Alice leaned forward. "Who had the house before Hattie?"

"The Pratters from California," Red said, and Gladys nodded again.

Alice didn't want to appear too obvious. "Don't a lot of old houses like that stay in the family for years? Seems like there was quite a turnover."

Gladys laced her fingers and placed them on the counter as she swallowed the last of her food. "Are you a travel person writing an article?" Gladys asked.

Alice quickly reached for her coffee. "Oh, no. No, just curious. It's such a beautiful place."

Gladys squinted, as if she were trying to see through Alice's face to find the truth. It made Alice ill at ease.

"That house was in the Harrison Wheeler family for many years—since the 1870s when it was built. Then after Albert Wheeler, the great grandson, passed on, his no-good son sold the place to pay off some gambling debts. I was outraged."

Red spoke up. "Gladys works at the local Chamber of Commerce. She can tell you anything you want to know about this town, going all the way back to the Revolutionary War."

Gladys passed him a disagreeable glance. "You make me sound like I'm over two hundred years old, Red."

He held up his hand in defense. "Now Gladys, nobody's saying anything like that. I'm just saying you're knowledgeable. Don't take offense where none was intended."

The man in the baseball cap turned to Alice. He was 60 or so, with a hound dog expression and a bulbous nose. "Don't get these two started. His son married her daughter and they were divorced 10 years ago."

Red's face reddened. "Horton, nobody needs to go around telling all they know in front of people who don't want to hear it. This woman isn't interested in these little bits and pieces of gossip."

"Horton, you talk too much and say too little," Gladys said.

There was an awkward silence. Alice picked at her muffin and gently cleared her throat. "Who had the house before the Pratters?" she asked, as casually as possible.

Gladys leaned forward, ignoring Horton and Red. "Now that's a sad story."

Both Red and Horton nodded in agreement. "Yes, ma'am."

Gladys looked up at the ceiling, as if to summon divine inspiration. She let out a deep sigh. "When the

Wheeler son, Bobby Wheeler, sold the house, he sold it to one of the true gentleman of the earth, Landis."

Alice straightened, rigid with interest. "Jack Landis…"

Gladys' eyes widened on Alice.

Red slapped the counter. "You've got that one right, Gladys."

Horton spoke up. "They don't come any better than Jack Landis."

Gladys shook her head, irritated. "The woman asked me a question!"

Red stepped back and Horton shrugged.

Gladys reached for her cup of tea and took a thoughtful sip, keeping the cup close to her lips. "How do you know Jack's name?"

Alice swallowed. "Oh, I guess Hattie mentioned it… or something."

That seemed to satisfy Gladys. "Well… when Jack moved into the Wheeler house, he breathed new life into it. He loved it and brought a kind of shine and pride to that place that it hadn't seen in years. Jack was a real worker and, just… just a good family man. He had two of the prettiest kids I think I ever saw, Kristie and Andrew. And Jack was a handsome man who didn't seem to know it. He was all neatly muscled—had a natural kind of muscular body, built on honest hard work. Had beautiful thick black hair that was over his ears; piercing, but real kind eyes. Jack walked around comfortably, like a man who was happy to be walking on the earth. Now that's rare, and that was Jack."

Red poured himself a mug of coffee, feeling energized by the story. Horton extended his cup and Red filled it as he lowered his eyes toward Gladys. "But his wife, Gladys, his wife was a real piece of work."

"A mystery," Gladys said. "A sad case."

"That's the right word, Gladys," Horton interjected, sheepishly. "Mystery. She was a walkin', talkin' mystery."

"What was she like?" Alice asked, riveted.

"Well, let's not get into love, with all its complications and mysteries and contradictions," Gladys said, with her fine, eyebrow-arching. "We'll be here as long as God keeps us alive trying to figure that one out."

"Well, I've been married three times," Red said, with a bewildering shake of his head. "And I still have not figured out all the ins and outs of the thing."

"You are too domineering, Red," Gladys said, sharply. "Pure and simple."

"Now let's be careful that the pot's not calling the kettle black, here," Red said.

"I'll not deny I have a forceful personality, Red, but I am not domineering!"

Horton turned to Alice, ignoring them both. "Jack's wife was a pretty little thing from Philadelphia, I think."

"Chicago, Horton," Gladys corrected. "Darla Landis was from Chicago!"

"Okay, Chicago. But she was remote, I would say, kind of a distant type of person who didn't have much to say to anybody. But she was pretty and ..."

Gladys interrupted. "... You already said she was pretty, Horton. Move on, now."

Horton did. "It was obvious that Jack loved her. Even worshiped her."

"I'd agree with that," Red said.

Gladys took over. "And she worked hard at it—I mean, that place. She and Jack really put their shoulders to the wheel and built a place that the whole town was proud of. Now... those California people were kind of lazy and let it go down again—expected everything to fall in their lap. Not used to hard work. Didn't know the basics of keeping a place like that."

Red moved toward Alice, stretched out his thick hairy arm and pointed out the window. "My first restaurant was right across the street and whenever I ran into any trouble, I called Jack. He could do it all. He could frame walls and roofs, do shingling, sliding and drywall, lay tile, do electrical or build you the most beautiful wood cabinet you ever saw. He had the gift, and he was generous with it."

Horton nodded. "That he was. He was always ready to lend a hand."

Gladys's expression darkened. "Until she left him."

"His wife?" Alice asked.

"Just walked off one morning. Left him, the house and her beautiful kids. Just walked off, and as far as I know, never came back."

Red grabbed a towel and blotted his forehead. "I never knew what he saw in her anyway. But, he did see something he loved, better than his own life. He obviously saw something there that none of the rest of us saw."

"It broke him," Horton said.

"It was a hard thing to see," Gladys said. "It was hard to watch him fall into depression, despair and bitterness. It was like he changed overnight. Wouldn't talk to you..."

"Hell, he wouldn't even answer you if you said hello," Horton said.

Red drained his coffee. "Wouldn't answer my calls. Whenever he came to town with those kids, he was no-nonsense. He was hard on them. He was hard on himself. I tried to talk to him once about it and he just told me, in no uncertain terms, that I was to mind my own business. He'd never talked like that before."

Gladys hunched over the counter, lost in thought. "He put that house up for sale within a couple of weeks."

"Got a good price out of it," Red said.

"The real estate market was booming then," Horton said. "And it was in such good shape. That kitchen was a showpiece, with all those maple cabinets and that utility sink and splash tile work. A real beauty."

"He had it sold in two months," Gladys said.

Alice spoke quickly. "Where did he go? What happened to him?"

Gladys massaged her forehead. "That was about 10 years ago. A long time now. About a year later someone told me he'd moved back to his hometown."

"Where is that?"

"Meadow Green, Pennsylvania. It's about 40 miles, south."

"Did anyone ever go up and see him?"

Red smacked his lips. "I was down that way once and was going to drop by, but by the time I found the house, it was late and nobody was home. I was shocked at the state of that house. I couldn't believe Jack Landis lived there. It looked haunted. An old broken down thing, dark and scary. There was no damned life to it. An eyesore."

Gladys swung off the stool and stood. "So that's the story of Jack Landis and that house. Thank God Hattie and John Drake took it over. I think Jack would be proud if he saw it now. They've done a great job."

Alice sipped her coffee and listened to Nat King Cole on the jukebox singing *The Christmas Song*. When it finished, Alice faced Red. "Something really strange happened to me last night during the storm. I picked up an elderly man. He walked right out in front of me and I almost hit him. He said he was a doctor, but when I asked Hattie about it, she said it couldn't have been Dr. Ainsley, the town doctor, because he's in his late 30s and rather short. This man was in his 70s, big, and, well, not very friendly. I gave him a ride to Hattie's and then he just sort of disappeared."

Gladys, Red and Horton regarded her first with suspicion, then with mild alarm.

"What did he say his name was?" Gladys asked.

"He didn't say. He just said he was a doctor."

Gladys, Red and Horton exchanged nervous glances.

"What is it?" Alice asked.

"Was he wearing black-rimmed glasses? Kind of a sandpapery type of voice?"

Alice nodded. "Yes."

Red wiped the back of his neck with the towel. "Did you notice if he had a little scar just above his right eyebrow?"

Alice brightened. "Yes! You know him. Who is he?"

Gladys stepped toward Alice with a grim, serious expression. "He *was* the town doctor," Gladys said, thickly, "but not Eden Grove's doctor. He was Meadow Green's town doctor."

Alice waited. "Yes... so what happened to him?"

Gladys continued, reluctantly. "Dr. Frank Landis was killed about 13 years ago. He was Jack's father. He'd come to visit Jack one Christmas, here in Eden Grove. He and Jack didn't get along. We all knew that. They got into a big argument one night. Dr. Landis had been drinking. I don't know exactly what it was about, but the story goes it was over Darla, and something about the kids... about how Jack had no business being a father when he couldn't support them. Something like that. Anyway, Jack threw his father out of the house. I guess the doctor went for a walk out along the road. There was a fierce winter storm that night, just like last night. Frank Landis was walking out on that road and was hit by a car and killed instantly."

Alice's anxious eyes traveled uneasily from Red's, to Horton's and then to Gladys' face. All three nodded at the same time, in tacit agreement.

Alice turned white.

CHAPTER 6

"It's obviously a mistake," Alice said. "We all know that. It was somebody else," she said, fretfully.

"He's been seen, but he's never talked to nobody before," Horton said.

"Be quiet, Horton." Gladys scolded. "Don't you see she's scared."

Alice turned sharply. "He's been seen? By who?"

"It doesn't matter," Gladys consoled. "Just tall tales and rumors."

Alice's eyes shifted distractedly here and there. "So you're saying I saw, spoke to and gave a ride to a ghost? I don't believe that."

Horton swiveled his stool away from her and Gladys folded her arms, considering a response.

Red finished ringing up a check, then came out from behind the counter and over to the others. "Listen, Miss... What's your name?"

"Alice."

"... Alice. None of the three of us have ever seen him, but we have heard stories. Now, that doesn't mean they're true. No ma'am. The Pratters claimed they saw him a couple of times, and they even called in some psychic woman from Philadelphia. She walked all along the property and on the road and inside the house and said she felt a presence—an unhappy presence—but that's all she said. She didn't really find anything. It made the local news shows four years ago, and it brought in a few curious tourists. As far as we know, there haven't been any other reported sightings... until now."

Alice struggled to center herself. She forced a strained smile. "Well, if nothing else, it will be a great story to tell at my wedding: how a ghost told me where to stay for the night."

The trio lit up at the news of the wedding and surrounded her with congratulations. Afterwards, when she asked for her bill, Red told her it was on the house; a wedding present.

Horton was preoccupied. He finally stepped forward. "Alice... what else did the doctor say to you?"

"Oh, just let it drop, Horton," Gladys said.

"I'm just curious, Gladys. She doesn't have to answer if she doesn't want to."

Alice wet her lips. "Nothing really... you know, just, well, nothing."

Horton slumped, disappointed.

Alice left, shaken and nervous. Back in her car, after a moment's reflection, she decided she'd leave for Holbrook after all. There was no reason not to. It had stopped snowing and the roads would be cleared in another couple of hours. As she traveled black along Main Street, she passed a final glance at the restaurant. Red, Gladys and Horton were looking at her through the window, their faces darkly private. Horton waved. She lifted her hand weakly.

A few miles from the bed and breakfast, Alice called Philip. When she got his voice mail, she left a message, saying she'd be in Holbrook sometime in the evening.

Back at Hattie's, the smell of cedar logs hovered like a living thing and drew Alice's eyes toward the glowing living room fireplace. Hattie was hanging some ornaments on the Christmas tree.

"Your room is all made up and ready for you," she said.

"Thank you, Hattie, but I've decided to leave after all."

Hattie turned to her, noticing the tension in her face. "Is everything all right?"

"Everything is fine. The roads are better than I thought they would be, so I might as well go. And now that the storm's passed, I'm sure you'll be able to rent the room tonight."

Hattie finished hanging a crystal icicle on an upper limb of the tree. "Yes, I'm sure I will."

Alice lingered for a moment and Hattie waited, noticing her posture was unnaturally stiff.

"You seem troubled," Hattie said.

Alice twisted her hands. "Hattie, have you heard about Dr. Frank Landis?"

Hattie's head tilted back and she shut her eyes for a moment. "Oh, my stars, you've been talking to those people in town."

"So you don't believe...?"

"It's a lot of nonsense. I have been here over three years and I have never once seen anything remotely like the ghost of Dr. Landis, or any other kind of ghost. It's a ridiculous story the townspeople like to tell tourists. I guess they think it helps bring in business. I hope that's not why you're leaving."

Alice's shoulders relaxed. "No... no. I guess it's just that... well I keep wondering what happened to that man—the one I gave a ride to."

"He went right back to where he came from," Hattie said, strongly. "That's what happened to him! Now you just put your mind at ease about it."

Alice smiled, briefly. "All right. I'll just go get my suitcase."

"Have a cup of eggnog with me before you leave," Hattie said. "I'll have it ready when you come down."

While she packed, Alice wrestled with her thoughts. Should she tell Hattie about the diary? Should she take it with her? It was Hattie's house after all. But then, to Hattie it was probably like all the other books around the place, and there were so many. Probably a bookshelf in every room. Hattie would almost certainly be happy to get rid of it. Get it off her hands. Keep the book-recycling ritual going.

And anyway, would Jack Landis really want someone else reading his diary? That was an easy one. Definitely not! Who would? What if it wound up in the local newspaper or, even worse, what if Hattie used it as some kind of advertising to help business? Perhaps turn it into a short promotional documentary of some kind about the house and the ghost of Dr. Frank Landis. Now that would sell! Jack would be horrified and humiliated.

Alice reached for the diary and slid it under the sweaters in her suitcase. But as she started out of the room, she stopped. What was she going to do with it? Hide it? Read it again? She didn't know. She just knew she had to take it.

Downstairs in the kitchen, Alice and Hattie drank egg-nog out of small glass cups. Since Hattie had been so dismissive and skeptical about "the ghost", Alice now felt less addled and more reassured. She could easily view the whole event as some over-reaction that was perfectly understandable because she was afraid and lost at night in a snowstorm. Whoever that poor man was, he was just that: a flesh and blood man who certainly had a home nearby.

Alice told Hattie about her wedding, and then they talked about Christmas shopping and how difficult it was to buy presents for men, and then finally they just talked about men: how predictable they are; how often they miss hints you give them about Christmas presents; how they have one-track minds and don't often see the obvious or better choice; how they can forget to pick up a quart of milk, but never forget an obscure sports statistic.

The longer they discussed it, the more Alice believed that Hattie was not happily married. She was lonely. Perhaps it was the way her normally engaging eyes dulled when she spoke her husband's name, or how her voice fell when she started a sentence about why they never had children. When she came back to the present, Hattie jolted back to life and smiled—but it was a smile that expressed more sadness than warmth.

"Men just have their ways," she said, more than once. "Ways of just shutting you out."

Alice couldn't mistake Hattie's sagging shoulders, her deliberate pauses, her lack of energy when she mentioned her husband and their nearly 25 years together. Alice began to wonder if Hattie's husband was really out on family business. Maybe he had left her, or was having an affair. What kind of love did they have? What kind of love did she have for Philip, or he for her?

Alice felt something push and nudge inside her, as if it were trying to awaken. It frightened her.

Hattie was perceptive. "Anything wrong, dear?"

Alice shook away the feeling and averted Hattie's face. "No... fine." But Alice was thinking of the diary—could see it clearly in her mind—could feel the power of its words and emotion. Jack knew he was in love from the first moment he saw Darla. Never doubted it. As Darla rode past him on her bicycle, she had looked back and smiled. Had she known, too? Was it destiny? Mystical love? Love at first sight? Mature love? If it was supposed to be mature love, it certainly didn't last.

"Are you sure you're all right, Alice?" Hattie asked again.

Alice nodded as she stood up. "It's just that I have to leave this cozy place and I dread the drive."

Hattie walked her to the car. "I wish you and your fiancé every happiness," she said.

Alice took her hand and squeezed it gently. "Thank you, Hattie, for everything and Merry Christmas."

As the road unraveled before her, Alice kept her eyes fastened to it, not allowing her thoughts to stray, corralling all her energies to the pinpoint certainty that her marriage to Philip would be one of commitment. Commitment was a reality—something she could understand, work with, and make practical through practice, sacrifice and understanding. It wasn't an elusive and mystical love. It was real. One thing she knew for certain: she did not love Philip in an elusive or mystical way.

She and Philip had once discussed this very thing. They were both acutely aware that their parents' marriages barely survived. Maybe their parents should have divorced, but they didn't. They had stayed together and made it work. They had stayed committed. She and Philip had no illusions about marriage. They knew they'd have to work at it. And by recognizing this and accepting it, their marriage would survive the challenging times. Of course, that didn't mean they weren't romantic or spontaneous. Philip had often brought her little presents or flowers, and she was famous for sending eCards and "real" cards to his office. They were simple, with phrases like "Thinking of You" or "Hey There, Sexy."

She had been on the road for almost half an hour when Philip called.

"I'll be on a three o'clock flight to Pittsburgh," he said. "That will put me at the house by probably 6 or 6:30."

"Me too," Alice said. "I'm on my way."

"Cool," Philip said.

"Do you ever say 'Cool' in a courtroom?" Alice asked.

"Once or twice. Judges think it's cool."

"Aren't you the clever one?"

"We've got lots of stuff to do, Alice."

She sighed. "I've got my list."

"My mother's been calling me every 2 hours."

"About?"

"Scotch talk."

"Which is?"

"Get married in a church. Move to Pittsburgh."

"… And don't marry Alice," Alice said. "... Because she's poor and…"

He cut her off. "She didn't say that. And, anyway, you have some good investments."

"That I'm going to have to live on for a while. Or, who knows, maybe reinvest in the shop," she said lightly.

Philip turned serious. "Don't even joke about that. You'll save your money and we'll live off mine."

"No thanks. We've talked about this, Philip. I need my own money. My own life." As soon as the words left her lips, she regretted saying them.

There was a long, cold silence. "All right, whatever," Philip said, flatly. "We'll talk about it on our honeymoon. I'll see you at the house around 6:30."

Before Alice dropped her cell phone back into her purse, she checked her messages and saw that her sister, Jacinta, had called. She'd call her back later.

Just ahead was a sign:

Meadow Green, PA - Jct. 2 Miles

Heat rose to her face. She abruptly hit the brake, thinking she'd missed the turn off. The car gently skidded. She quickly realized her mistake, released the brake and adjusted the steering wheel. Fortunately, no one was behind her. She took a breath and returned to the speed limit.

She drove apprehensively, unsure why. She rolled the window down and let the cold air wash over her. But the air filled her with unease. The rush of wind seemed to bring a mounting confrontation. The white landscape was suddenly a blur, the pavement slushy, the shoulders of the road piled high with dirty snow from the snowplows and frequent traffic. She rolled up the window and leaned back into her seat.

"How far is Meadow Green?" she asked herself, aloud.

The closer she came to the turnoff, the more nervous she became. She dropped below the speed limit, and when cars zipped by, heads turned toward her with annoyed expressions. She arrived at the junction to Meadow Green, winced, then took the turn. How far could it be?

A mile later she saw a green sign that announced the distance: 35 miles. Not that far! She glanced into the rearview mirror and saw her eyes. They held anxiety, and lots of questions.

CHAPTER 7

Meadow Green was in south central Pennsylvania. It was a short hop away from Blue Knob Mountain, the second highest mountain in Pennsylvania, and about five miles from the Mythic Ski Resort.

In contrast to Eden Grove, Meadow Green was a town of designer shops, stylish cafes, bookshops and plazas. Most of its 19th-century buildings had had a complete makeover, enhancing the lively and busy Victorian buildings with their turrets, gables and archways. The streets had been widened and were lined with antique streetlights and wooden benches to accommodate and manage the swell of tourists during the summer, autumn and winter holiday peaks. Despite the changes, traffic was still heavy and slow, the streets filled with shoppers, kids and pedigree dogs. Alice began to wonder if anyone ever went skiing. But, as an entrepreneur herself, she found the energy exhilarating.

The snow, the gleaming Christmas decorations in the store windows, and the 20 foot Colorado blue spruce in the town square all greatly added to the town's picturesque charm and holiday atmosphere. It was a town that had been redesigned for tourists, for people anxious for a good time and willing to spend money to experience a Hollywood-style celebration where Bing Crosby would have been proud to sing *White Christmas*.

It took her 20 minutes to find a parking space near a fudge and ice cream shop. She switched off the engine and sat utterly still. She shuddered. What was she doing? She was solving a mystery. That's all. She grabbed her purse and dug out her phone. She glanced about nervously and carefully googled JACK LANDIS, waiting as the screen refreshed. She swallowed, feeling her heart thrumming. She focused. There were several Jack Landises on Facebook and LinkedIn. There was a racecar driver, a judge, an accountant; and all were in, or near, Meadow Green. Her eyes froze on an obituary. That Jack Landis was 83 years old. Alice relaxed a little and kept scrolling. Nothing.

She stepped out of the car, struggled into her coat, stretched, and then strolled down the snow-shoveled streets, window shopping and soaking up the atmosphere. People smiled and moved easily in a shared subtle pleasure of the season, lighthearted, already "in the zone" of Christmas.

Alice entered a blue and white café, with wrought-iron table and chairs, and ordered a turkey sandwich and cappuccino from the blue-vinyl-jacketed menu. When she had finished the sandwich, she asked the 20s something blond woman behind the coffee bar where the local Chamber of Commerce was. Alice figured that, like in Eden Grove, Jack Landis' reputation had surely spread in a town like this where he'd grown up and where his professional skills and talent would be in constant demand. And if Gladys, back in Meadow Green, was any indication of where the seat of local information resided, then the Chamber of Commerce was the place to begin her search. If that didn't work, she'd find a phone book or call information.

The Chamber of Commerce was two blocks away. She walked and sipped the still-warm cappuccino, feeling a humid breeze with fitful currents of colder air. Sporadic sunlight broke through and glared off windshields, snow-covered rooftops and distant mountains, ghost-like in the lowering sky. Was she really going to do this? Find Jack Landis? Why not? What's the harm? None. For the first time in weeks, she was having fun. It was a great diversion from her hectic life and, anyway, she still had plenty of time to make it to Holbrook by 6:30. It was only 12:50.

The Chamber of Commerce was in a circular plaza on Main Street. It was a two-story brick building with a large picture window and a shingled roof. Inside, a woman behind the desk was in her late 60s or early 70s, small, frail-looking and fidgety. Her manner was awkward, but she seemed willing to help. She reminded Alice of an English teacher she'd had in high school.

"Hi. I'm looking for someone and maybe you can help me."

She gave Alice a proud, confident look. "If they're from around here, I know them. I've lived here my entire life. What's the name?"

"Jack Landis."

The woman's little gray eyes expanded. "Sure, I know him."

Alice tipped up her chin and breathed in a happy impatience. "Is he close by?"

"Well now, that depends."

"Yes...?" Alice asked.

"Jack Landis is a contractor, and he gets around. He doesn't let any grass grow beneath his feet in summer—

or snow melt under his feet in winter. Jack is a worker—a doer—and he could be right next door working on a project or up on Mythic Mountain working on that new dining room that some other contractor, whose name I will not mention, messed up."

Alice smiled, faintly. That was the Jack Landis she'd heard about! Anticipation swelled.

"I hope you don't have a job for him, because he's always booked up months ahead."

"No, nothing like that."

"Are you a relative?"

"No..."

The woman studied her. Alice saw the gentle suspicion in her eyes.

"Well, I mean, I might have a project. I've heard how good he is... you know with projects. Do you have his address by any chance?"

"Where are you from?" the woman asked.

"New York. I have a little candle shop there."

"And you're thinking about opening one down here?"

The question surprised her. She was grateful for the suggestion. "Well... I... don't know... maybe."

"You've looked at real estate?"

"... I'm just sort of... looking."

"So what do you need Jack for?" the woman persisted. "Do you have a house here?"

Alice fortified herself by switching her purse from her left shoulder to her right. "Friends... I'm staying with friends, nearby, and they need some work done."

"Well you can call him, but I doubt whether he's going to have any time." The woman reached under the counter for a business card with Jack's address and phone number. Alice thought the woman had a playful glimmer in her eyes when she slid the card toward her. "His office is in his house, but he won't be there."

Alice took the card. "Thank you."

"I was Jack's English teacher in high school," she said, softly, squinting.

Alice lifted her head and couldn't hide her astonishment. "Really?"

"A curious, persistent student, and what a smile." Her face darkened. "He's barely said ten words to me in 10 years, but then..." Her voice faded. "If you reach him, don't expect him to talk much."

Alice leaned in closer. "Did you know his father? Frank Landis?"

"Did I!" she said, sharply. "He was a good doctor, but a lousy man and a worse father." Then she caught herself, and her lips tightened in guilt. "May God forgive me. Especially at Christmas." Her eyes narrowed on Alice's face. "You're not a friend of the family, are you?"

Alice backed away, wanting to cut the conversation short. "No... thanks again for the card." She turned to leave, but the woman's voice stopped her.

"Do you know where Cyprus Way is?"

Alice looked down at the address. "Well, actually, no."

The woman reached for the phone. "If you really want to get a hold of Jack, don't waste your time calling him. I'll call the ski lodge and see if he's there."

Alice shifted her weight awkwardly onto her left foot. "That's not necessary... I can..."

The woman ignored her and dialed the number. "No trouble. No trouble at all."

Alice lingered, suddenly feeling foolish and adolescent. She felt like some high school girl trying to get a date with the star quarterback.

She went to the reception table and leafed absently through a brochure. She tossed it down and reached for a magazine that showed models with blank or haughty expressions wearing Helmut Lang dresses. A second magazine had catatonically bored models in Givenchy gowns, staring despondently into the distance. "Why don't they smile?" Alice thought, as she leaned an ear toward the woman's phone conversation.

The woman spoke loudly, as if the lodge was right next door. They could have heard her without the phone.

"This is Beatrice Mellon, at the Chamber of Commerce. Who is this?" She waited a moment and then shook her head. "I don't know you. You must be new. No. I know everybody in this town and I don't know you. You must be seasonal, dear. Well it doesn't matter. Do you know who Jack Landis is? … Good. Is he up there?"

Alice pretended to be preoccupied with a brochure, but a nervous moment later, replaced it on the table and glanced out the window.

She froze. He passed by the picture window, walking briskly. It was the same man she'd picked up on the highway the night before! Dr. Landis! His dark clothes fluttered in the wind. His hair was blowing wildly. He looked about warily, like an animal searching for something. Then he saw her. He stopped, waved and flashed a crooked gash of a grin.

Alice's heart beat wildly. She hurried to the door, yanked it open and burst outside. As she stepped down onto the sidewalk, the world fell into a dizzying silence, as though she'd been dropped from a great height into a bottomless canyon. She could almost feel the world spinning on its axis. She saw a merry-go-round of blurry images.

86

Then he was gone! He just disappeared! The streets were silent, as if the life had been sucked from them. Completely empty. No crowds of people, no cars, no blinking Christmas lights. Just blowing snow.

A cold blast of wind whipped across her face, scattering her hair. She jerked her chin in the direction of the sound of the retreating resonance of his footsteps, gradually trailing away into silence. But he wasn't there.

She closed her eyes, feeling a throbbing fear.

When she opened them, Beatrice Mellon stood in the doorway, looking at her, perplexed and concerned. "Are you all right?"

The crowds had returned, the cars, the blinking lights, the distant sound of *Jingle Bells* wafting out onto the streets from the bookstore nearby.

Alice swallowed. "I'm... yes... I'm fine."

Beatrice looked doubtful. "Are you sure?"

Alice was still distracted. "... Of course. I'll just go..."

Alice walked away, numbly, leaving her half-consumed cappuccino and Jack's business card on the reception table next to the brochures.

She gradually pulled herself together. She wanted to get out of town as quickly as possible. Get to Holbrook and to safety. Her pace took on urgency, and despite the cold, she was perspiring.

Inside her car, she rested her forehead on the rim of the steering wheel, struggling to come to terms with what had just happened to her. Was she ill? Was she hallucinating? Perhaps it was her blood sugar. She hadn't had a physical in over a year. Maybe it was the stress she'd been under. Maybe it was the one hundred things she had to do before the wedding pressing down upon her. The details—so many details—just with food alone! It seemed as if everyone had e-mailed her with their dietary restrictions and requests. The vegetarians, the vegans, the fish eaters, the garlic lovers, the garlic haters, the lactose intolerant, the diabetics, the meat eaters who hated the vegetarians, the vegetarians who hated the meat eaters, the kosher meals, the meals for the kids: spaghetti with meat sauce, spaghetti without meat sauce. Pizza without cheese! Pizza with extra cheese and no meat. And Philip wanted the adult food to be gourmet, no matter what the dietary restrictions were and who had requested them. She was so tired of looking at menus! And then there was the shop. She had to make a decision about that, and soon. She was so tired of thinking about it! She tried to take a deep breath and exhale slowly, but even that didn't help. She had to stop worrying!

She started the car and edged out of the tight parking space into lethargic traffic, purposely not looking at the sidewalks. She didn't want to know who the man was. She didn't want to know why he kept showing up! She just wanted to get back to Philip.

She followed the signs to the highway, relieved when, in her rearview mirror, the town slowly faded away and traffic thinned, as vehicles withdrew to roads leading to the ski resort or their homes. It would be easy driving now. No more turnoffs. No more exploration. No more solving mysteries. No more detours.

A few minutes later, Alice saw a young girl hitchhiking. Alarmed, she slowed down to get a better look at her. She was 14 or 15, wearing a short black leather jacket, tight jeans molded to her hips, and a brown cowboy hat, with long blond hair spilling out from it. Alice had hitch-hiked once when she was that age, desperate to get to a friend's house, and an older man had picked her up. He started caressing her arm as soon as she got in the car, asking her where she'd like to go, in a creepy seductive voice. She could still remember the panic and the nausea she felt... and then the relief when he finally stopped at a light and she could bolt from the car. She ran back home, swearing she'd never hitchhike again.

The hitchhiker turned her back to the oncoming traffic and kept walking, unaware that Alice had decelerated. She was tall and loose-limbed, walking with her left arm extended up and her thumb pointed at the sky.

Alice passed her, pulled over and stopped. The girl hurried toward the car and opened the door.

"Hey," she said, poking her head into the car. "How far you going?"

"I'm going to Holbrook."

"Oh, good." The girl climbed in and closed the door. "I'm just going to Tylerville. About ten miles up."

Alice turned back onto the highway and accelerated.

"Cold out there," the girl said, folding her arms tightly.

Alice glanced over, noticing a little diamond stud in the side of her nose and three golden earrings in her left ear. "Do you do this often?" Alice asked.

The girl looked at her with the cold, bored eyes of the young.

Alice got the message. "You live in Meadow Green?"

"Yes... trapped like an animal."

"It's a pretty town. Must be gorgeous in the spring and autumn," Alice said.

The girl shrugged. "Where are you from?"

"New York."

The girl lit up. "New York City!?"

Alice nodded.

"That's so cool. That's where I'd like to live. Did you grow up there?"

"No, Cincinnati. But I've lived in New York for about seven years."

"As soon as I get out of high school, that's where I'm going. This town is such bullshit, you know. Tourists everywhere... Rich people with their big houses and big money showing off and shit."

"You have friends in Tylerville?"

"Yeah, my boyfriend, Evan. He's sixteen."

"How old are you?"

Alice got the look again. "Whose mother are you?" the girl asked, with an edge.

Alice swiftly studied the girl's pretty, thin face. There was something about this girl that touched Alice. Maybe it was the golden eye shadow and snappy blue eyes that flashed with recklessness and innocence, or the projected cool aloofness that Alice recognized and knew so well, since she had practiced it herself for many years—still used it sometimes. The wind had whipped up the pink in the girl's cheeks, but her skin was pure white; lips full, glossed with light red lipstick and slightly puckered with indifference.

Alice turned away from her and smiled. "I'm nobody's mother. Does your mother know you're seeing this guy?"

This time Alice got the look of impatience. "I need a ride, not a lecture. Okay?"

"... Okay..." Alice paused. "Why didn't your boyfriend pick you up?"

"His parents won't pay for his car insurance. Costs a fortune. He's working at a used car lot to make money."

"Aren't there buses to Tylerville?"

"I hate buses." She examined the car. "Nice car."

"Thanks."

"Is it yours or your husband's?"

"Mine. I'm not married… yet."

"Smart."

"Why?"

"Marriage is so bogus."

"Bogus?"

"Most of my friends' parents are divorced, or they never married."

"And yours?"

She lifted her left shoulder. "What do you do?"

"I have a shop. A gift shop."

The girl's eyes glittered with engagement. "Cool. That's nice."

Alice smiled. "Yes… nice. What do you want to do when you move to New York?"

The girl didn't hesitate. "Write. I want to be a poet and novelist."

"Really. Are you writing now?"

She nodded, shyly. "Poems and some stories."

"Do you have any poems memorized? Any you want to recite?"

The girl shifted her weight uncomfortably. "No…"

"I studied the piano when I was young," Alice said.

"I love music," the girl said. "I play the guitar some."

Alice felt a growing affection for the girl. "How do you plan on getting back to Meadow Green tonight?"

"I'll hitchhike."

Alice held her tongue, even though she wanted to give this girl a lecture. She felt nervous for her, and now that she had taken her on as a passenger, somewhat responsible. Alice glanced out the window. Shadows darkened under skies scattered with broken clouds. "Is your boyfriend comfortable with you hitchhiking like this?"

She shrugged, then nodded, silent.

Alice faced the road, uneasy, lowering her eyes. "By the way, my name's Alice."

The girl looked over, dropping some of her wary stiffness. "I'm Kristie."

Alice turned sharply. "Kristie?"

"Yes," Kristie said, noticing the sudden alarm in Alice's eyes.

"What's your last name, Kristie?" she said, struggling to keep her eyes on the road.

"… Landis..."

Alice's eyes clouded over. When Alice focused on Kristie, it was as if she were seeing her for the first time.

"What's the matter?" Kristie asked.

Alice shook away her anxiety. She could not believe this. How was it possible that of all the teenagers in this town, Alice had picked up Kristie Landis? "What time are you going back tonight? What time is your date over?"

"Why?"

"… It's just that… well I planned to have the car looked at, and I was going to do it in Tylerville anyway, then maybe look around at shops. How about if I give you my cell number and when you're finished with your date, call me… If it works out and I can take you back to Meadow Green, then I will. I was thinking of going back there anyway."

Kristie studied her, trying to understand.

Alice stumbled over words. "… For my shop. I mean, I might want to open a shop there. Here, in Meadow Green."

Kristie stared in disbelief. "Are you serious?"

"Yes…" Alice paused. "... And besides, I don't think it's a good idea for a girl like you—a very attractive young woman—to be out hitchhiking, especially at night."

Kristie sighed, angrily. "You are like... I don't know. It's like none of your damned business, you know! I've done this before!"

Alice kept her voice steady. "I don't care how many times you've done it. It's still dangerous." She paused. "I had a very scary thing happen to me when I hitchhiked once. It can be very dangerous. You're old enough to know that. Your parents would freak out if they knew."

Kristie looked away. "Bullshit! I can take care of myself."

"Okay, fine, bullshit, but do me a favor. Call me. If the timing is right, I'll take you back."

Kristie shook her head. "Hey, whatever. You want to give me a ride, so fine. Cool, I'll take it. It's cold out there. And the buses stop running at six. Fine."

Alice settled back into the seat. "Okay. I'll give you my number." She paused for a moment, wondering what she was doing and what she was going to tell Philip.

Alice turned into the gas station and parked away from the pumps, near the bathrooms. She took a pen and some paper from her purse and jotted down her cell number on one of her business cards. When she handed it to Kristie, she looked at the girl with cautious warmth. "So you'll call me...?"

"Sure... I guess so. Why not?"

Kristie got out and closed the door. Alice watched her serpentine across the damp cement, past the lusty, wandering eyes of three 30s or so gas station attendants, toward two awaiting teens: a boy and a girl. The girl, probably 16 or so, wore bell-bottom jeans and a maroon oversized jacket. She was a lithe beauty, with short, dyed, bright red hair, long golden hoop earrings and an aura of corrupted innocence. She smoked as if it were an act of rebellion.

The boy was a study in black: black hair, eyes, clothes. He looked back at Alice with dark suspicion. His hair was swept sloppily to the side; his eyes hard, a little bored; his energy full of unpredictability and unrest. There was no denying that he had a seething sexuality that young girls always seemed to find attractive. Alice remembered Vic Sharp. He had been the same type and when Alice was 16, he made her weak in the knees, as well as the head.

Alice drove away reluctantly. What would Jack Landis do if he knew his daughter was with those two "friends"? Did he know? Would he care? Should he know?

Alice started back to Meadow Green, to the Mythic Ski Resort, not even trying to make sense of it all.

CHAPTER 8

Alice found the two-lane meandering road to the Mythic Ski Resort, driving past dairy farms, covered bridges and clear streams, finally climbing into high mountains. Golden light from pierced clouds bathed the road and slid across the coated forests, revealing distant ski trails, rolling hills and pastures below. As she looked ahead, she could almost hear the soft grinding whistle of the ski lift. She remembered skiing with Philip in Colorado last winter, trying new trails that were groomed and gnarly, feeling her tired knees and the icy cold wind across her face. She recalled the exhilaration of speed, danger and excitement as she sliced through glimmering snow, plunging down to the pasture below like a wild thing escaping from the restless hands of everyday life. There were no thoughts, no obligations and no time, just reactions and play. Though she wasn't a great skier, she had improved quickly in the two years she'd dated Philip, and he'd been surprised. She wondered if Jack skied.

The wind moaned past her window and she turned up the heat, suddenly feeling a twittering anxiety. It was after 3 o'clock. She hoped Jack would still be there when she arrived. Then, on second thought, she hoped he wouldn't. That way she wouldn't have to decide whether to tell him what Kristie was doing.

Twenty minutes later, she entered the resort's congested parking lot and found a narrow space behind the main lodge. Outside, she stepped carefully toward the lodge, finding a shoveled path that led around mounds of plowed snow, past boisterous young men with skis swung over their shoulders, and a family of four searching the lot for their parked car.

She arrived at the grand porch, supported by massive brown Doric columns. It was strung with white Christmas lights, as were the gutters and the eves of the Great Clubhouse and all the surrounding trees. Two large wreaths with red velveteen bows hung on either side of the great oak door, where a steady stream of people emerged and entered, wearing red, yellow and white ski jackets and colored caps. Alice ascended the stairs and slipped inside.

The Great Clubhouse was modeled after a vintage ski lodge with high thick crossbeams and a raging stone fireplace. An elegant Douglas fir, flashing colored lights, stood in a room that was filled with memorabilia, including a flexible flyer sled, wooden skis, and hand-painted 1950s ski murals of downhill racers and mountain landscapes. The atmosphere was sharply festive. Groups sat near the fire in swallow-you-up chairs and couches, sipping drinks, bantering about the day on the slopes, absently watching others shuffle in and out from the nearby ski shop and restaurant. Kids danced and bounced about like rubber toys and no one seemed to care.

Alice went to the front desk; she was met by a young, short-haired blond, with tired eyes and a flash of horsy upper gums.

"Hello," she said. "Can I help you?"

Alice unbuttoned her coat and glanced about, uncertainly. "Yes... well... I..."

"Yes?" the girl asked, a bit impatiently.

Alice hadn't thought about what she'd do when she actually arrived. Her only game plan had been to find Jack. After that, she hadn't a clue. But somehow, asking for him now didn't seem quite right. What if this girl knew Jack? It would be very awkward if she called for him. What then? What would Alice say? I've read your diary. Your daughter is hitchhiking and running around with lowlifes?

Alice pointed toward the restaurant. "That's the restaurant, isn't it?"

The girl scratched her pug nose. "Yes, that's the Nordic Restaurant."

Alice pretended surprise. "Oh, the Nordic Restaurant. Thank you. I'll just go over there... have a bite," she said with an apologetic smile.

The girl turned away toward a male colleague and gently rolled her eyes.

The Nordic Restaurant was nearly empty, with just two or three tables finishing a late lunch. The walls were knotty pine, the tables and chairs oak; tall windows offered a clear view of soaring woodlands, ski trails and a far-off mountain lake.

A stout man in his late 40s, with a heavy face, a sad-looking mustache and patchy dark hair, approached her. His dark pants sagged; his red ski sweater, with embroidered Santa Claus, was tight and unflattering. "Having lunch?" he asked, slightly curt, with green elsewhere eyes.

"Well... just some coffee?" Alice asked.

"There's a snack bar downstairs," he said. "Plenty of coffee and eats down there."

Alice decided to be creative. "I thought I heard pounding or something?"

"Pounding?"

"Yes, construction or something."

He turned defensive. "Well, yes… I mean, there's always something that needs work around here… I can't help that."

"I understand," Alice said. "I have a little shop. Same thing."

Her words gave him grateful permission to vent. "I was mopping up water this morning as it spurted from a hole in the second-floor ceiling of a room across the way. Just had the damned room renovated. By the time I got there the water had had plenty of time to ruin a beautiful brand new parquet floor. It also took down part of the ceiling. What a damned mess! Damned contractors messed up the plumbing. Don't want to own up to it."

"What a shame," Alice said, genuinely concerned.

He was lost in an intoxicated frustration. "So I call the contractor, 'cause he's a licensed plumber. Not that he will ever actually show up or send another licensed plumber: no, no, no… he's too busy. He's gonna send me the plumber's assistant. Doesn't matter how small or big the job, the assistant is guaranteed to come and do the job then hand me a bill that buckles my knees. But I'm not just paying for the work he did but for the boss's overhead—his insurance, payroll tax, office supplies, coffee, snacks, whatever. But I'm not payin' for this one. They're gonna eat this! These guys drive me nuts! So I told them to go to hell. I got my own man and I'll send them my bill."

Alice backed away, and the man suddenly "came to." His face fell into an apology. "I'm sorry, Miss… I didn't mean to go off like that. It's just been a bad day. This is our busiest season… and…" He pointed to the ceiling, to some brown water streaks. "And now I've got a big problem on the roof that has to be fixed before this roof caves in." He threw up his hands. "What-a-ya gonna do?"

"I understand," Alice said.

"But you're here for a good time, not to hear my complaining." He extended his hand. "I'm Stan. I'm one of the owners."

Alice reached and they shook limply. "Alice."

He indicated toward a table near a window. "Have a seat over there, Alice. I'll bring you some coffee."

They started toward it. "So you found someone to fix the problem?" Alice asked.

"I was lucky… I got the best guy around. He knows everything and has the best people. Can do it all. I would have had him do the work in the first place, but he's always booked up. It's costing me big time, but I know it'll be done right this time."

"What's his name?" she said, offhandedly.

He was gently surprised by the question. "… Jack Landis."

Alice nodded, took off her coat and sat at the table. "Well, good luck, Stan," Alice said.

Stan suddenly seemed to see her for the first time. His eyes filled with pleasure and he stood with adolescent awkwardness. "Yes… thank you Alice. You just take it easy now, and I'll get you some coffee."

After he'd returned and poured her cup, he hesitated. Alice's cell phone rang. It startled them both. She retrieved it from her purse as Stan turned and shambled away.

"Alice? It's Roland."

"Roland! I was going to call you. What's up?"

"I just wanted to let you know that we're busy as hell. People are buying candles like there's a blackout! You should have left a month ago."

"Thanks. Does this call mean you need help?"

"Yeeesss! I can't handle it alone."

"Okay, call your friend... Juan. You didn't have to get permission for that."

"Hey, I know we don't need to be paying another salary, but…"

She cut him off. "Do it, Roland! Call him!"

"He'll want a whole day. Not just a few hours."

"Give it to him!"

"Okay. You doin' good?"

"I have no idea. I'm like… I don't know," Alice said.

"Have you lost your focus?" Roland teased.

"Oh, shut up!"

After Alice hung up, she took a sip of her coffee, cheered by the good news. Maybe the shop would make it after all.

As she was draining the last of her coffee and listening to tinny Christmas carols over the scratchy overhead speakers, she grew progressively edgy. Nothing she was doing was rational. And she was a rational person. She prided herself on being rational.

She got up. She'd find a room somewhere for the night and wait for Kristie's call. On the way back to Meadow Green, she'd warn Kristie again about the dangers of hitchhiking and leave it at that. The rest was up to Jack. Kristie was right. It was none of her business. She'd leave for Holbrook at sunup.

The dining room was empty when Alice paid the cashier for the coffee. She left, passing the ski shop. It was swarming with people, but she decided to take a quick look around, so she squeezed in and started for the rack of skis, examining the snowboards, poles, jackets and goggles along the way.

A tall, attractive, long-haired blond man in his 30s eased toward her, with a loose, confident smile and lean athletic body. His fitted white sweater and tight jeans were effective in projecting a sexy whimsy. "Can I help you find anything?" he asked.

She looked up, uninterested. "No, just looking."

"I can get you a great deal on anything. I know the owner."

"Really? So do I."

"You do?" he asked, surprised.

"Sure. Stan."

He was undaunted. "Okay. I can get you an incredible deal on skiing lessons. Forty percent off."

"No thanks."

"Free first lesson and fifty percent off the rest."

"Stan may not approve."

"Stan's got nothing to do with it. I'm the ski instructor," he said, proudly.

Alice looked away. "I see…"

"We have some great trails. No better alpine skiing in the state. And it's fantastic exercise."

Alice heard a soft deep voice from behind. "Nordic is better for you physically, Dan."

Alice turned to gaze up into the smooth dark eyes of a man well over six feet with wide shoulders, a square jaw, and medium black hair which curled over the top of his ears. He wore jeans, brown Timberland boots and a red and black flannel shirt. There was an earthy, dusty look about him, as if he were a cowboy just back from a day of riding the range.

She was caught by an unexpected excitement. Trying for a blank but friendly expression, she stared at him. His eyes, clear and cheerless, held her for a time, exploring her, before he looked away. All at once she was self-conscious and fluttery, as she watched him examine a set of skis.

"That's a lot of bull, Jack. Nordic is a lot of hard work, without the thrills."

Jack shrugged. "It's the ultimate cardiovascular workout, there are no lift fees, the scenery's beautiful, and it's easier on the environment."

Alice's eyes widened, almost imperceptibly. "Jack?" she asked.

Jack turned. "Yes…"

"Jack Landis," Dan said.

Alice was slightly startled, as if awakened from a dream.

Dan stepped between them. "I'm Dan Wallace," he said, turning jittery with concern that he was losing Alice. He waited for Alice's response.

She ignored him and faced Jack. He wasn't what she had expected. Nothing like she'd pictured him. She remembered a line from the diary. *"Kristie is a beauty, like her Momma. Sure didn't get it from me."*

This Jack had a kind of sturdy elegance, like a tall tree that bends easily in the wind and achieves grace in stillness and solitude. But there was a contradiction: his expression was somber, his eyes alluring but disconnected. She sensed a reserved energy that restricted him. And yet, there was something electric about him that stirred her; restless fireworks went off in her chest. She turned away, feeling absurd.

"You ski here often?" Dan asked Alice.

Alice wiped her damp forehead. "No… It's my first time."

"Really," Dan said. He looked at Jack. "When's the last time you skied, Jack?"

"... Long time."

"I see your son up here snowboarding. He's good."

Jack nodded and reached for a thin set of blue skis, made for Nordic. "I'm thinking of taking my daughter on a cross-country trip. Maybe buy her these for Christmas." He looked directly at Alice. "What do you think? Think she'll like them?"

Alice folded her hands, avoiding his eyes. "... I don't really know your daughter."

Jack sighed. "Well, she's not much on outdoor things. She's at the age where everything I suggest is stupid. She just makes an ugly face and says NO."

"She's a pretty one though, Jack," Dan said, with a frisky expression.

Jack's severe eyes pinned him with disapproval.

Dan retreated, folding his arms. "I... I mean for a young girl."

"I've never gone cross-country skiing," Alice said.

"You'll hate it," Dan said. "Wait until you get to that first big hill. You'll wish you had a ski lift or a rope."

Jack replaced the skis.

Alice said, "Coming from her father, I'm sure she'd love the skis. I would have."

Jack gave her a last unhurried glance, but was mute. To Alice's disappointment he turned and edged his way out of the shop.

"Jack doesn't talk much," Dan said. "I'm surprised he spoke at all... and especially about his daughter."

Alice shifted her weight, thinking.

"I'll take you," Dan said.

Alice blinked, watching Jack's retreating figure. "What?"

"I'll take you cross-country skiing. You'll love it."

"You just said I'd hate it."

"You can't believe everything I say."

"I believe that," she said starting for the door.

Dan followed her. "I didn't mean it that way."

"I've got to go," Alice said, picking her way through the crowd of customers.

"How about dinner tonight? I know a great place."

"I have plans."

"Tomorrow or next week?"

"I'm getting married."

Dan laughed. "Yeah, right, like I can believe everything you say."

Outside the shop, Alice stopped and faced him. "I really do have to go, Dan. It was nice meeting you."

He screwed up his lips in frustration, lifted his hands, and then dropped them to his side. "Okay. If you change your mind, I'll be in the ski shop, pining away."

Alice looked at him in mock pity, then swung into her coat and left the lodge.

Outside, a light snow was falling across a gray world. Descending the stairs, Alice thought of Kristie and the menacing-looking boy she'd left her with. She felt a bleakness, an irrational twist of fear that tugged at her. She dearly hoped Kristie would call her for the ride back home.

As she approached her car, she saw Jack a short distance away, loading tools into the back of a blue GMC Safari Van. She saw LANDIS CONSTRUCTION printed on the side in black letters. She paused, hoping he'd notice her. He did and nodded, then turned away preoccupied, returning to work.

Alice opened her car door and stopped, suddenly getting an idea. She closed the door and walked toward him. "Finished for the day?" Alice asked.

"Nope."

Alice waited for more, but it didn't come. "I'm looking for a place to stay tonight. Know of any?"

"What about here? Stan probably has an extra room somewhere."

"I was hoping for some place a little more quiet."

Jack scratched his head, thinking. "I'm going over to The Broadmoore now. It's a twenty-four-room Victorian mansion that's been turned into a bed and breakfast. You might get lucky. I can call Nora Taylor; see if she can take you."

"Don't bother. Since you're going anyway, can I follow you?"

He considered her words. "Okay... but she may be all filled up."

"Then I'll find something else close by."

He closed the back door. "All right."

Jack was easy to follow. He took the curves carefully and let the more aggressive drivers pass, decreasing his speed if Alice fell behind. Despite the steady flow of traffic and the many thoughts sliding in and out of her mind, she felt the peace of the mountains as she drifted in and out of shadows. She was comforted by the old bare trees and protruding rocks, quiet witnesses to the relentless passing of humans and their many dramas. But, ironically, they also made her feel vulnerable—and as fragile as the tiny snowflakes that blew randomly and shattered into her windshield.

At the base of the mountain, a helicopter rattled over them and drifted away into a smudge of gray clouds, lying heavy and low on the horizon. It startled the stillness and seemed out of place.

They drove another 5 miles until they turned left onto a secluded winding drive between tall, snow-covered pines, and then continued until they arrived at a beautiful salmon-stoned Victorian mansion, with extensive porches, soaring gables and many bay windows. The white and burgundy sign in front said *The Broadmoore.*

The parking lot at the rear of the house was nearly full, but they managed to find two parking spaces. Jack came over as Alice emerged.

"It's beautiful," Alice said, taking in the wooded surroundings, gazebos and quiet pond.

Jack shoved his hands into his dark blue parka and nodded. "Looks full," Jack said. "Hope there's room."

They started toward the entrance against a cold wind. As they walked, Alice felt a pleasurable agitation; a combination of guilt and exhilaration that made her a touch light-headed.

"This place was built in 1895," Jack said. "Master craftsman from England, Italy and the U.S. helped construct it. It's about 10,000 square feet." He pointed to the woods. "Over five acres of woods, gardens and lawn. It was restored in 1986. The Taylors did a great job."

As he spoke, Alice saw his eyes glitter for the first time; his face came alive.

"You work here often?"

"As much as they'll have me. I'm helping to restore one of the five bedrooms. Nora rents out the other rooms for private parties, wedding receptions, business luncheons, that sort of thing."

"You have people working for you?"

"Only six. They're good. I can trust them. And I have my son."

"Your son?" Alice asked.

"Yeah. Andrew. He's here, laying some tiles in the bathroom we're working on."

Alice turned, surprised. "Here?"

"Yeah. He's at that age where he hates everything except computers, skateboarding and snowboarding—anything where he can show off. He thinks construction work is beneath him."

"How old is he?"

"Thirteen."

Alice looked away and tried to sound casual. "And your wife?"

They approached the stairs. Jack frowned down at the ground. "She's dead."

They climbed the stairs and entered the marble and alabaster foyer, strung with pine and holly garlands and decorated with poinsettias. As they entered the main hall, Alice was spellbound by the broad, two-story black walnut grand staircase and the collection of elegant Victorian furnishings.

Nora Taylor, a plump woman with a toothy smile and a generous mound of black-and-gray-beauty-shop sculpted-hair, came through pocket doors from the Library. She wore a long burgundy and cream dress, lots of rings and flat brown shoes. She greeted Jack warmly and then turned to Alice.

"This is Alice, Nora; she's looking for a room," Jack said.

Nora's brow knotted. "I'm sorry, but we're completely full."

"Well, it was worth a try," Alice said, resigned. "It's such a beautiful place. Can I look around?"

"Sure!" Nora said, her face coming to life. "Jack, take her for a little tour on your way upstairs. And be sure to show her the beautiful loveseat in the Sitting Room."

Jack hesitated, and then he wiped his lips with the back of his hand, unzipped his jacket and led Alice toward the dining room, across parquet floors. He pointed out the splendid oak paneling, a built-in buffet, a window-seat and a tile fireplace. Alice commented on the stunning crystal chandelier and stained-glass windows, depicting nymphs, shepherds and fat little cupids, wings fluttering, bows cocked, arrows in flight toward the heart.

In the plush Sitting Room, with velvety burgundy walls, Jack gestured toward the Victorian couch and loveseat. "The frames of the sofa, loveseat and chairs are solid beechwood," he said.

Nora had followed them and cut in swiftly. "Jack did all the finishing on the sofa and loveseat... hand-finishing. He sanded, stained, hand-rubbed and sealed. He did a fantastic job, didn't he?"

Alice went to them, running her hand along the luxurious burgundy upholstery. The crests and arms of the sofa and loveseat were intricately carved with the traditional Victorian rose and leaf design. "Yes, he did. They're beautiful."

Jack turned his uncomfortable gaze toward the fireplace.

"Take her upstairs, Jack," Nora said.

Jack hesitated, standing awkwardly, a little off-balance. His eyes darted about, nervously. "Yeah... Okay," he said.

He took her to the third floor first. They stepped across thick red carpet and passed one of the suites that had an open door. It was decorated in vintage Victorian style, with a king-sized bed, two private balconies and a state-of-the-art Jacuzzi.

"All the rooms have beautifully carved mantels, built-in armoires and marble sinks," Jack said proudly, as if the place were his own.

On the second floor they entered the unfinished maple bedroom he was restoring. The furniture and floor were covered with drop-cloths; the walls were half-papered in a quiet green and white floral pattern. There were paint cans pushed in the corners.

"Andrew?" Jack called.

Andrew came yawning out of the bathroom with a weary glumness. He was tall and trim like his father, even in floppy clothes. His black hair was stiff, his blue eyes transfixing, his regal face chiseled and proud. He looked like Jack. He ignored his father and, when he leveled his eyes on Alice, his body suddenly lost its lethargy.

"How's it going?" his father asked.

He shrugged.

"What does that mean?" Jack said, with the flavor of a command.

"It's done," Andrew said, barely opening his mouth. "Just finishing up. The bathroom door isn't hanging right. It's getting stuck."

"Maybe too much moisture in there. Did you plane it?"

"Yeah. Off the top."

"What about the hinges? They have to be lined up perfectly. Have to be absolutely perpendicular or gravity's going to pull the door off balance."

"Okay, I'll fix it."

Jack gestured toward Alice. "This is Alice."

"Hi Andrew," Alice said, reaching for his hand. They shook.

Andrew's eyes moved slowly, unsure. He looked at his father for some explanation.

"I'm showing her around," Jack said, quickly. "She was looking for a room here, but Nora's booked up."

Andrew looked down at his feet. "She could stay here."

"Here?" Jack said, surprised. "It's a mess. Not finished."

"Wouldn't take much. All we have…"

Jack broke in. "Andrew, there's no way she…"

Andrew blushed.

Alice cut in abruptly. "I would love it," she said.

Jack looked at her. "But…"

"I'm sure Nora wouldn't mind having the business."

Jack ran a thoughtful hand along his shadow of a beard.

Andrew looked pleased with himself and then went for humor. "Hey, you got brand new tiles in the bathroom."

Jack lifted an eyebrow. "Okay… if it's all right with Nora, it's certainly okay with me."

As they started downstairs, Jack turned to Andrew. "You heard from Kristie?"

"No."

"She was supposed to call me an hour ago. Can't reach her on her cell. You talk to her?"

"Tried. Got her voicemail."

Jack looked worried.

Alice descended the stairs in mute indecision. She could tell them both right now that she had just picked up a hitchhiker named Kristie, and then ask, very casually, if it could be *their* Kristie. But then maybe Jack already knew that Kristie hitchhiked. Maybe it wasn't a big deal to him. Maybe it was safe in this area.

But maybe it wasn't, and Jack would get very upset and go looking for Kristie. Maybe he'd over-react. And how would Kristie respond? Being independent and rebellious, she might do something even worse, like run away.

Alice's mind settled on a final hunch: Kristie seemed to trust Alice; they'd made a connection; she felt it. She'd wait, and if Kristie called her, then she'd warn her that she was going to tell her father, for her own good. And if she *didn't* call her, then she'd find some way to tell Jack; maybe even call him anonymously.

As they stepped onto the landing of the first floor, Alice struggled with doubt and contradiction. What was she doing? She felt as though parts of herself had shattered and pieces were falling away. Unglued, is the word that arose. She felt unglued! How could she ever pick up those pieces and glue herself back together? She felt helpless with indecision. After taking some deep breaths, she gathered her thoughts.

She'd return to the gas station, meet Kristie as planned, and then drop her at the house. That would be the end of it! That would be the end of this whole silly, adolescent adventure. She had no business being here in the first place and certainly no business getting involved in the lives of this family.

But Jack? What about Jack?

She heard him call her name.

"Alice...?"

Their eyes met.

CHAPTER 9

After Jack and Andrew explained the plan to Nora, she agreed to let Alice stay in the partially renovated room. Alice registered while Jack and Andrew rolled up the drop-cloths, stored paint and varnish cans in the closets, moved furniture and repaired the bathroom door. Nora sent her 17-year-old niece, Shannon, to dust, vacuum, make the bed and clean the bathroom. She was a nervous girl, slouchy and thin, with reddish hair in a sheep dog haircut. She was unwittingly careless and noisy, especially in the company of two attractive men, and she stumbled about the room like an artless dancer. Between the three of them, the house took on the sounds of battle, with pounding, vacuuming, scraping and thumping.

In the gold parlor downstairs, curious guests cast upward glances as they snapped out newspapers and magazines or flicked through iPads, registering mild irritation that their peaceful retreat was being disturbed.

After Alice had checked in, Nora invited her to have afternoon tea and cookies in the plush sitting room. "Since your room isn't ready, we can get to know each other," Nora said. Alice was a bit distracted at first, but soon became engaged in Nora's narrative about the history of the house. But Alice also noticed that Nora seemed preoccupied and anxious, as if their conversation were only a distraction from her real subject of interest, and she was waiting for the perfect moment to gush forth the true passion of her heart. Finally, that moment seemed to come, perhaps because Nora felt she'd prepared the ground with enough "filler" to feel comfortable "shooting from the hip." She leaned forward, conspiratorially, placed her hands in her lap and locked her small, earnest brown eyes on Alice's face.

"Have you known Jack long?" she asked.

"Oh, no," Alice said, quickly. "I just ran into him at the ski lodge."

Nora nodded knowingly. "I see..." She seemed to be searching for words. "Now please don't think I'm just an old gossip, although I am, but I've known Jack for a long time, about 10 years and, well, it's just that, in all that time, as far as I know, he's only been out two or three times with a woman and it never came to anything. I've even tried to set him up a couple of times myself. My husband, Leonard, God rest his soul, did too, but Jack just didn't seem interested in any of those women. So, naturally, when I saw you come in with him, it was just kind of a surprise."

Alice took a sip of peppermint tea. "Like I said, I just met him."

"But he's comfortable with you, Alice," she said confidently.

"Comfortable?" Alice asked, unsteadily, her eyes blinking fast.

"You have to understand, Alice, I'm the mother of three boys and two girls, all grown, most happy, except for one girl and one boy. God help them, and me. Anyway, my point is, as a parent you want your children to be happy, more than you want breath for yourself. And I knew right off when they brought that 'special someone' home whether there was a true match or not. I knew when that girl or boy was the right one for my kids. Call me psychic. Call me odd. I don't deny it's a talent. I don't deny it's a gift. I was dead-on with all five of those kids and I told Leonard. He was, by the way, a believer in me because he'd seen the results. Even said I should go into the matchmaking business, which I've since considered—you know—with all the guests that come and go. Maybe set up a website. I love computers. Could sit behind one all day just clicking away at nothing." She threw up her hand, as if to stop herself from blathering on. "But listen to me, just an old windbag, quacking like a wild duck."

Nora drew even closer, so that Alice smelled the rose hip tea on her breath. Her voice was breathy and private and there was a merry twinkle in her eyes. "Jack likes you."

Alice straightened.

"Oh, he may not know it himself yet, but he does. You can take it to the bank. I've never been wrong. Never. Not once."

Alice took in the thought, and then carefully lowered her rose-colored tea cup to the saucer, pretending to be admiring a picture on the wall. But her hand trembled and Nora noticed.

"Are you enjoying the sugar cookies?" Nora asked.

"Yes."

"Kids from the high school sent them over to thank me for a donation I made to the glee club. And the fudge. Very rich, that fudge."

114

Alice turned her face toward the window, where daylight was fading into dull gray. The snow had stopped. She stood and looked toward the ceiling. The room had fallen into a sudden silence. Alice took the opportunity. "They're probably finished up there. I think I'll go lie down for a while. Thanks for the tea."

Alice started out of the room. Nora pushed up and started after her. "Alice…"

Alice stopped, but only partially turned.

"Have I upset you?"

"… I'm just tired."

Nora folded her chubby hands, penitent. "Alice… It's just that I think Jack's pretty special. He's a good man. So generous with his time and skills. Been a good father to his kids. You should see Kristie, his daughter. What a beauty. But Jack's just kind of closed off his heart. Closed off a big part of himself. I've tried to talk to him like a mother, but he won't listen. Something happened to him years ago… something very sad and he's never really recovered. I think he's tried, mostly for the kids, but I can see, he just can't seem to shake off those old ghosts. When I see you with him, well, I think there's a chance."

Alice faced her. "Nora, I'm… I'm getting married in five days."

Nora's face sagged in disappointment. Finally, she nodded resigned, turned and went back to the office.

Alice climbed the stairs slowly, feeling like she'd suddenly doubled her weight. The whole thing was just too weird, she thought. Too fast, too unclear and too upsetting. What she needed was a nap and a little private time to sort everything out.

When Alice entered the room, she was astonished by the change. There was no doubt that the room was still a work in progress, but the unfinished quality somehow added a magnificent charm, like an incomplete masterpiece by a gifted artist. Even though there were bare patches of white on the walls and ceiling and a gentle smell of plaster, none of that really mattered. The room was filled with a kind of grace.

The soft colors were soothing; the thick down comforter on the canopied queen-sized bed beckoning; the glossy surfaces and deep green carpet, rippling from a fresh vacuum, were welcoming. Shannon, Andrew and Jack stood before her looking pleased and hopeful. Jack seemed to be the most nervous, and, unfortunately for Alice, that added another layer of appeal to his already magnificent good looks.

"I hope this will do," Jack said.

Alice smiled. "It's beautiful. I'm so glad you suggested it, Andrew."

Andrew grinned, shyly. "I think it looks pretty good," he said.

"Andrew can get your suitcase," Jack said.

"Thanks, but he's done enough. Nora said she has someone."

Shannon was the first to leave. She ducked and left like an intruder. Alice gently touched her arm and repeated her thanks as she passed. Shannon beamed.

Andrew gathered up a partially opened cardboard box filled with leftover tiles, passed his father a quick searching glance, then left.

Jack tucked the rolled up drop-cloth under his arm and started for the door. He stopped at the threshold. "I hope you'll be comfortable."

Alice's smile came and went too fast. She was sure it hadn't look sincere, and she'd wanted it to be. She tried to speak; the words got trapped.

Jack glanced at her with cautiously interested eyes, then left the room, closing the door behind him. Alice stared at the door for a moment, then raised her fists, threw back her head and yelled silently. "Ahhhh! What am I doing?" She began pacing the room frantically, worried and conflicted. "Here I am, staying in another room that is permeated with Jack Landis' desirable energy. How did that happen?"

When her bags arrived five minutes later, she had the presence of mind to find a tip for the wanting-to-please high school boy with wild blond hair that reminded her of an alfalfa field.

"My name's Ozzie," he said, as he dropped her suitcase near the armoire and placed her garment bag on the bed.

She smiled and handed him two dollars. "Thanks, Ozzie."

"Thank you!" he said, looking proud to have been of service.

Alice calmed herself by emptying the garment bag, and then lay down on the soft, deep comforter, puffed up on two pillows. For fifteen minutes, she resisted the temptation to reach for the diary, but her mind was playing possible scenarios with Jack; outrageous and guilty possibilities. Finally she gave in, got up, went to her suitcase, released the latches and rifled through it until she felt the smooth leathery texture. She extracted it slowly, as if it were some buried vice she was reluctantly raising from the dead. It was like a Pandora's Box that, if opened again, would surely spew out confusion and change— lovely, wonderful and awful change? She wondered.

She wilted a little. This silly diary was challenging her safe and planned life. Her "unexamined" life, her mother, the psychologist used to say. "Remember the old weird man Socrates," she would add with a wink. "The unexamined life is not worth living."

Alice stared up into the light-green canopy, remembering part of an old conversation she'd had with her mother a few months before her death. A conversation she'd long forgotten. But now their heart-to-heart talk was easily reproduced, in every detail, as if she and her mother had spoken only yesterday.

"Alice, why do you insist on living an unexamined life?"

"Mother, my life is fine. I don't need to analyze every action, thought and word. I just want to live my life."

"And how will you do that?" her mother asked.

"Look, mother, I know what I want out of life. I want to keep it simple. You always say to keep things simple. You always say Dad complicates his life too much."

"Well, I shouldn't say that about your father, but he does. Anyway, simple is good. What does that mean to you?"

"Oh Lord, Mom, I'm not one of your students or patients. I'm your daughter."

"Don't duck the question."

"Simple for me is being independent. I want a good paying job. I never want to be broke or have to depend on someone else for money."

"I can understand that. What else?"

"I want to be healthy."

"Of course you do. You shouldn't eat so many sweets."

"I've cut back."

"What else?"

"Oh, Mother!"

"Come on, Alice!"

"Okay, I want to meet a guy someday and get married."

Her mother stood. She'd been a tall, stately woman with rich, long, red hair, a broad face and deep green eyes. It was an open, honest face, brave to the very end, even when her once sturdy body broke down into quivering flesh and protruding bones. She laughed easily, and she had laughed then.

"What's so funny?"

Her mother arched back, laughing, and continued laughing, finally breaking into a cough because she was sick with cancer then, but the family didn't know it. "Allergies" two doctors had said.

"What's so damn funny, Mom?"

"Meet a guy and get married? Ha! Simple? Ha!" She waved a finger of warning in the air. "Love, if it comes, will never be simple."

"I didn't say love. I said meet a man and..." Alice stopped, realizing the trap. "Love is implied, Mother."

"Never implied! Never! Love wakes you up, disturbs you, frightens you. Demands of you! If it's real, it opens you and fills you with new life every day. It forces you to meet yourself every day. Meet a man? Yes, simple! But if you haven't taken the time to examine your life—to experience your own true worth—you won't recognize or understand love in yourself, or in anyone else. Maybe you'll get married. But it won't last. Perhaps you'll settle for someone safe and, since you won't really know what love is, you might mistake your love for real love. But then, in a short time, you'll realize your mistake. You'll soon be just another married couple, confused by what has happened. 'How could this happen?' you'll say. I see them every day, Alice, not communicating, not caring and not really loving. At the first true test, they crumble and run away, either literally or emotionally. And if it's emotionally, you'll live the life of the dead."

Alice lay back on the bed, drew the diary to her chest and kept it there until it grew warm. She blushed at the thought of having Jack close; could nearly feel his breath on her. She was dangling close to the edge of a precipice: she was a child in her mother's arms—a mother who was standing by the edge of that precipice. One part of her was the mother trying to keep her from danger while another part, that warm and anxious and exhilarated part, was doing her best to leap from those arms and plunge down the cliff.

"He's comfortable with you, Alice," she kept hearing Nora say.

Alice opened the diary to a random page. To her surprise, she noticed two pages were stuck together, near the middle. How had she missed that? She sat up and slid her thumb along the seam of the pages, gently separating them. She began to read.

Where does love come from? I never thought about stuff like this before I started writing in this thing. Certainly not before I met you. Stuff? (Find a better word, you'd say) Okay, how about "things" or "concepts"?

Love happened, that's all I know. I saw you then, and I see you now and I feel natural, with a kind of restless and happy "bigness", like the sea or the sky, that never seem to settle on completion because they're always too busy rediscovering themselves with light, color and clouds. You're my light, color and clouds, Darla.

I can just see my old high school English teacher trying to make sense out of that last sentence. I dare you, Ms. Mellon!

In an argument the other day, Saturday, you said I had ruined your life. I had trapped you into marriage, into giving me our children out of guilt. Later, you said you'd only said all that because you were angry; because you were tired and hadn't slept well.

I wonder if I captured you, perhaps put you on a pedestal where you'd rather not be. I wonder sometimes if I am even capable of inspiring you to be the kind of woman, the writer, you want to be. Is my love too stifling, too young, perhaps too adolescent for your mature inner life and ambitions? I don't know, Darla. Probably. I don't think so much, like you. Work is my thinking. Connecting to my work and the earth is my art.

Late tonight, as you finally drifted off to sleep, it finally came to me that maybe my love has been and is so selfish and all-consuming that I just assumed you loved me as much. I just assumed it! Thick-headed guy that I am! Then I really started to think… I mean, really think back a few years.

I thought about your father, who was so disappointed that you married me and not Thomas, the doctor from Chicago, that he wouldn't speak to me at the wedding. About your mother who had always believed that moving to Meadow Green from Chicago was the biggest mistake they ever made, and your marriage to me confirmed it. Then I thought about your terrible and awful relationship with your father. You only talked about it once, down by the pond on that hazy rainy April day, a few months after Andrew was born and sick with one of his many ear infections. You were so quiet and pale when you whispered out the whole painful event. It made me sick.

As hard as it is to write this, I do believe now that you wanted to run away from your family and I just happened to be there. I didn't believe it then, but I do now. And we both know you despised Thomas the doctor. I guess you probably thought I wasn't a bad sort. (You said that on our second date.) Not the brightest light on the Christmas tree, but maybe not too bad to look at deep into the night, like tonight. A very black night with no moon. Just bugs scratching and whistling in the dark.

Of course, I'll never tell you this and will never admit it to another living soul. I couldn't. I couldn't handle the truth out loud. But here... it stays a secret.

I will always love you and I will never apologize for that or feel sorry for myself that you don't have the same love for me. I don't care. My love for you just is, and nothing will ever take it away. And when I look at Kristie and Andrew, there's no joy or pleasure that can equal it—no heaven or paradise I can imagine that can come close.

As to your love for me? I'll take whatever you have to give. I have to. I can do no less. It keeps me breathing.

Where can I hide this damned diary, so no one will ever find it?

Alice closed the book slowly, wishing she'd never found it—never intruded on Jack's personal and intimate thoughts. She laid the diary aside, stretched her legs out and lay back, closing her eyes. Had Darla really died or did Jack just say that to close the door on any possible discussion of her?

God, how she needed a nap. Philip would call soon and what would she say?

To shut off her mind, she began counting from 1 to 6 repeatedly, until she drifted off to sleep.

It was Mozart's 40th Symphony that awakened her: her cell phone was ringing out tah-ta-tah, tah-ta-tah, tah-ta-tah-ta. In the darkness she rolled, reached, struggled and finally found her purse. Clumsily, with great effort, she snagged the phone and answered in a foggy, sleepy voice.

"Hello..."

There was a long pause.

Alice pushed up on her elbows. "Hello?"

"This is Kristie..."

Alice swung her legs to the floor and found the light switch. "Kristie! Yes. How are you?"

"Did I wake you?"

"No, no... well, yes I was just taking a little nap."

"I wasn't going to call. I mean, I was going to get the bus, but I missed it. I'm really late and my father's really going to be pissed off."

"What time is it?" Alice asked.

"Six-thirty. Are you still in Tylerville? Can you give me a lift?"

"I'm nearby. Just tell me where you are and I'll come get you."

Fifteen minutes later, Alice was driving toward Tylerville, wiping her still sleepy eyes, listening to her growling empty stomach, and peering into the darkness at the line of cars ahead, all probably on their way to Meadow Green for dinner or a movie.

At a stop light, she reached for her cell phone and was just about to call Philip when it rang. She looked at the lighted LCD and didn't recognize the number.

"Hello."

"Hello... Alice?"

"Yes," she said, not recognizing the voice.

"It's Jack Landis."

Alice felt a euphoric rush.

"Alice? Are you there?"

"I'm here, yes. I'm here... Jack." Just saying his name excited her.

"I hope you don't mind that I called you. I tried your room, but Nora said you had left. She got your number from the registration form. I know that's not proper, but..."

"No... fine... no problem."

She heard Jack clear his throat. "I'm just sort of... well... taking a wild chance that maybe you don't have anything planned for tonight and... well... wondered if you might like to have dinner?"

Alice was processing this disturbing and wonderful thought when she heard two beeps, which meant she was receiving another call. "Jack... can you hold just a moment? I'm getting another call."

"Should I call you back?" Jack asked.

"No, I'll just see who it is and call them back."

She pressed the gray button and answered. "Hello. This is Alice."

"Hey, sexy lady, where the hell are you?"

It was Philip! She struggled for composure. When she answered, her voice was much too forced and exaggerated with glee. "Philip... I was just thinking about you!"

"I'm glad to hear it."

"Where are you?" Alice asked, fighting anxiety.

"Where I thought you would be. Home. The roads weren't bad at all."

"Well, I'll be there soon," she said, immediately realizing she was headed for trouble.

"Good. How far away are you?"

Her voice became meek. "Well... I won't... be able to make it tonight."

Silence. "What?"

She suddenly remembered that Jack was on hold. "Philip, can I put you on hold a minute?"

She was just able to hear Philip's irritated voice saying "Alic..." when she switched to Jack.

"Jack?"

"Yes, I'm here."

His voice instantly calmed her and she felt a wonderful warmth in her chest. But then she also felt a throbbing, run-away guilt. She felt too many things! Where was her focus? Her mind was like a mass of gnarled wires. "Just make a decision, Alice," she thought.

"Alice?"

"Jack... I'd love to have dinner with you."

She heard him sigh gently into the phone. "Good... there's only one thing. My daughter's not home yet. I don't want to leave until she gets here. Can I call you back with a definite time? She should be here soon."

Alice squirmed. "Sure."

"Okay... Good. I'll call you."

Traffic fizzled away and the highway to Tylerville expanded into four lanes. She swerved into the left lane and raced ahead, checking her mirrors for police and traffic. She switched back to Philip. He was annoyed and flinty. "Alice, what is going on?"

Alice hunted for words, slouching in her seat. "I'll be there tomorrow, Philip. I'll tell you all about it."

"Tell me now. What the hell's going on?"

"I can't explain it on the phone. I'm leaving first thing in the morning and I should be there by eleven o'clock at the latest."

"We have things to do, Alice. The caterer wants a final count. We have to meet with the florist. All this snow is messing up the travel arrangements."

"I know. I know."

"Have you been drinking?"

"What!? No, of course not."

"This is the kind of thing my mother does. When times get the least bit challenging, she starts drinking. Trying to escape from everything."

"I'm not your mother, Philip."

"Then get over here. Jacinta keeps calling."

"I'll call her," Alice said. She heard the two beeps again. Someone else was calling. It could be Jack or Kristie. She grimaced. "Philip, can you hold for just a second? I have another call I have to take."

Philip exploded. "No, I'm not holding. The hell with it!"

He was gone.

Alice pulled into the right-hand lane and decelerated, collecting herself before taking the call.

"Hello?"

"It's Kristie. Are you almost here? My father is freaking out. My brother just called and told me that my father has a date or something. He hasn't been on a date in three years and he's like losing it! Can you please hurry?"

As panicky as she was, Alice couldn't help but smile. "Yes, Kristie, I'm hurrying. I'm almost there."

CHAPTER 10

Kristie was waiting at the same service station, alone, cowgirl hat on, hunched and still. As soon as she spotted the car, she broke for it, yanked open the door before Alice had come to a full stop, and threw herself inside, shuddering from the cold.

"Let's go!" she said, in an anxious voice, slamming the door.

Kristie's sweet perfume flooded the car. Alice reacted instinctively by wiggling her nose.

Kristie noticed. "My boyfriend gave it to me..." she said in quick defense. "He made me put it on. I didn't want to." Her mouth turned French-like: pink and puckered.

They drove for a while in silence. Kristie seemed listless, lost in her thoughts.

"How was the date?" Alice asked.

Kristie shrugged.

"Who's the other girl?"

"A friend."

"Does she have a boyfriend?"

Kristie's voice was strident. "You ask a lot of questions that are really none of your business!"

Alice retreated into silence. Kristie was obviously upset about something.

"So you were going to take the bus?" Alice asked, trying again.

"Yes."

"You weren't going to call me?"

"No."

"Well, at least you're honest. And I'm glad you didn't hitchhike."

She flicked her eyes at Alice then turned away again.

"Your father's pretty angry at you, huh?"

"Big deal. Just because he's like socially stunted, he thinks I should be too."

"Tell me about him."

"What about?"

"Anything."

"He's like at war with the world except when he's working. So he works all the time, and he wants us to be studying, or working around the house or on some boring project with him. I can't believe he's like going on a date tonight. I can't wait to find out who this woman is."

Alice's hands tightened on the steering wheel. She decided to probe a little. "What's your mother like?"

"My mother's dead," she said, heavily.

"I'm sorry."

"Don't be. It's life. It happens."

"What was she like?"

Kristie took her cowgirl hat off and rested it on her lap. "I don't remember much. She left us when I was five." She thought for a moment. "I mostly remember her gorgeous blond hair and breathy voice."

Alice waited for more.

"She was a writer, you know," Kristie said proudly. "She had a book published."

"Really. What's the title?"

"*Improvisations.*"

"A novel?"

"Yeah. I've read it about 10 times."

Alice could see that Kristie liked talking about her mother. Her defensiveness began to melt. "What's it about?"

"It's about a woman who just disappears: leaves her family, past, everything and moves out west to a small town. She meets and marries this older guy, who raises mules. She tries to live simply, but feels all this guilt about leaving her family. One day, she finds her husband dead on the back porch. So now she's alone and lost— feels like she's being punished for her past, because she really loved the old guy. She wants to go back home, but doesn't because she was so unhappy. So she sells the mule farm and moves to California where she meets this younger guy, a painter. She has a baby girl, then feels trapped again. She realizes that she has to go back and face the family she left, or she'll never find any peace."

"And does she?"

"Yes... but she does it in secret. They don't know she's around. She just watches them from a distance; her children, her husband. And then she writes about how much love she has for them and how she wished things could be different. Wished she could be different, but she can't."

Kristie swallowed, then continued. "When they're not home, her old family, she slips in and brings them presents and flowers and leaves a poem on the kitchen table. Then she leaves town, driving off into this like gray hazy rain, and she talks about how unclear life is sometimes and how you just have to make it up as you go. That's the end."

"It sounds wonderful."

"The critics liked it a lot."

"What was the poem? Do you remember it?" Alice knew she would.

Kristie looked at Alice. Her eyes drifted up and down her, pleased to have been asked. "This is the last part of it." She spoke slowly, in a lilt.

> *There is only a moment to love in pain*
> *Before it flees on sighs of regret.*
> *There will never be tonics that clean the stain*
> *Nor wages enough to pay the debt.*

Alice sat silently for a time and let the poem settle. "I like it," she said. "How did you know your mother wrote the novel?"

Kristie chewed on her thumbnail and spoke softly. "Daddy told me. He said she came by once, a few years back."

Alice suddenly felt uncomfortable. It wasn't a level playing field. She knew much more about Kristie's life, her mother's and father's lives, than the girl would probably ever know about Alice's. If the roles were reversed, and if Kristie had learned the intimate details of Alice's past and played the dumb card, digging and probing like some aggressive and tactless reporter, she would be furious if the truth were ever revealed. She decided to change the subject.

"Would you like to hear some music?"

Kristie looked over. "Sure."

"What do you like?"

"Whatever. I like some rock. I like Norah Jones."

"Me too."

Alice punched through the channels and stopped when she heard Joni Mitchell singing her latest version of *Both Sides Now*. "This okay?"

She smiled. "I like Joni Mitchell. I play this on my guitar."

They listened to the music without speaking. When they passed the green sign announcing entry into Meadow Green, Alice felt the tension return. She knew Philip well enough to know that he would be calling her again at any moment, demanding explanations and details. He was a detail person. He was a curious and jealous person, who often walked away from an argument, but only for strategic purposes: he always returned, swiftly, fully armed and ready for battle. It was as if he were cross-examining a witness and, when answers he wanted or needed were not forthcoming, he'd whirl around with a dramatic flair, take a few heavy steps forward, gather his thoughts, then spin and attack with a renewed ferocious resolve to get at the truth. It was both admirable and intimidating. In the legal circles he ran with, he was known and respected for it. She reached for her cell phone and turned it off.

Then there was Jack. She wasn't proud that she had read his diary, but if she hadn't, she wouldn't be going out with him. But how could she be proud of that, especially since she was literally traveling down the road to marriage? She was going out with a man who hadn't been on a date in three years, knowing full well that it wouldn't and couldn't come to anything, because she was leaving for Holbrook the first thing in the morning and she would never see Jack Landis again!

But there was no denying it—she was as excited as a girl on prom night. Eager, fantasizing like a teenager. Feeling a rush of sudden heat. What should she wear? She'd have to wash her hair. Did she have time? Why was he attracted to her? Did Nora tell Jack that Alice was getting married?

At dinner, what should she talk about? Her shop? Why she was in Pennsylvania? She tried to remember her last date with someone other than Philip. She hadn't been "on a date" in over two years!

Kristie jarred her out of her inner movie. "Are you dating anyone?"

Alice was as still as a statue. "… Yes."

"What's he like?"

Alice ignored her. "I'm lost. You're going to have to give me directions to your house."

Kristie pointed the way down a narrow two-lane road, past towering black trees and new homes with shrubs and porches strung with Christmas lights, until they came to a quiet single lane road, with deeply cut wheel tracks in the snow. Alice turned left and drove for about 100 yards until she saw the shimmer of lights through a mat of moving trees, coming from a large three-story colonial-style house ahead. In the front yard, stood a ten-foot pine tree glowing with white Christmas lights. She stopped. Jack would surely be waiting for his daughter and any car driving along this back road would be an easy target.

Kristie gave Alice a helpless look. "Oh boy…"

"I don't want to face your father," Alice said.

"Neither do I."

Alice reached for Kristie's hand. "Promise me something, Kristie. Promise me you won't hitchhike again."

"I'm not going to promise that," Kristie said, crossly, yanking back her hand. "No way. I've got to see my friends."

Alice leaned back against the door. "Then you're very foolish. And eventually, someone who knows you will see you hitchhiking and tell your father."

Kristie took one slow blink, as if to erase the statement. "Thanks for the ride."

After she left, Alice watched until she entered the house, then drove away, not sure how she should tell Jack about Kristie.

When Alice reached the main highway and started back to The Broadmoore, she turned on her cell phone. Sure enough she had a message from Philip. His voice was low, seething with anger.

"Call me when you get this, Alice. I'm very upset. We need to talk. We need to talk now! Call me!"

She didn't call him back. She was about to turn into The Broadmoore parking lot when Jack called.

"Hi. My daughter finally made it home," he said, in a somewhat agitated voice. "If I didn't love her so much I would strangle her. I grounded her instead."

"'Grounded' is one of the most frightening words in the entire teenage vocabulary," Alice said.

"She'll put up a fight."

"I always did."

Jack lightened his tone. "I can be there at 8:30. How is that for you?"

Alice pulled into a parking space and stopped, glancing nervously at the amber-lit clock on the dashboard. It was 7:25. "Yes... I'll be ready. How should I dress?"

"No jeans. It's a nice place. I'll wear a sport coat. What is that? Upscale casual?"

In her room, Alice stripped clumsily, unlacing and kicking off her boots, stumbling and hobbling out of jeans, sweater and undergarments, slinging clothes in all directions, leaving the bedroom for the bathroom, running across the blue, newly tiled floor to the shower. She turned the silver lever right, and the water shot out in hot, pneumatic bursts. She leapt away. Steam rose and rolled like fog. After several gallant attempts, avoiding a scalded arm, she managed to find the optimum temperature, step inside and draw the blue and green pastel plastic shower curtain around her.

The stream was strong. Almost punishing. "You deserve this pain," Alice said to herself aloud. "You should have called Philip back. You should be on your way to Holbrook."

Shampoo/conditioner and soap, supplied by the hotel, were an easy hand-reach away on a white, eye-level shelf. She lathered her hair in light speed and rinsed it briskly. She usually used a separate deep conditioner, but didn't have time for that. She'd have to leave it to the hair angels.

She washed thoroughly with a thick navy blue wash cloth that seemed the size of a hand towel, then shut off the spray of prickly water and stepped out, refreshed and tingling.

As she was blow-drying her hair before a fogged up mirror, wrapped in a generous blue towel, she began to wonder what she would do with the diary. When she left town, should she mail it anonymously to Jack? Should she burn it? Should she send it back to where she found it: to Hattie in Eden Grove? She certainly couldn't take it with her to Holbrook. Philip could find it and she'd be forced to explain everything.

Speaking of Philip, what would she tell him? She had never been a very good liar and yet how could she tell him the truth? How could she not? Lying is not a good way to start a marriage. Her shoulders slumped. Philip didn't deserve this. She shut off the dryer. She had never been unfaithful to Philip; had never even thought of it. As far as she knew, he had never been unfaithful to her. Being faithful and truthful were virtues she believed in and respected.

But was this really being unfaithful? She was just going out to dinner with Jack. It was innocent. Harmless. She was doing it out of curiosity, because she had read the diary. That's all it was: because of the diary. Surely Philip would understand that. He would understand curiosity and investigation; a sense of fun and adventure. That's really all this date was and nothing more.

Satisfied, she nodded, convinced. She switched the hairdryer back on, raking the long, wet strands with her fingers, adjusting the focus of heat and allowing her thoughts to wander into risky realms. What would it be like living in Meadow Green? What would it be like dating Jack, learning to mix into Kristie's and Andrew's lives? Would they accept her? Would she even like being a "stepmother"? The words "stepmother" sounded distasteful and old. Would she and Jack fall in love?

She stopped, gently toying with the ON switch as if it were a loaded gun. She finally turned it off.

She stood stiffly, her guilty eyes staring at nothing. Philip would not understand. No way. He'd see that vague and dreamy quality in her eyes when she spoke about Jack. The same quality she was now seeing in the small circle she'd cleared in the mirror with a washcloth. She opened the bathroom door. The fog cleared. Now she saw a hopeless resignation. She leaned forward into the sink. "Don't kid yourself, Alice."

She sat on the edge of the bed, wrapped in the towel for ten minutes, unable to make a decision. Twice she'd reached for the phone and then retracted her hand. The first time, she was going to call Jack and cancel the date. The second time, she was going to call Philip and tell him that she was on her way. She didn't make either call. She was paralyzed with doubt and disappointment in herself. What would Kristie think of her when she found out that she was *the date?*

The clock was ticking away, like a taunting adversary. It was a quarter after eight.

CHAPTER 11

Jack felt the flare of nerves, the unraveling of volatile emotions and a terror of the unknown that he hadn't felt in years—and had never wanted to feel again. He stood before a full-length mirror in his bedroom, clumsily tucking in the dark blue striped shirt-tail into his chocolate brown wool pants, examining himself with a raised chin and uncertain, insecure eyes.

Kristie was locked in her room, still angry from their argument, playing loud rock music that shook and thumped the house. Andrew was hovering downstairs, waiting for a glimpse of his old man about to go out on a real live date, so he could snicker and mock him with his radiant mischievous eyes.

Jack thought about this. "No matter how much love you have for your kids, sometimes they feel like the enemy," he said aloud.

Jack looked hesitantly at the dark blue blazer with its glossy gold buttons, hanging smartly on a broad wooden hanger to his left, looking back at him with a challenge. "Leave me out of this," it seemed to say. "You wear me and she'll think you're trying too hard. Blue blazer... Who the hell do you think you are? Mr. Country Club?

Be yourself, for crying out loud! Wear the brown corduroy jacket with the green pants and yellow shirt."

Jack frantically obeyed the blue blazer's instructions, grateful for the suggestion. But the brown corduroy jacket didn't want to go either. It said, "Corduroy on a first date? Yellow shirt? Come on, Jack, autumn's over. Besides, yellow makes you look pale and old."

Jack struggled out of that outfit into another and another and then another, until finally all the jackets' and blazers' voices got swallowed up into "that damned rock music."

"Turn that damned music down, Kristie!" he shouted.

The volume dropped immediately, then crescendoed, thundered, and shouted louder than before.

Jack threw up his hands. "The enemy!" he yelled.

He stripped, slinging away the final outfit.

He stood looking at himself tragically, helplessly, dressed only in his underwear and dark blue socks. His hair was askew; his eyes were bewildered, dark bulging circles. Shirts, jackets and trousers lay scattered and rumpled on the smooth blue carpeted floor and queen-sized bed, like victims of a massacre. Why was he putting himself through this!?

Ever since he'd first seen Alice in the Ski Shop, he'd felt a little off-balance, as if he couldn't quite find his center of gravity. Inside, some "thing" had awakened with a fury; it was like a storm, a heartbreak, a wild rush of insistent new life pushing through the center of his heart. It was a stabbing thing that opened old wounds, broke new ground and released wells of fear.

Of course he thought of Darla. Of course he compared the feelings, because at his age, and after all the time that had passed, he knew it was rare to feel those strong things, where words got stuck in your throat, then fell into your heart, where no word survives. Those "every-thing-at-once" feelings that nature produces effortlessly in the change of seasons or in the complex world of a shallow pond, where water, mud, animals and light play in a perfectly constructed "house", where no twig, leaf or fish is out of place. But that is uncommon and exceptional in the world of people. Things and feelings often come in pieces and have to be sorted out or put together like a puzzle. Nature is simple. People are complicated.

He stared at his nearly naked body, muscled and hairy; studied the blue corded veins in his arms. He'd always been naked and honest with Darla. Always. Harboring no secrets. No lies. No hidden emotion. Naked! He had believed in that love. Believed in her. Believed in him. In them. The commitment of marriage. It seemed a perfect house.

The old anger rose again; he saw it in his clenched jaw. But it wasn't enough. It wasn't enough to give everything. It wasn't enough to trust, believe and love so completely that you got lost in the depths and currents of it, like a silvery fish swimming in blue rippling water. Of course all things die at their right time. That was the way of nature. Nature is about death: to support the cycle of life. But not before its time! Not that way! Not a senseless, unholy death!

He went from anger to elation at the thought of his date with Alice, and that disturbed him. His stability seemed to have vanished, but he cooled at the thought of her. What was that? "Where do such things—feelings—come from?" Jack asked aloud in a hopeless, brittle voice. Then he thought, "Alice is like a wind! Like a sudden quick wind that kicks up dust, ripples lakes, and stirs the trees."

It was a series of unexpected things about her that had surprised him. The quickness of her step when she'd entered the shop. The easy elegance of her walk; so feminine with light steps, even in boots. The slow flutter of her long lashes as she viewed the rack of skis. The lazy turn of her head and the unexpected refinement of her long neck. Her voice was low and a bit breathy. He'd expected high, somewhat girlish. The pure white skin was natural, not overly made up, and then there was that appealing beauty mark just above the left side of her mouth that just rattled him. He'd lost his concentration as he'd examined the skis—the ones he had planned to buy for Kristie for Christmas. Her thick hair was the color of autumn, his favorite season—and he, uncharacteristically, almost reached for it. He longed to reach and touch it!

But it was her chocolate brown eyes that had moved him the most. They held secrets and intimacy, almost as if they (she and Jack) had at least once been intimate! That's when he'd first noticed the shakiness; and a little unexpected intrusion, like a tiny punch, in the center of his chest.

It was why he'd left the shop abruptly, believing he'd never see her again. But when she approached him in the parking lot, he felt surprised and constrained by her prettiness. That's when he saw an invitation in those intimate brown eyes, and though he first questioned it, he saw that beckoning again after they arrived at The Broadmoore and started up the stairs.

He'd had no intention of asking her out. Absolutely no plan. So why did he? He could barely remember picking up the phone. He didn't believe for one moment that she'd agree, but when she did, he wasn't surprised. None of it made sense.

But he was still in his underwear, staring at himself in the mirror, smelling the cedar from his closet, staring at the rack of hanging shirts and one remaining sport jacket: it was brown and he'd outgrown it. He still had to find something to wear. He still would have to think of conversation at dinner—interesting, stimulating conversation—because, surely she was college- educated. Nora had told him she was from New York. What would she expect? His biggest fear was to see the intimacy in her eyes turn to boredom as soon as he opened his mouth. Why would she be interested in going out with him anyway? A woman that attractive and intelligent surely would have a boyfriend—should have a boyfriend—or a husband!

He turned away from the mirror, slouching into apprehension and worry. What would she expect? The last woman he'd dated, Mira Fields, was attractive and buxom, with the electrified artificiality of a TV game hostess. Her favorite subjects were TV court/cop shows. On the second date she made it obvious what she wanted, by using the word sex as frequently as possible. "Sexy car. They allowed sex tapes in that trial. I think summer is sexy, because it's hot. This restaurant has sexy colors. I think contractors are… like sexy in flannel shirts. Do you have any?" There was no doubt that she was attractive, in a game hostess kind of way. But Jack couldn't seem to find the "center" of her. In mid-sentence, she'd slide away from topics of conversation about her work or his kids, which were undoubtedly boring, into a half- remembered plot of Law *and Order* or some damned thing about *Dancing with the Stars*. She'd repeat the plots of movies he'd never seen, but forget logical sections, so that by the end, Jack was confused and speechless, and she was silent, straining to recall.

At her place, the sex wasn't sexy. Afterwards, she smoked aggressively and Jack left at the best possible and most sensitive moment, feeling the weight of failure in every eager step toward the front door.

He'd learned a few months later that Mira had made a bet with some of her co-workers at the elementary school (she taught 5th grade) that she could "make it happen with Jack." A year or so after, Mira married the Sheriff, Al Bledso, and they now have a 2-year-old daughter who Jack thought was gorgeous. Whenever Jack ran into her, at the supermarket or in town, Mira ignored him.

Jack glanced at the clock and grimaced. It was just after eight. If he didn't hurry, he'd be late and send a clear signal that he was an irresponsible schmuck. He was desperate now. He straightened out from his fever of anxiety and stretched to his full six-two height, coming to a dreaded conclusion: he'd have to ask Kristie for help. He simply couldn't make a decision.

He reached for his navy blue terrycloth robe, fought his way into it and belted it snuggly with a final forceful yank, as if to say, I'm still in charge. I'm the father. He marched out of his room across the glossy oak wood floor to Kristie's room. He paused, drew a deep breath and knocked. No response. The music was deafening. He pounded. No response. He shouted and pounded.

When the door opened, Kristie stood slackly in jeans and a bright red halter top that revealed her taut flat stomach and a little blue tattoo etched incredibly in it that said "OH YEAH!" How Jack hated that tattoo. But he couldn't think of that now. They'd already fought that battle—many times.

Kristie's blond hair was brushed to a gloss, her lips ruby red, her half-hooded eyes circles of disinterest and annoyance. But in that light, she looked like her mother, and that melted some of Jack's irritation. He looked past her into her room and noticed how immaculate it was. They'd never fought about that. Everything else, but not that. Kristie liked order and neatness.

"I need your help," Jack said, pointedly.

Kristie stuck her fist against a long shuddering yawn.

"Will you shut that music off!?"

Kristie reluctantly turned and drifted lazily to her boom box and shut it off. The sudden silence hurt and Jack rubbed his ears. She looked at her father and crossed her arms, silent, holding the power of the moment and loving it. She knew that her silence kept her in charge.

Jack searched for words, lifting his hands helplessly. "I don't know what to wear... to dinner tonight. I just..." His voice trailed off into bleakness.

Kristie nodded, lifting her drowsy, all-knowing plucked eyebrows as if to say, "I know, you poor ding dong," but she didn't speak.

"I'll try on a couple of things and you just give me your opinion. You know what women like. I haven't done this in a long time."

Kristie seized the moment. "If I help you, will you drop this stupid grounded thing?"

Jack's chill was obvious. "Kristie... don't push this. I'm fed up with your secrets and your running around with kids I don't know and you won't tell me about. I don't know when you're coming home—because you say you'll call and you don't—and I don't know what the hell you're doing out there half the time!"

Kristie scowled at him. "When are you ever home?"

"I'm not getting into this again, Kristie," he said, looking nervously at his watch. "I'm already late."

"It's no, because you always want it your way."

"I don't know what that means."

"It means you're only a father when it's convenient."

"Kristie. For once, let's not fight. Not tonight. Okay?"

"It's true. I never see you at home for more than an hour or so."

"I have to work, Kristie! You know that. I have a demanding business."

"You work all the time, Daddy! All the freakin' time! I have secrets because you're never home to talk to, or you're tired or like depressed, so you go off to your work-shop downstairs and work again. You're like always run-ning away from us."

"Don't start with that again, Kristie. I've never, ever wanted to run from you and Andrew. Never!"

Kristie continued, her voice growing in strength. "Don't you think it's pathetic that you haven't been out on a date in three years!? That you don't even freakin' know how to dress for one? What the hell is that!? These are like basic things that people know. It's like ABC."

Jack felt the sting of her words. It weakened him; Kristie saw it in his eyes. She wanted to stop, but she also wanted to go in for the kill. "There are so many women in this town who want to date you but you're like too good for them or scared or still thinking Mama was the angel of angels and no one is or ever will be a saint like she was."

"That's enough!" Jack snapped.

"She ran out on us, Daddy! She left! Okay!? What kind of a mother leaves her kids!? Huh? How could you love her?! How could you even miss a person like that!?"

Jack moved toward her, flushed with anger. "You don't know what you're talking about!"

"Then you left, too!"

"I've always been here for you and Andrew. Always!"

Kristie twisted up her lip in distaste. "Bullshit!"

Kristie dropped her arms and stepped aggressively toward him. The tempo and the violence of her words increased. "Did you know Andrew hates skiing? Did you know he hates doing that stupid work you give him whenever he has a free second, but he does it without complaining because he wants to please you? Did you know that he's started stuttering again when he's called on in class? Did you know he doesn't have any friends and thinks there's something wrong with him and he even thought of killing himself a month ago? Did you know he saw granddaddy two or three times in the last week?"

Jack stared back, solemn and troubled. "What are you talking about? He saw granddaddy?"

Kristie crossed her arms and lowered her voice to a smooth, sharp edge. "Were you really ever there for him except when it was something you needed or wanted? He needs help. He's been crying for it, but all you can do is remodel somebody's freakin' kitchen, fix somebody's plumbing or lay some stupid foundation!"

Jack leveled his furious eyes on her. "That's enough, Kristie! I'm your father, not some low-life punk you hang around with."

"The low-lifes I hang around with are there for me!" she shouted.

Kristie watched her father's features slowly fall apart: first his face, then the drop of his broad shoulders and then the lowering of his weary eyes to the floor.

His voice was hoarse with defeat. "You'll not leave this house for a week."

He turned and left. Kristie heard his door close quietly. Then there was only a painful, ringing silence. She had finally defeated him. Every word was like a bullet that had hit the target. Every inflexion pitched just right and artful—real poetry—each snap of her tongue, venomous, like a snake. She stood there trembling.

But instead of feeling strong, with a sense of release and triumph, a slow heavy sickness descended upon her. Weakness shook her limbs. Her stomach knotted up, her throat tightened, and she felt stabbing pains of immediate regret, as if her own words came back seeking vengeance and restitution. How could it be? He deserved it. Someone should have said it long ago. She should have said it! But pangs of remorse came in waves; she shook her head slowly with shame and paced her room for a long time.

Suddenly, she noticed Andrew was standing in the hallway staring back at her, accusingly, slightly startled, as if he didn't know his sister at all.

"What are you lookin at?!" she shouted. "Get out of my face!"

He shoved his hands deep into his jeans pockets and ambled away.

Jack sat on the edge of his bed, staring vacantly, wondering how the simple act of loving Darla could have spawned so much pain, disappointment and confusion. As a practical man, he should have reasoned that love and hate were connected like heat and cold and night and day, but for some odd reason he'd believed that love—real love—was set apart somehow—an exception—a miracle that was protected from the obvious dualities of life: love and hate. It was silly, of course, but loving Darla for him was, in reality and in fact, that way. It was devoid of duality—even through the arguments, the differences and many complexities they passed through. Love for Darla had no hate attached to it. No other or dark side. Even when she left him and the kids, there was no hate for her in him. Disappointment, yes, a sense of loss, yes, certainly confusion, but not hate. He still loved her—even now—and there was no room for hate for her anywhere in his world.

For a brief moment he remembered the diary she'd given him. He recalled the pleasure in her happy impatient face as he'd peeled away the gold wrapping paper. Perplexed, he'd stared dumbly at the soft brown leather cover and a burgundy silk ribbon bookmark.

"It's a diary," she'd said, giggling a little. "You write down your thoughts, feelings and anything else that comes to you. You reveal your inner, hidden world."

He had shrugged and scratched his head. "Okay..."

How could he forget her contented sigh when he'd looked at her lovingly, thanked her and said he'd write in it. What he'd say, God only knew.

How he wished he hadn't lost the diary. He still felt guilty for losing it. How he longed for it now and wished he had the presence of mind and the courage to start a new one. It had helped him to document and explore his feelings. He had to admit it, although he'd never admitted it to Darla, at least not that he could recall. Now, he wished he had. After a few weeks of writing in it, he began thinking of it as a friend he could talk to and discuss things with. Darla had been right: "Give it time, Jack, it'll grow on you."

He folded his hands and dropped his head. Whatever that budding feeling was that he felt for Alice, he didn't want it to grow. He didn't want to go through those suffering feelings again. Never. No way. He'd kept his life simple. And it was working—at least until now. But he had his work. He had his kids, and they came first and would always come first. He stood and went to the mirror. He studied his face. His sad eyes held questions. He didn't feel properly present in his skin. What was happening to him? And what had he done to alienate his kids when he loved them more than his own life?

He glanced at the phone. It was time to call Alice and tell her he couldn't make it.

CHAPTER 12

It was Sunday morning. Andrew was outside his father's room, his ear pressed tightly to the walnut bedroom door. He was still disappointed and mad at his father. He gradually peeled his ear away; Sunday morning silence rang in the house. No human sounds. Was his dad still asleep? Andrew glanced down at his worn, brown, leather house shoes, floppy pajama bottoms and old T-shirt, working on his plan. It was time to go. He padded to the landing of the solid walnut winding stairs and spiraled down to the first floor, skimming the top of the railing with the flat of his hand.

In his room he dressed quickly in jeans, a blue and red flannel shirt and a gray sweatshirt that had AWESOME printed across the chest. He laced his Timberland boots, lost in the smoke of thought and composition. A communication was forming. At first just the sound of words and ragged sentences; a desperate tangle of ideas, rejections and images. He was not that good in English, like Kristie was. All her teachers praised her talent. "A gifted poet" one of her old pop-eyed teachers once said. "Surely a great writer lurked behind those brooding eyes", her latest English teacher had said.

But Andrew was a good idea man and had good fol-low-through. His father had said so many times. Hell yes! he thought to himself, feeling galvanized by that thought. And then, like mystical magic, the idea that he'd been working on most of the night came to him like a karate chop to the head. He dropped down into his swivel desk chair and stared into the blue MacBook Pro computer screen, feeling a rush of energy. He closed the *Tera* computer game and launched his word processing software. He drummed the desk impatiently while he waited, afraid he was going to lose the words. Finally the electric white empty page lay before him like a wide sheet of snow, waiting for his footprints.

He lifted his head and began to type. The words flowed easily. They were a brilliant collection of senti-ment and poetry. When complete, Andrew read them over twice, did a spell check that found two typos: "spe-cail" and "misteak." He corrected them and printed the letter.

The only pen he could find was a leaky one. He frowned but snatched it, careful not to spill any blue ink, make any smudges or any other goofy mistakes. This had to look professional. His printing was precise and large. It seemed to take forever as he pressed and grimaced and worked. The letters were large. You couldn't miss seeing it. Good! That's the way it had to be. He read the letter once more, smiling victoriously. He creased the letter twice, into a meticulously flat and perfect rectangle that satisfied his sense of design, and reached for a letter-sized envelope. He printed the name ALICE on it. He insert-ed the letter into the envelope, licked and sealed it. Good! The first part of the mission was completed!

He got up, reached for his cell phone and pocket Leatherman, picked up the letter and left the room, throwing dramatic darting glances. He crept like a "special ops" soldier across the sandy brown carpeted living room and paused in tense vigilance to slant a look up the staircase. That sturdy staircase he'd helped his father build. Not an easy job. He recalled one of their conversations while they were building it. "Spiral and other winding staircases are tough to build," his father had said. "They're tricky to design, which is the reason I got this one already designed. And if you don't know what you're doing, they can be wobbly and unsafe."

"Then why do it?" Andrew had complained.

"Because it will be fun and it will look great."

Andrew pinned his chin to his chest, making an ugly face. "I don't see much fun in this. And what if it's not safe? Then what?"

"Ours is going be safe, Andrew," his father had stressed, with a sharp determined nod of his head.

It was not only safe, but it was also beautiful. It gave Andrew pleasure to look at it, and he was proud every time his dad told anyone "Andrew helped me build it."

Andrew heard the shower. Kristie was up; she would be down in five minutes, making her usual breakfast: OJ and toast followed by a jelly donut and chocolate milk. She hadn't changed the menu since she was seven. He was still mystified that she stayed so thin.

He hustled off to the kitchen, searching the maple cabinets for anything he could grab and eat, shuffling through coffee filters, bags of nuts, packages of chocolate chip cookies (his dad's favorite), and cans of soups; finally he found one of his father's Clif Bars. Crunchy Peanut Butter! He loved peanut butter! He stuffed it into his jeans pocket, next to the Leatherman, swerved around the breakfast bar and hurried to the hall closet, hoping for a clean get-a-way. The shower stopped, just as he snatched

his forest green parka, red ski cap and gloves. He carefully inserted the letter in his inside coat pocket and wrestled
into the parka as he skipped down the cement stairs to
the garage, circumventing the black GMC Jimmy, and his
father's work van, to get to his 3-speed trail bike.

He guided it around the snow blower and the box of
Christmas decorations to the metal outside door. He
turned the knob and kicked it open. He was too forceful.
The door slammed hard against the outer cement wall,
making a dull BANG that echoed. Panicked, he pushed
the bike outside and closed the door securely, tense, looking back stealthily. All was quiet.

He was immediately surprised by the cold, gray morning. Icicles hung from the eves; the snow was tight and
crunchy; black trees were drizzled white from a light
overnight shower. A light snow still fell. Andrew felt as
though he was inside a giant freezer—and that he could
easily become frozen food.

Gripping the handlebars, he broke into a run, swinging
his left leg over the seat, planting himself securely, and
pedaling vigorously down the driveway, puffing white
vapor from his mouth and dodging ice patches. The
wind stung his face, bringing tears. He balanced the bike
with his legs and, with his free hands, tugged the cap
down tightly over his ears and forehead. The bike wobbled and swerved, nearly pitching him, but he seized the
handlebars, regained control with a victorious grin and
soared into the glassy morning with a wild sense of adventure and freedom. He was on his way! On his way to
a secret, dangerous mission! He felt bigger, older somehow, and he wondered if it was because he felt hopeful.
Maybe hope and a sense of adventure make you feel bigger and better, he thought.

His plan was a simple one, but it would take daring and maybe a little skillful acting. The acting he'd practiced the night before after his talk with his father: a conversation that had irritated him.

"I just thought we should talk a little," his father had said, coming into Andrew's room and plopping down on the edge of the bed, looking sorrowful.

"I thought you were going out with Alice," Andrew had said, turning away from his computer screen and facing him

"Alice?" his surprised father said.

"That's her name, isn't it?"

"Yes. It just seems..." He spread his hands. "I don't know, awfully familiar."

His dad was dressed in paint-spotted brown khakis and a faded denim shirt. His hair was combed carefully and moussed, something his father seldom did; only when he made them go to the Methodist church, because of some new guilt or old conflict.

"Aren't you going out to dinner with her?"

His father signed heavily. "No. I canceled."

Andrew shot up, feeling an old bitterness and disappointment. "That's bullshit!"

Jack threw him a burning glance. "You know better than that! There are better words to use!"

"You say it. I hear you!"

"Okay, so I shouldn't and you shouldn't. Pick better words."

Andrew stiffened. "Did you cancel because of Kristie? Because of what she said?"

"No... well, maybe, but it's true, we haven't spent much time together lately. We haven't talked... or gone anywhere. I've been working a lot of hours."

Andrew pivoted, jamming his hands into his pockets, staring angrily at the poster of Britney Spears hanging over his computer. She was dressed in hip-hugger jeans and a tight V-neck red halter top that showed nipples. She stood hipshot, head back, teased blond hair framing a glossy face, wet lips and half-hooded eyes set in a lusty invitation.

"Andrew?"

Andrew was silent.

"Andrew?" Jack said, louder. "Turn around."

Andrew obeyed, but his burning eyes wandered, finally resting on the far wall.

"You like her, don't you? Alice?"

He shrugged.

"Speak up, son."

"She's all right."

"I like her, too, Andrew, but it's not like we can have any kind of relationship or anything. She's just passing through. She's leaving in the morning."

Andrew shrugged again. "So why did you ask her out then?"

Jack scratched his head, uncomfortable. "I don't know. I liked her, thought she was attractive... You know." He decided to change the subject quickly. "So I thought maybe we could do something tonight. Grab some pizza and go see a late movie. Give Kristie time to cool off."

Another shrug.

Jack stood. "Come on, son..."

"Are you afraid of women?" Andrew blurted out. "I mean, you never go out with them."

"No, I'm not afraid of them. Of course not."

"You never go out."

"I've been out."

"What! Three years ago?"

"You want me to go out?"

"Whatever. I just think it's weird. Here's this woman, and she looks good and seems, you know, nice and everything and you ask her out, she says yes, and then you cancel. I really just don't get that. Charlie Banks' dad got married again two weeks ago. He was only divorced for a year or something. Charlie said he went out with a lot of women—all kinds."

"Okay, well, that's good for Charlie Banks' dad," Jack said defensively. "But he's a lousy electrician, in my opinion, and he and his new wife drink too much."

"Whatever, Dad. You know what I mean."

"So you want me to get married? Is that what this is about?"

Andrew turned away. "Just forget it."

"No, really, Andrew, is that what you want?"

"How do you know Alice wouldn't stay for another day or two? She might if you asked her. I heard her tell Nora she really likes this town. And why do you and Kristie have to fight all the time anyway? And why do you listen to her?"

Jack frowned down at the sea-blue carpet. "Which question do you want me to answer first?"

Andrew gave another frustrated shrug.

"Do you want to go to the movies or not?"

"I've got things to do," Andrew said.

Jack pocketed his hands and looked at his son warmly, with some sudden new recognition: could it be that Andrew was growing up? Jack decided to try for another approach. "Son... Andrew. Finding the right woman is... tricky. It's not easy. You'll learn that when you start dating."

"Whatever."

"Andrew, what's this about you seeing your grandfather?"

Andrew slung an angry hand toward Kristie's room. "She should just keep her damned mouth shut!"

"Andrew, calm down! Take it easy."

Andrew sat.

"Was it a dream? Have you been dreaming about him?"

Andrew slumped. "No." He shook his head.

Jack waited patiently. "So…"

"So, I saw him near The Broadmoore. In the woods."

Jack massaged his eyes, struggling. "You saw him?"

"Yes. I saw him," Andrew said, firmly.

"Son… How do you know it was your grandfather?"

"Come on, Dad, I'm not an idiot! I know what he looks like. I've seen the pictures in your album. There's a picture of him on the mantel downstairs."

Jack searched for words, trying not to overact or let his rising agitation show. "Andrew… okay… okay… Did he say anything to you?"

"Not the first time."

"The first time? When did you see him the first time?"

"On Thursday night, as I was leaving The Broadmoore. I saw him standing at the edge of the woods."

"What did he do?"

"He waved."

"Just waved."

"Yeah."

"And you immediately recognized him?"

"Yes!"

"Were you scared?"

"Hell yes… I mean, yes. It freaked me out big time. I thought I was like, going crazy or something."

"Then what?"

"He turned around and walked back into the woods."

"When did you see him the second time?"

"Friday night when I left. He was there again."

"And he talked to you this time?"

"Yes. He said 'Don't be afraid.' Then he said he was going to make everything all right."

Jack mumbled back Andrew's words, mystified. He stammered to get the next question out. "Andrew... Your grandfather has been dead for thirteen years! You were just a little over a month old when he was killed."

Andrew turned almost apologetic. "I know... I saw him, Dad, that's all I know. I mean ghosts and things like that... well... I don't believe in them... but I saw him."

Jack was still not convinced. "Why didn't you tell me?"

Andrew eyed him pointedly. "You don't believe me, do you? I knew you wouldn't, so why would I tell you?"

Jack lowered his eyes. "Okay... okay, son. Will you tell me if you see him again?"

Andrew wiped his nose.

"Andrew!?"

"Okay, yes!"

Andrew turned left on Chestnut Street and pumped hard for more speed, whizzing past Caroline Wolpert's house, a single-level ranch with a plastic snowman in the front yard, still illuminated. Tall, honey-blond Caroline was 14, and she had remarkable "stats". She was known at school as "Caroline and her two big Wolperts." She'd never given Andrew the time of day, but he'd had at least two "most impressive" dreams about her, where she claimed he was "the coolest guy in the school." She even wanted him to kiss her. Yep, most impressive!

Past the old cemetery, Andrew took a steep hill, braking, releasing, braking, to keep from skidding out of control. He bounced along the elementary school parking lot toward a shortcut, and through a row of trees that would eventually take him to The Broadmoore grounds.

There was no doubt he was nervous. He definitely did not want to see his grandfather the ghost again, and as he approached the area where the old man had first materialized, he kept his saucer-like eyes moving, his body crouched, ready for flight. He wouldn't stop and talk to the old booger under any circumstances. Despite the valiant front he'd presented to his dad, the whole incident had made him sick from fright, and he hadn't slept well since.

But he arrived at The Broadmoore without incident and parked his bike behind the house, near the service/delivery entrance where he always parked. No one was around.

Inside, as he stood in the long, narrow hallway that led to the back stairs, a wave of heat instantly warmed him. His face and fingers tingled back to life. He smelled sweet muffins, coffee and bacon—and felt a sudden wrenching hunger. But eating would have to come later. He glanced at his watch: 7:23.

He crept quietly up the brown carpeted back stairs, unable to avoid the occasional squeak, cringing each time, and pausing before moving on. At the top of the stairs on the second floor landing, he stopped, unzipped his parka and slipped his bare hand into the inside pocket. With inner glee he drew out the letter, looked at it proudly, and went to the heavy oak door that led out into the second-floor hallway. Now, he was home free. He reached for the doorknob and pulled.

It swung open too quickly. He nearly took it in the face. Nora appeared in the doorway, startled and rigid. "Mercy, Andrew! You nearly scared me to death. What are you doing here?!?"

Andrew fought for his mind. "I... I forgot something... yesterday."

"Couldn't it wait? It's so early."

He dropped his head. "No, couldn't wait." He brushed by her into the hallway and turned left away from Alice's room. Nora watched him pass, shaking her head.

Moments later, Andrew walked briskly down the hallway, dimly lit by Victorian mother-of-pearl lamps, feeling his heart thunder in his chest. At Alice's room, he stopped and glanced up and down the hallway. No one. He leaned over and slid the letter under the door. He bolted for the back stairs.

Under the main staircase was a service/storage closet. He knew from experience that, in this closet, he could hear most conversations that took place in the foyer, living room and stairs. That closet was his destination. That's where he'd eat the Clif Bar and wait for Alice's response.

CHAPTER 13

In her hotel room, Alice eased down in the ladder-back chair near the bay window, crossed her legs and stared blankly, resting her eyes on the far dark mountains. Sunday morning came shyly, in shades of dull gray and with frigid temperatures that inspired the most religious and ambitious of humans to indulge in more sleep. Slow, dark, chubby clouds covered the sun, and inky shadows crawled and stretched across the snowy mountains and lakes. Deer crept from beneath dark pines and gazed, with heads held high, seemingly grateful for a sleepy world, where rare quiet and safety emboldened them to move away from the trees to open ground. Birds seemed reluctant to fly through cold ripples of air and stayed perched close to the chimneys, silent and motionless, near the rise and curl of smoke.

Alice hadn't slept more than four hours, and she wasn't looking forward to focusing her bloodshot eyes on the highway to Holbrook. She was up at 4:30, showered and dressed in comfortable black wool slacks and an emerald cashmere turtleneck by 5:15. She'd made her mouth up carefully, applied light makeup, created a ponytail and tied a paisley silk scarf artfully around it, the scarf Philip had given her on her last birthday.

She had done her best to look "awake" and ready, but her eyes were puffy and raccoon-like, her skin wan, her energy vacillating from passivity to agitation.

She saw the deer, the birds and the breaking clouds, where occasional slivers of sunlight cast the distant lake in an artificial metallic sphere.

She played back the brief conversation she'd had with Jack the night before.

"I don't quite know how to say this," Jack had said, in a low contrite voice. "I'm not going to be able to make it."

Alice was still seated on the bed, wrapped in the towel and shivering. She began chewing on a thumbnail, feeling her heart sink. "Oh..." was all she could say, even though she tried for more.

"Personal things... you know? Bad timing."

"Oh, sure. Yeah... No, I understand."

"So, you're only staying the night?" he said softly.

"... Yes. I'm leaving in the morning."

There was a long silence before Jack spoke. "Do you come this way often?"

"No... not often."

"If you do..." his voice trailed off.

"You'll take me cross-country skiing?" she blurted out, surprised she'd said it.

Silence.

"I'd love to," he finally said.

Alice released trapped air from her lungs, feeling a rush of child-like glee, but then just as quickly, sorrow weakened her posture. She knew full well that it would never happen. "... Well, then, I guess this is good luck and goodbye."

More silence.

"It seems like a long time," Jack said.

"What?" Alice asked.

"… Knowing you. I feel like I've known you for a long time. Goodbye doesn't seem, I don't know, quite right somehow."

His words warmed her, pierced her, hurt her.

"I'm not making much sense," he continued.

"No, you're not," Alice said, almost breathless, although she knew exactly what he meant. She just wanted to hear more.

"Okay… Alice. Safe trip, then."

She slouched further. "… Yes…"

At 7:30, Alice finally went downstairs for breakfast. Mr. Dog, the German Shepard in residence at The Broadmoore, was languishing in his LL Bean Scottish colored bed next to the stone fireplace. She studied his golden, lazy eyes and his ears, that were as pointed and still and tall as church spires.

At the breakfast buffet, Alice chose a blueberry muffin, coffee and a banana. Nora joined her at her table, bringing a second muffin and her own cup of coffee. She was wearing a royal blue dress with a scoop neck, and a choker of soft pearls that she fingered as she talked. Alice avoided Nora's probing eyes and just listened to her rather pointed conversation about TV dating shows and the wonderful marriages that had been held in the house. Then there was the upcoming Christmas Eve party that Nora promised "would be bigger and better than ever this year. I've hired a chef from Philadelphia and you should see the menu. I'm not going to tell you anything else about it, except that this party is going to be the talk of the county."

Back in her room, Alice gripped her cell phone tightly, squeezing it until her fingers hurt. She paced. It was nearly 8:25. Philip would be furious. Who could blame him? But he seemed a lifetime away, in the past, and they the players in an old grainy black and white movie, with dark shadows, melodramatic expressions and echoing dialogue, like "Don't you love me anymore, Alice?"

"Of course I do," she answers much too quickly. Then she turns away, concealing an obvious painful secret.

"But what?" he asks, pleading. "Look at me, Alice. What is happening?"

"I don't know," she says, not meeting his eyes. "I feel scared, confused. It's the damned diary! I should have never opened it! Never read it! Now I can't forget him!"

"Diary!? What diary? What him?!!" he asks, his eyes wide, his body stiffening with anger.

Alice sat again in her chair, picking absently at her turtleneck, looking out the window. Suddenly she saw Mr. Dog break from the side of the house, barking and scattering in all directions, lunging after a squirrel that was fleeing and flicking a desperate path to the nearest tree just outside her window. In the nick of time, it leapt, seized the tree and pivoted out of sight, leaving a disappointed and frustrated Mr. Dog in a circular, raspy-bark frenzy.

Alice turned from the window and stared into the room, awkward and self-conscious, as if it were filled with accusing eyes and pointing fingers. She had still not called Philip, something she dreaded more than an IRS audit.

She shut her eyes and dropped to the bed in a bounce. She gripped her phone, turned it on and pressed Philip's number on speed dial. It rang three times before Philip answered in a deep, flat voice. Alice leaned forward, wincing.

"Where are you, Alice?"

She kept her eyes closed. "I'm still in Meadow Green. I'm leaving for Holbrook as soon as I get off the phone."

"Are you going to tell me what this is about?"

"Nothing to tell."

An icy quiet.

"Alice... you're not a liar, unless you've just discovered a new talent. But I'm not stupid. Your voice is different. Your actions speak volumes. Something is going on."

"Nothing to tell."

"You're not on trial, but the guilt in your voice says you are. Talk to me."

"It's not guilt, Philip. Don't play lawyer with me. It's nothing. Really. I'll tell you all about it when I get there."

"... You will get here?"

"Of course."

"I mean, you're not just saying that again, to put me off?"

Alice shot up. "I'm leaving now! Okay?!"

"Okay," he said, softly.

"I'm packed. I'll be there in, I don't know, two or three hours."

"If you're not here by then, I'm going there."

Alice gave a huff of a laugh. "Don't be silly. I'll be there."

"By the way, your father called. He's bringing a girl-friend to the wedding."

Alice pressed the phone forcefully into her ear. "What? He didn't tell me anything about it the last time we talked."

"When was the last time you talked?"

"I don't know, maybe a week ago."

"She's 46, and guess what? She's an attorney. Medical malpractice."

Alice shook her head, overwhelmed. "Okay, okay, look, I'd better get going. I'll see you soon."

"I love you."

Alice swallowed. "I'll be there before you know it."

After she dropped her phone into her purse, she reached for the diary that was lying on the nightstand next to the bed. How she wished she had never found it. She nearly tossed it on the unmade bed, but then thought better of it. Nora would delight in presenting it to Jack and Jack would no doubt be angry and hurt. She shoved it down into her purse.

Ozzie, the same alfalfa-haired boy who carried her bags in, rolled them out, looking dazed and lethargic from lack of sleep. He stopped when he saw an envelope on the floor lying to the left of the threshold. He saw Alice's name printed on it in blue ink.

"I think this is for you," he said, turning to Alice.

She saw it, walked over and picked it up, curious. After the boy had left, she slid her thumb along the sealed flap until she found a space and opened it. She removed the letter, shook it out and read.

Dear Alice:

I made a mistake last night. A big mistake! I didn't sleep at all. I thought of you. Please stay another day. Let's do something special. Let's get to know each other.

Sincerely,
Jack Landis

Alice read it three times, feeling a tightening in her chest each time. She thought the style peculiar, given that his diary entries were more poetic, but she didn't dwell on it: the message was honest and to the point. The impact was effective, wonderful and awful.

She glanced around, conflicted. When would he have delivered it? When she was at breakfast? Was he downstairs, waiting for an answer!?

Nora was waiting for Alice at the foot of the stairs. Her hands were folded, her expression reflecting the soft concern of a pious nun. Alice's back straightened while she expanded her peripheral vision, to see if Jack was nearby.

"And so you're off," Nora said, meekly.

Alice stopped on the last step and extended her hand. "I am. Thanks for everything, Nora. You have a delightful place."

They shook limply.

"Thank you. I only wish you could have stayed longer. I'll pray for you in church this morning." She patted her hand, slanting a look of grandmotherly wisdom. "You be happy now, Alice. And remember that true happiness comes from being honest and true to yourself."

Alice retrieved her hand and managed a strained smile and only slightly annoyed tone, though she had wanted to speak cordially. "I *am* happy, Nora. I'm going to be married on Christmas Day and that makes me happy."

"Of course it does," Nora said, obviously unconvinced.

Alice took a last glance around, trying not to appear anxious. She saw the roaring fireplace, the gentle comfortable rooms, the glowing Christmas tree topped with a Victorian angel with broad silky wings; the glossy wood

surfaces and the buffet of freshly baked bread and muffins. She didn't see Jack.

"Will you do me a favor, Nora?"

"Of course."

"Will you tell Jack that... well, just tell him thanks, but
I had to leave."

Nora nodded. "I'll tell him."

"Merry Christmas," Alice said, glumly, then started for
the front door.

Andrew was still hiding in the closet under the staircase, holding a flashlight with the beam pointed at the
floor. With his back pressed tightly against the wall, he
listened until the conversation faded. He heard the front
door open and close. Alice had left. He slowly slid down
the wall, coming to rest next to a yellow plastic mop
bucket and hamper filled with clean rags. He pulled his
knees up into his chest, switched off the flashlight and
dropped his head.

Outside, a gentle snow fell. Nora told Alice that the
weather people were predicting another snowstorm. "But
not until sometime tonight," she added. "You should
have an easy, comfortable trip to Holbrook."

Once the bags were loaded in the trunk of the car, Alice got in, gave Nora a final wave and drove away beneath
the pines and out onto the two-lane highway.

About a half-mile down the road, she wrenched the
diary from her purse and sat it next to her on the seat.
Perhaps the best thing to do would be to sling it out the
window sixty or seventy miles up the road. It would
probably never be found and that would be the end of it.
With the diary finally gone, Jack, Kristie and Andrew
would slowly fade from her consciousness like a dream.

Alice drove leisurely, fighting her distracted mind. She
looked out on a morning that was now white and wild,

with bursts of wind, drifts of curling, blowing snow and swift-winged birds darting across wide fields to secluded black trees. The day seemed a perfect combination of uncertainty and possibility. Would the snow continue? Would the sun appear? Would the wind continue to agitate the hungry winter land or blow itself into exhaustion? Would winter ever end? Did this land ever feel the warmth of a gooey summer sun that spread itself out into daisies, forsythia and corn that was "as high as an elephant's eye?"

An old tractor lay in a field, half-covered with snow, pitched left, as if it had been trapped in the web of the snowstorm and couldn't escape. A long silver train lumbered across the unraveling countryside moaning, struggling, it seemed, to climb into the rising mountains, on a pilgrimage to some town where friends, family and Christmas were waiting. Along the road were tall snowy pines. The wind stirred their crests, spraying white dust into the air. As Alice took a sharp curve, she pierced a scattering cloud of it.

That's when she saw it through a scrim of haze: a massive brown body, brutish and beautiful, a crown of antlers like bare limbs rising from his head. The deer stood commandingly across the yellow line in the center of the road, his liquid eyes fixed and fearless.

She slammed on her brakes. The tires screeched like a wild animal. The car lurched and skidded forward for an eternity, and Alice braced for impact. The front bumper finally stuttered and bounced to a halt, only inches from the deer's resolute body.

Reality returned slowly, in a cold silence. The deer was dead still, his magnificent brown eyes radiating a cool, proud confidence. No fright!

Alice recovered, peeling her stiff fingers from the steering wheel, dropping her shoulders, and releasing quick breaths. She studied the deer. It watched her. White vapor puffed from his nostrils.

They were alone on the road. No other cars anywhere. Neither moved. It was a moment of extraordinary splendor.

A long moment later, a car approached from the opposite direction. The deer still didn't stir. The black SUV slowed to a crawl and then stopped. Alice craned her neck to see the driver, but she didn't have a clear view. The deer blocked her vision.

The driver quietly opened his door and eased out. Alice shifted left until she could see him. She stared in silent confusion, barely breathing. It couldn't be! It was Jack! She reached for the door latch and gently lifted it. She got out, looking first at the deer then at Jack, feeling the wind blow sharply across her ears. Gathering thick clouds over the mountains were heavy with snow.

Alice reached for her coat and put it on, not taking her eyes from the deer. His liquid brown orbs shifted as he watched them, while Alice and Jack studied him in hushed astonishment. Jack's eyes strayed to Alice. He lifted his chin, his gaze intent and searching, his hands stuffed into his brown leather jacket.

The deer tilted his head, as if hearing silent music. When he moved, in a slow delicate prance, his muzzle high and probing, Alice held her breath. Then the lightning of urgency and freedom struck. He bolted and didn't seem earthbound, as he sprang across the pavement, off the shoulder, plunging down a gully into the darkness of the trees, out of sight.

Alice and Jack followed him with their eyes. Then, slowly, they turned. Their eyes met. It was a fragile moment.

"I've never seen that before," Jack said.

Alice nodded, turning away from the wind. "I almost hit it. Him?"

"You okay?" Jack asked, quickly.

"Yes."

"... Yes, that was 'a him' all right, and he was big."

"Why the antlers?" Alice asked.

"They fight with other deer. Competition for mates."

"He was beautiful," Alice said.

Jack looked toward the trees. "That he was. Strange, he stayed so long and... no traffic in either direction. Maybe that's why."

Alice crossed her arms and looked away, so he wouldn't see the vulnerability and hopefulness in her eyes.

Jack ran his hand through his hair, mussed by the wind, seeking the right words. "I really did want to see you last night."

Alice didn't speak. She continued to avert his eyes.

"I was on my way just now to see you. To tell you that. I had a kind of disagreement with my daughter, Kristie, last night and... well, it just didn't seem right somehow to leave... And I needed to talk with my son."

"I understand. Really. I got your note."

"My note?"

"Yes, the one you left under my door."

Jack appeared confused.

Alice saw the confusion, but figured it was because she hadn't contacted him in response. "I told Nora to tell you I had to leave."

Jack zipped his jacket up to the neck, and pointed to where the deer had fled. "Without him, we would have passed each other without knowing it."

"Maybe."

"I called you about ten minutes ago... left a voicemail," Jack said.

"I turned my phone off. The battery is low. I forgot to charge it last night."

Alice trembled. Jack noticed. "Look, Alice... I'd love to take you cross-country skiing today. It's supposed to clear up around noon. It would be perfect."

Alice toed at the ground. "I'm sorry. I can't."

"Can't you leave tonight? Tomorrow?"

She shook her head. "No."

"I'll even take breakfast... coffee... anything."

She looked into the brilliance of his handsome face, his full lips, his pleading eyes, his raven hair scattered into a perfect art. She wanted to move into him, dance with him, brush his cheek with her hand. She knew him well at that moment. Yes! Of course she did! They had shared moments, undocumented by experience perhaps, but the diary had introduced him to her and revealed the man—a man filled with honesty and conviction. A good man. Her body had awakened and responded to his words, to the first sight of him, to the sound of his voice.

Jack stood waiting for an answer, as the wind came in little bursts; as snow stuck to her coat and frosted Jack's hair.

But it seemed obvious now that their time had come and gone. Last night might have changed everything; might have cracked open the world to the possibility of a new life, but it didn't happen, and Alice was sure that it didn't happen for a darn good reason: because it wasn't meant to happen.

And there was Philip, who loved her. Was she being fair to him? No. Nor to their commitment. She and Philip had a history, a real history, with confidences and trust; arguments that had hammered out the dents of differences and conflicts into smooth workable models of relating and sharing; they had strategies for the future; they had long intimate nights that had endeared and excited. They had a past, present and future. They had a sure thing. Their new life was planned and ready to begin.

Her body relaxed in relief. She'd made her decision. "I have to go, Jack."

He shrugged in disappointment. "Someone else?"

"Yes. Someone is waiting."

"It had to be." His chest rose with a breath, then fell. "I guess you could say you're like that buck deer out there."

Alice lifted a questionable eyebrow.

"It came as a great surprise. It woke me up to things I hadn't felt in a long time, and it showed me the wonder of life again—even if it flashed away too fast." He looked at her deeply. "I wish I could have known you better, Alice."

She melted away into his eyes. She would have to go, NOW, or she would stay, and never leave him again.

She returned to her car, belted herself in and closed the door. She drove by Jack slowly, allowing her eyes to linger on him and rest in his gaze. He nodded, and in that last look of longing, he gave her the most unspeakable pleasure and agony that she'd ever felt—or knew she was capable of feeling. It took all her strength to keep going, watching him through her rearview mirror grow smaller until she rounded a curve and he faded from sight.

CHAPTER 14

Minutes later, Alice looked right and saw the diary lying on the seat next to her. She'd forgotten about it. She whipped the car to the side of the road and stopped. Cars passed. Time passed. The wind whistled. She agonized, arguing with herself. The diary seemed almost alive! She shook her head at the absurdity of the thought.

It's Jack's, and he should have it! She should have handed it to him and then the whole thing would have been over. Did she keep it because she didn't want it to be over? Who was she kidding? She checked her mirrors. The road was clear. She made an abrupt U-turn and raced back to Meadow Green.

At the same curve in the road where'd she'd left Jack, the black SUV was still parked on the shoulder, driverless. Alice pulled over and parked behind it, shut off the engine and reached for her phone. She called Philip.

When he answered, she couldn't find her voice.

"Hello... Hello?"

"It's me, Philip," Alice finally said, in a tight, thin voice.

"You sound funny. I can barely hear you."

Alice lowered her head. "Philip... I'm having doubts."

"What? You're breaking up, Alice. I didn't hear you."

She spoke up. "I'm not sure... I mean... Philip... I think I need more time."

"Time for what?"

"I'm confused or something. I don't know... I need time to think about everything."

Philip's voice turned cold and stern. "Are you with somebody?"

"No. But... Look, I'm trying to be honest with you and with us. I'm just, I don't know. I'm not sure I can go through with the marriage right now."

"Not sure? Where are you? I'll meet you."

"No..."

"Alice, I know you. I may know you better than you know yourself! Tell me what has happened. Something has happened to you between Friday night and today. What is it?"

Alice switched the phone to her left ear, glancing down at the diary. "I just need time, Philip, that's all. Just a little more time to try to figure everything out."

"Dammit, Alice, you've had two years! Level with me! You're not being fair!"

Alice cleared her voice. "You're right, Philip... I'm not." She struggled to push out the words. "I met someone..."

"You're breaking up again. What?"

She spoke louder, "I met someone..."

Alice felt the cold, like a liquid, fill up her body.

When Philip spoke, his voice was edgy and remote. "I thought so. You just met him, or has this been going on behind my back!?"

"No! I just met him... Oh, God... I don't know what happened. I don't know!"

"Okay, Alice. Fine! You call the guests, the vendors, and the families and *you* tell them your happy news! I'm certainly not going to!"

"Philip, please, I just need…"

"And you should know me well enough to know that I won't give up without a fight!"

"Philip, just give me…"

But he was gone.

Slowly, painfully, Alice lowered the phone.

Five minutes later, when Jack appeared from the woods, Alice was still sunk in sadness behind the wheel of her car. He saw her and stopped, caught between surprise and delight. He started toward her. As he approached, Alice reached for the diary and quickly slipped it under her seat. She'd had all the bare truth she could handle for one day. She rolled down her window and flashed a half smile, but she was on the verge of tears. "You're still here."

"Yeah… I was looking for the buck. Thought he might have hung around, but he's gone."

He looked at her directly, seeing sadness. "Are you all right?"

Alice looked down. "I don't really know what I'm doing…"

"Is that someone still waiting?" Jack asked.

"Yes, Jack, he's still waiting… and I don't know what to do."

Jack looked skyward, then toward the mountains. When he spoke, his voice was hesitant and low. "What do you want to do, Alice?"

Alice let out a long breath. "I'm tired. I'm tired of thinking about all this. I want someone else to make my decisions. I want to be the person I was two days ago, before…" She stopped, her voice trailing off.

Jack caught her eyes as the thunder roll of a jet passed over. He waited until the silence returned. "Maybe this is our time, Alice. Maybe we've each lived a long, searching life—a lonely life—and now it's time for us."

His words brought tears. Alice leaned away, wiping her damp cheeks. When she faced him, her eyes were red-rimmed. "Jack... I don't want to leave."

Alice followed Jack's car up into the mountains. The world shimmered with hope and terror. Alice felt as though she were experiencing a death and rebirth; about to break through the crust of a hard crinkly skin and wiggle away from it, like a snake, free and exposed. Her volatile emotions changed with the weather: happiness to despair. Bright optimism to fear.

The sky shed thick clouds, forcing them to the edge of the horizon. Then there were sporadic bursts of sunlight revealing winter lakes, tree stubbled hills and ski trails. Minutes later, a raw wind blew in a foggy cluster of clouds that hugged the mountains and spewed frenzied snow.

As she traveled down the far side of the mountain, Alice saw sloping valleys, and sunlight winking off distant cars. A bulky, blue-square log cabin loomed out ahead, surrounded by rising land and endless rows of sugar-coated evergreens that stood in formation, like soldiers with a firm patience.

Jack turned into a narrow winding drive and she followed him, viewing the countless sizes and varieties of trees, some standing at arms' length from her window: Douglas fir, Fraser fir, Balsam fir, white pine and Scotch pine.

They parked in a gravel lot outside a cozy, log cabin-style warming hut, strung with Christmas lights. Alice stepped out and took a deep breath of the cold lively air, filled with the scent of pine. Jack wandered over.

"Beautiful, huh?" he asked.

"Where are we?"

"Gosser's Tree Farm. It has great cross-country ski trails and horse-drawn sleigh rides. I've known Mike Gosser and his wife, Nancy, for years. We went to high school together. It's time we went cross-country skiing."

They started for the hut. Inside, they were met by Mike Gosser, a short, stocky man with a bald, domed head, stubby arms, a whitish gray beard and a face filled with ruddy happiness. Dressed in a bright red ski sweater and loose jeans, Mike resembled a modern version of Santa Claus.

He hugged Jack like an aggressive bear, then bear-hugged Alice, as if she'd been a part of his family for years. Alice struggled for breath as Jack introduced her.

"You're gonna have a helluva time!" Mike bellowed in a deep base voice that rumbled. Then he released her, throwing his hands to his hips. "Look at you, Jack. Look at this guy," he said to Alice. "Still handsome, still fit, still with hair and now with the prettiest girl I've seen since I saw Nancy, a-hundred and one years ago, it seems." He swept in close to Alice's face and his mischievous eyes enlarged. "She's my wife. She's as fat as me and twice as smart!" He laughed deeply. "She's up at the house pounding out the bills and fighting the vendors!" He laughed again.

Alice smiled timidly, turned and warmed her hands at the wood stove that crackled and soothed. Firewood was stacked in a wood box near a cluster of cushioned benches and a deep worn, brown couch. The room was lit by some track lighting as well as by various-sized gas and kerosene lamps. Mike told her that drinking water was

177

available from a pump out the back door on the deck. "Comes from a well with the freshest water you've ever drunk," he said. "The kitchen is equipped with a gas stove, pots and pans, dishes and utensils for ten people, who can spread out sleeping bags or whatever," Mike added. "Jack helped me build this hut. That's why it's so sturdy. The deck is a work of art."

"It's got some flaws," Jack said. "You didn't give me enough time on it."

"Listen to Mr. Perfectionist here."

Jack looked around. "Where is everybody?"

"A big group just left about fifteen minutes ago. Two of them have never done cross-country before." He slapped his bold and bountiful belly with both hands. "Big old sons-a-bucks like me. From Kentucky."

"Business good?" Jack asked.

"Yeah, real good this year." Mike turned his attention to Alice. "When this guy called me a few minutes ago and told me he was coming, and not with Andrew or Kristie (that heartbreaker daughter) but with a woman, I almost dropped to the damned floor!"

Jack shifted, uncomfortably. "Yeah... a Mike, you still have that morning rate?"

"Stop it, Jack. Ski as much as you want. I think I still owe you a thousand or so for this hut."

"Mike, you paid that two years ago."

"Whatever. You also helped me cut eight miles of trails and built that hut up near the pond."

Jack's eyes shifted awkwardly, feeling Alice watching him. "Mike, we're going to need some equipment and..."

Mike pointed toward the back room, to a small ski shop, where rental and retail equipment hung from the walls in neat rows. Alice turned. A teenage girl with spiked blond-and-green hair, freckles, granny glasses and a confident expression, nodded from behind a mahogany counter. "That's Carly, my daughter. She'll set you up and put you on your way. Jack, you know where the hot drinks are on the honor system: hot chocolate, coffee, and tea. And then there's eggnog in that little fridge over there, no booze inside." He squinted sheepishly. "... Except when Nancy's not around, which means that today, it's loaded." He guffawed. "Hot damn, I'm a funny son-of-a buck!"

Jack helped Alice retrieve her suitcase from the car and carried it to the hut's dressing room in the rear of the shop. She went to work, rapidly changing into her long underwear and then pulling on some ski pants Carly had helped her choose, as well as one of her own white wool sweaters.

Meanwhile, Jack ripped the top from a package of hot chocolate, shook it into a white mug and poured steaming hot water over it. He wandered to the couch, stirring, preoccupied. He sat and continued to stir with a wooden stick, lost in thought. Mike was watching him, while sipping a generous cup of eggnog.

They began catching up on business and family news, both lamenting the mysterious ways of their teenage daughters and how glad they'd be when they grew up to be "Daddy's Girl" again.

"Kristie looks so much like her mother sometimes, but she has my father's biting tongue. She can slash you to pieces with it," Jack said.

Mike lowered his voice and threw a coy glance toward Carly. "I can't get Carly to talk to me at all. I ask her a question and she just bats those long lashes and says 'I don't know... We didn't go anywhere. I don't smoke, Daddy. I don't do nothing.'" Mike shook his head, frustrated. "Yeah. Right!"

Jack looked down sorrowfully. "Yeah, one day they're five or six and will only eat cold pasta and ketchup, hugging you with those fat little arms and then, suddenly, they're nearly grown, and it's like you don't know who they are, what they want or what to do with them. Kristie used to talk a lot about her mother, now she almost never mentions her and, when she does, it's all... well..." Jack squared his shoulders. "... You know... angry."

Mike was anxious to move the conversation along, and he soon managed to steer it toward Alice and how she and Jack had met.

"So, tell me everything, Jack."

Jack was reticent and fidgety. "This is our first date, Mike, give me a break."

Mike dropped to the couch next to him and Jack felt the floor shake. "I ain't giving you no break, Jack. I saw it in your eyes as soon as you came in. You're caught. And, hey, I'm all for it, buddy."

Jack nearly drained the cup of chocolate. "The water wasn't so hot, Mike."

"So sue me. And don't change the subject."

"I don't know her at all, Mike. I like her, yes. But... she has someone else."

Mike's eyes widened. "What? Married?"

"Not yet, but almost." Jack straightened with gentle alarm. "Do you really believe a woman with her looks and intelligence wouldn't be with somebody?"

Mike drilled him with his eyes. "She's with you, ain't she? I mean, Duh! With you and not with that 'somebody'? Actions always, ALWAYS, speak louder than words, my friend. I saw the way she looked at you. Like you stepped off her own private dreamboat."

"Dreamboat?"

Mike shrugged. "Okay, so it's something Nancy would say. See what eighteen years of marriage does? There was a time I wouldn't have been caught dead saying something like that. But over time, part of me has morphed into Nancy and her into me. We're like two Christmas candles that have kinda melted into each other over the years. My point is that Alice likes you BIG-time!"

Jack stood, staring nervously. "I'm scared, Mike. Scared I won't know what to say to her; scared she'll think I'm stupid; scared I won't do the right things. I mean, I haven't been with a woman—a woman I've really liked—since…" He paused. "Since Darla."

"I know. Believe me, I know! Way too long."

"I don't know where the years have gone, Mike. I don't know what happened. It's like, when I saw her, I just sort of woke up from a long, long sleep."

Alice opened the dressing room door and walked past Carly into the main room, where Jack and Mike looked on admiringly. The Gore-Tex waterproof pants and wool sweater drew easy attention to her breasts, hips and slim waist. Under the glimmer of the track lights, her auburn hair was full, burnished and fetching. She stood stiffly, feeling on stage.

Jack finally found an elusive breath. "Well, let's get outfitted and hit the trail."

Carly quickly fitted them with boots, skis and poles. Mike brought out a blue, fleece-lined parka with an elastic waist drawstring and hood, and he assisted Alice into it. Carly handed her a blue ski cap and some thick gloves, while Jack slipped into a red, black and gray jacket with a storm collar and hood.

Alice felt jumpy and excited, but she didn't allow it to show. She moved slowly, spoke softly and avoided Jack's eyes, because she knew they would give her away: they would hold tenderness and invitation; they would tell the story of her heart; a heart wide open and burning. He would see a woman who suddenly wanted to praise the world. Perhaps he'd also see a woman struggling with guilt and confusion.

Jack looked at himself in the mirror, zipping up the jacket and noticing an odd reflection in his eyes. The deep sorrow he'd been seeing for so many years was replaced by hope, anticipation and fear. When he took a deep breath, he could almost feel himself expand out into the world like a hot-air balloon. He looked at Alice's reflection in the mirror, and the joy of "taking her in" filled him with pleasure and vigor.

He turned and their eyes met—a brief, courageous glance. A rush of desire made them quickly disengage.

Alice and Jack carried their thin skis outside and Mike strolled along with them toward a trail leading from the hut through a row of soft-needled Balsam trees, into relatively open snowy land. They trudged against a cold gentle wind and sporadic snowflakes, hearing the muted echo of birds and the distant growl of a snowmobile. The clouds parted, then gathered and closed off the sun again, making the distant hills and winter landscape appear beautifully desolate and challenging. Mike looked toward the sound of the snowmobile. "The most difficult trails are groomed by snowmobiles. Otherwise, we don't allow them on any of the trails."

Mike lowered his sunglasses against the sharp glare of the snow, while Alice and Jack adjusted their goggles.

"Do you sell a lot of trees?" Alice asked.

"Oh, I guess we harvest about twenty to thirty thousand trees each year," Mike said. "Of course we plant new trees to maintain the perpetual tree growth. We also donate a lot of trees to various charities. That was Nancy's idea."

"I've never seen so many Christmas trees in one place."

"Well, we plant about 2,000 trees per acre. Only about 1,000-1,500 survive. Then we've got to shear them to give them the Christmas tree shape."

"How long does it take a tree to grow?"

"Oh, about six to ten years... that's fighting wind, heavy rain, hail and drought, employees and equipment. It's a helluva business. My father started it. My real passion, though, is managing the cross-country skiing business. Nothing like it."

They approached an old stone bridge arching over a noisy splashing creek, and stopped near a wooded hillside where the trail began.

"Okay, kids. I'll leave you two here. Jack's been on this trail. It's my favorite. Give me a shout, Jack, when you get back to the hut. I'll come down and say goodbye."

After Mike ambled away, Jack and Alice placed their narrow skis on the snow, clicked the boot toe pieces into the bindings with an easy snap and passed each other a quick tentative smile.

"Since I've never gone cross-country before," Alice said, "it might take me awhile to get the hang of it."

"Take all the time you need. We're in no hurry."

They checked their skis once more before gliding off, free-heeling their way along the well-groomed trail. Their thin skis slid easily within the set of tracks made by previous skiers, and they heard far-off laughter to their right, where a group of skiers were struggling to conquer an intensive uphill.

Neither spoke as they skied over quiet rolling pastures, down modest hills and through peaceful wooden paths. A short time later, the trail dropped swiftly down the side of a mountain and Alice lost her balance and nearly fell, recovering quickly, by bending and leaning left. They slid down the side of the mountain through trees crackling in the wind, and at the base near a wildlife pond, they had a gorgeous view of the distant snowy hills. They stopped to rest. Jack pointed across the lake.

"There's a bench over there, if I remember correctly. Would you like to rest?"

Lack of sleep the night before had diminished Alice's strength. She nodded.

They skied around the lake, scattering a couple of puddle ducks, who flapped wildly, complaining in staccato quacks. They slapped across the top of the water, webbed feet dragging, finally lifting skyward into the slant of the wind, gliding over a bank of trees.

"Most of them go south," Jack said, fascinated. "Don't see many of them around here in the winter. I'm glad these stayed around to keep us company."

Alice smiled. It sounded like the Jack she had read about in the Christmas Diary.

They raked newly fallen snow from the bench and sat down, both enjoying the intimacy while trying to appear casual.

"If the sun comes out, it'll warm up," Jack said. He quickly realized the utter obviousness of the statement and he dropped his head, feeling a small humiliation. He tried again. "So how do you like cross-country skiing?"

Alice nibbled on her lower lip. "I like it, very much. Makes me feel peaceful."

"Yeah, I'd almost forgotten that," Jack said. "Kind of brings you back to yourself."

Alice paused. "Jack... There's something I wanted to tell you. I have to tell you."

She hesitated. Jack looked skyward.

"... I'm supposed to get married on Christmas Day." She paused, hearing the regret in her voice, feeling the sting of surprise in her stomach that she had blurted it out. "I just felt I should tell you that."

Jack was silent for a moment before lifting his goggles to his forehead and straightening. Her words changed the quality of silence. They sat staring.

Finally Jack spoke. "Yeah, I guess I figured that. Nora told me that."

Alice studied him. "So I guess what I'm saying is, I don't feel very good about myself right now. I should be with him, finalizing menus and travel plans and music and... a hundred other things. I shouldn't be here."

Jack looked ahead, nodding a little. "Alice... Sometimes things just hit us, just like that storm hit us the other night. It shakes us up—changes us and sends us down a new road; a road we wouldn't have seen and didn't know was there. It doesn't make us bad or good. Sometimes, it just happens."

He faced her. "I'm glad you're here, Alice. Whatever you decide to do. I'm glad you're here."

She smiled, ruefully. "The truth is, Jack, I think I'm scared of this marriage."

Jack nodded. "I was married once—a long time ago, it seems now. It was a good thing. A real good thing."

Alice lifted her goggles. "Did you know you loved your wife when you first met?"

He didn't hesitate. "Yes. I knew. Right off."

"Did she know?"

Alice studied his reaction. He stared, soberly. "I don't know."

"If it's not too personal, what happened to her?"

He clasped his gloved hands together. "Well, that's a long story. To make that long story short, she was killed in a fire out west, about four years ago.

Alice was surprised and saddened. "I'm sorry."

"... Thank you. Yes... it was tragic. Hard on the kids, even though she'd left us many years back. She was a writer—not when we were together—but after she left. Sold a novel and was working on another. She was living with an older man, a famous painter, but I don't know that much about art, so I'd never heard of him. He died only a year or so before the fire."

The sun broke through the clouds and shadows washed the mountains. The snow stopped.

Jack continued on in a fragile voice, lost in old sorrow. "She thought I hated her for leaving us, but I didn't. I didn't really understand it, but I didn't hate her. She said she felt lost and trapped. Not always," he added rapidly, as if to preserve some dignity. "Sometimes she was happy. And she loved the kids. I knew that. Know that. She was a good mother. When I think back on it now, I see that I just didn't see things so clear." He quickly corrected his English. "I didn't see things clearly. Well, I was young. What do you know about love when you're so young? After so many years, now, I wonder if I really loved her at all. I hurt a lot for a while but, I don't know, maybe I thought that was love." He lifted his hands. "I thought I could love for the both of us, no matter what, but I didn't always understand her the way I should have. She was secretive and lived a lot on the inside. I've always lived out... outside where you can see and understand things. The truth is, I was just young, and I believed things were simple—one way—when they weren't. I should have seen."

"Aren't you being a little hard on yourself?" Alice asked, softly.

He took off his right glove and wiped his mouth. "No... I don't think so. I mean, the kids... kids never really understand. Andrew worries me. He's inside like Darla. I don't know what he feels or thinks most of the time... not really. He went off somewhere early this morning, but where? I don't know. That's what happens when you work a lot of hours. Your kids get independent."

"What about Kristie?"

Jack looked over, uneasy. "Am I boring you?"

"Not at all."

After Jack saw the sincerity in her eyes he continued. "Kristie's more like my father, I think. Rebellious, independent. Talented like her mother though. Don't think she got much from me except maybe some stubbornness... and she doesn't mind hard work. Her grades are good and she's the opposite of most teenagers when it comes to her room: it's spotless, everything in place."

He paused for a moment and rubbed his eyes. "I don't know, Alice. I don't know if I'm the father I wanted to be. I'm always questioning that, especially now as they're growing up and showing themselves in new ways. Surprising ways. It's scary sometimes. I probably should have remarried but..."

Alice's stole a look at his face, then looked away. "Why didn't you?"

Jack stared at her for a moment, finding her irresistibly alluring. "Yeah, that's a big one. I don't know. I meant to, for the kids. I tried to... But after Darla left, I just couldn't think straight, couldn't work; just couldn't put two thoughts together that made any sense." His eyes wandered with the shadows.

"I hope I've done the right things for them," he said.

Alice found his eyes. "You know what my mother once said. She said, 'I know I made mistakes, but I figured as long as my kids knew I loved them, that was the most important thing.' And we knew she loved us, even though she wasn't always perfect, at least in our eyes."

Jack considered her words and then nodded. "I like that. I hope my kids know that. Anyway, that was a nice thing to say, Alice."

Alice looked into the moving sky. "I'm getting a little cold. Maybe we should ski for a while," she said.

"I know a good trail back to the hut."

They stood and, while Jack lowered his ski mask, Alice's attention was suddenly caught by a sudden movement in a cluster of trees near the pond. A raw wind punched the crests of the trees, spraying a shower of snow which fell like a shimmering wave. And then Alice saw him: Dr. Landis was standing there! In a sudden burst of wind, his wild hair exploded up like white fire. His taut, ravaged face was stamped with conflict and surprise.

He waved hopefully.

In a desperate reflex, Alice pointed and screamed.

Jack whirled toward her pointing finger.

Dr. Landis had vanished.

CHAPTER 15

They skied swiftly, silently, through a late morning that had turned treacherous. The restless gray sky seemed agitated. The fierce, bone-chilling wind punished their backs and nearly sent them para-gliding down steep hills. They ducked and poled themselves forward until they finally came to a low-lying, sheltered trail that was hemmed in by stone walls and tall pines, where pastures once met an old stagecoach road. After a brief but silent rest, they braced themselves again and moved on into open land with a stunning view of the high eastern hills.

Jack was certain he must have said or done something to upset Alice, but for the life of him he didn't know what it was.

She refused to talk. "It was just a deer or something," was all she would say after she screamed and pointed into the trees. But she was noticeably shaken. She had paled and she trembled.

They skied on.

Inside Alice's body was a raging storm. She could no longer dismiss it or rationalize it; she couldn't pass it off and wish it would go away, or that it had never happened. Whatever or whoever that madman was, she had to face the fact that in some inexplicable way, he was "real" and that she was in the grip of something terrifying and weird. She'd been ignoring the signs and coincidences right from the beginning, even before she'd found the diary. The premature snowstorm; the barren lifeless landscape, where she'd become lost and disoriented; the man materializing from nowhere, leading her to Hattie's Bed and Breakfast; his mentioning the bookshelf: "Browse the shelves," he'd said. "Take a real good look, even at things behind the books… in the very back of the shelves."

She sought rational possibilities. Was the man a ghost or was he some psychological projection? Perhaps he represented her father or her deepest feelings of insecurity and unresolved issues from childhood? Perhaps the "sightings" had been brought about by fatigue, stress or fear of marriage. It was also possible that she was mentally unstable. As chilling and upsetting as that was, she had to consider it. But then, the folks at the diner in Eden Grove had described the doctor in every detail; had said he'd been seen by others.

She felt Jack's eyes on her as they crested a hill and paused, gazing down at the main hut. They pressed on. Alice's legs were wobbly, her arms weak, and she was heaving in gulps of cold air that burned her lungs.

But it had all accelerated when she'd found Jack's diary and read it. All of this wouldn't have happened if she hadn't gone looking for Jack. Why did she do it? She had no one else to blame except herself. She was responsible. So the question was: what was she going to do now?

After she had changed clothes, Alice entered the communal room and took a mug of hot chocolate from Jack, who seemed to be working on a complex thought.

The fire was alive and crackling. Alice and Jack shared the hut with eight other skiers, some hugging the fire, others seated on the couch and chairs, drinking from mugs and bantering about their skiing adventure.

"Feeling better?" Jack asked.

Alice nodded. "Some."

"Hungry?"

"A little. Still thawing out."

"Yeah, it was cold. The weather people missed that one. I heard it's supposed to snow again—about five inches."

Alice frowned. "That's not good."

Jack breathed in his angst. "Would you like to have lunch?"

Alice took a drink and felt the warmth gather in her chest. Despite the warmth, she shuddered. "I think I'm going back to The Broadmoore. I didn't get much sleep last night and I have some things to do. Calls to make."

Jack tried not to show his disappointment.

"But, if you're free, we could meet for dinner," she said, subdued. "I mean, if you can arrange it with your kids—with Kristie and Andrew."

Jack stood taller. "Yes. I'm sure it will be fine with them. We can make up for last night."

Alice turned serious. "Jack, I need to discuss some things with you tonight."

"I'd like that. I'm sorry I talked so much back there. I guess I..."

Alice interrupted. "... I enjoyed listening to you, Jack. I really did." She made a vague gesture with her free hand. "It's just that, I need to... well, tell you some things about myself."

Jack was relieved. "Alice... I can tell you're really going through something, and it's none of my business, but

I just want you to know that I really like your company and if I can help you in any way, I will."

Her eyes glided out over the room and suddenly filled with tears. It irritated her! She wasn't one of those women who cried at the drop of a hat. She sat the mug down, wiped her glistening eyes and then placed a hand over her mouth. "Damn! I should go."

She left to retrieve her coat. When she returned, she'd recovered, but didn't look directly into Jack's eyes. "I can be ready at seven."

"I'll be there," Jack said. "Can you find your way back all right?"

"Yes, thanks. Please thank Mike for everything."

When Alice entered The Broadmoore, Nora came from the living room and met her. She was still wearing her Sunday dress, all smiles and hand-patting, her bright eyes reflecting the lights of the Christmas tree. "I'm so happy you came back! How long are you going to be with us?" Nora asked.

"Probably just the night," Alice said, in a crisp business-like manner, noticing three new, elaborately wrapped Christmas presents under the tree. "You know it's going to snow five more inches and I really don't want to drive in that." Alice was trying to keep her self-composure.

"Of course you don't," Nora said.

Ozzie appeared and lugged Alice's bags back up the stairs and into her room, looking blunted and world-weary. He said he was working a lot of hours to save money for Christmas presents.

"Have you finished your shopping?" he asked.

"I'm afraid not," Alice answered, nearly depressed at the thought.

The boy's impressive hair was spiked stiff and shooting out threateningly, like a porcupine. Alice turned away from him and suppressed a surprising urge to giggle. She needed to laugh and was grateful to him for that. Before she tipped him, she ordered a ham and Swiss cheese sandwich on whole wheat and a cup of the soup of the day, which Ozzie said was vegetable beef.

"I had some, and it's pretty good, although it's kinda backed up on me, probably because I was carrying some heavy things," he said. "I have a hiatal hernia."

Alice suppressed another grin.

When he returned with her order, Alice had not moved from the end of the bed where she'd been sitting, staring out the window at the snow flurries. She ate slowly, working and re-working conversations she'd have to have with Jack, Philip, her father, her sister and her friends. By the time she'd finished lunch, her mind had locked up. She was exhausted. She spread out on the bed, covered herself with the down comforter, and fell asleep.

She awakened on the third ring of the hotel telephone and clumsily reached for it.

"I tracked you down," Philip said.

Alice blinked around, disoriented. A dream about her candle shop catching on fire still clung to her eyes. "What?"

"But then it's not a big town and I know how much you love to stay in the local bed and breakfast. Remember the one we stayed in last fall in Vermont?"

"Yes."

"You sound asleep."

"Because I am," Alice said, hoarsely, getting up and leaning back against the headboard and rubbing her glassy eyes.

"I'm coming to see you," Philip said.

Alice snapped awake. "What? No, Philip!"

"Do you think I'm going to sit here and wait for you to make all the decisions? Do you think we're going to discuss this—one of the most important decisions of our lives—on the phone!? No, Alice. No way. I'm sick of this. I'd have left already if I didn't have to finish the draft of an oral argument I have to e-mail this evening to Howard in New York. This is a case that could really do it for me, Alice. It could do it for us. I can't discuss it with you now, but believe me, it's a story that's going to hit the media after Christmas. Anyway, we've got to talk about this—*us*—face to face. Whatever is going on, we can work through it. I know we can."

Alice massaged the bridge of her nose. "Philip... okay. Look, there's no need for you to come here. I'm leaving tomorrow."

"Yeah, right! Forget it, Alice. I've heard that song before. I'll be there by eight tomorrow morning. Don't leave! We're going to get closer because of this, Alice, you'll see. I don't care who this clown is you think you're in—whatever—attracted to. Once we talk this through, calmly and clearly, once we're together again, you'll forget all about this whole incident. I promise you. I'll see you tomorrow. I'm armed and ready for battle!"

Alice held the phone limply in her hand until the ear-piercing screech of the busy signal shattered the air. She hung up. The clock read 4:07. She'd slept almost 3 hours!

She called her father but he wasn't there. She didn't leave a message. Her sister didn't answer either. Everybody was probably out Christmas shopping. Alice left a message.

"Hi, Jacinta. It's Alice. I know Philip has probably called and told you everything, and you haven't called because he told you not to, because that's the kind of thing he does, but look, everything's fine. I'll tell you all about it in a day or so. Call if you want to, or you can wait. On second thought, maybe waiting is better. I'm just real confused right now. Anyway, hope you're all well. Say hello to Chris and the kids. Love you."

Next she dialed the shop and waited for Roland to answer. He did on the third ring. "Not as busy as yesterday, but we're not doing bad," he said. "Are you getting those wedding day jitters?" he asked, chuckling.

"Roland… You have no idea."

"I'll be there, baby doll, pushing you on. Don't worry. Don't sweat it. Just don't ask me to spend any time with that…"

Alice cut him off. "… Don't say it!"

"Philip!" he said, cackling like a witch.

"Roland…" Alice scolded, "That's enough!"

Then in a calm, insincere voice, Roland continued… "Okay, okay. He's a lovely person. He just hates me and I loathe him."

"Yes, Roland, I know. I know. I'll keep you separated at the wedding, somehow."

After hanging up, Alice shuffled into the bathroom. She turned on the water and dropped two orange oil beads into the churning water, watching them slowly melt and drift. They released the scent of fresh oranges.

Moments later she was in the tub, stretched out, resting her neck against the back rim, feeling the swirling, soothing warm water. If only she had more time to sort out her feelings! But tonight, she could focus on Jack. Her hands scooped and drifted, her toes wiggled happily and her heart fluttered whenever she thought of having dinner with him.

At one point a song came to her: *Have Yourself a Merry Little Christmas.* She hummed and sang and thought she sounded pretty good, at least in the bathroom echo chamber.

Ten minutes later, while shaving her legs, she noticed her fingernail polish was pocked and faded. She drained the tub, then switched on the shower and washed and deep-conditioned her hair. She stepped out, turbaned her head with a white towel, and then went to work removing the old nail polish, finally apply new polish. Red, of course.

As she was blow drying her hair, she wished she had those big fat rollers she'd kept at Philip's house. Her hair was thick and stubborn and she was growing increasingly concerned that, if she wasn't careful, she could end up looking like the bellhop kid, Ozzie.

She finally had to walk away from the hair struggle and start the makeup. She applied foundation and powder while watching the weather report on TV. The heavy snow hadn't started yet. It would come within the next few hours, bringing freezing rain and high wind. Would Philip make it, she thought? She quietly answered herself aloud. "I hope not." She quickly clarified what she really meant. "I hope he sees the report and doesn't leave Holbrook."

She stared into the mirror and applied lipstick and lip liner, feeling an irrepressible buoyancy, noticing her eyes were made larger by a sense of anticipation and hope; her face was relaxed and youthful. It was an unfamiliar expression; she stopped for a moment to study it, as if she were a stranger. Her mind wandered into fantasy: life with Jack and the kids, then to self-delusion: "This date is no big deal. We're just going to talk."

While she wandered the room in her bra and panties, oblivious to the rambling TV newscaster, she inserted a pair of small diamond stud earrings and continued to daydream possible dinner scenes and conversations. Back at the mirror, she posed and examined her figure, her long legs and short, trim waist. She leaned and turned in a slow laziness, lifting her sharp little nose, playfully teasing her hair, gently thrusting her full breasts, going for erotic innocence. Next she made her mouth prim, portraying a blend of brooding intensity and chilly emotional distance. The double knock on the door sent her pivoting toward it, startled, awakening her sharply from her sexy award-winning performance into a self-conscious embarrassment.

"Yes," she called, grabbing for her bathrobe.

"It's Ozzie."

"Who?"

"The bellhop, Ozzie."

"Oh, yes, Ozzie."

"I have flowers for you."

"Flowers!?"

"Yes."

She hesitated before opening the door a foot, pinching the bathrobe at the neck and giving Ozzie a slow guarded take.

Ozzie grinned through gapped front teeth, pleased. "They're roses! I can smell them."

Alice could smell them, too, so powerfully rich and intoxicating. They were wrapped and folded in lavish red and green decorative cellophane and topped with a broad red ribbon and bow. Ozzie presented them to her gingerly, base first, and when she gathered them up into her arms, she felt a solid vase. She tipped Ozzie five dollars.

After Ozzie left, she tore her eyes from the wrapping long enough to switch off the TV. She placed the flowers on the coffee table, unaware that she was smiling, and slowly peeled away the cellophane, allowing it to fall carelessly onto the floor. The roses burst out ecstatically, instantly filling the room with joy. Alice reached for the card, excited and impatient. She opened the cream-colored envelope, pausing briefly to read her name, printed on it in bold careful letters. She retrieved the card.

Alice:

> *Drove past the flower shop and it*
> *just seemed right. I guess that means*
> *I'm looking forward to tonight.*

> *-Jack*

Alice didn't have to glance at the mirror to know she was flushed. Her eyes flicked around the room for a place to display the flowers. Next to the bed! She placed the lead crystal vase on the night table, spread out the delicate half-opened roses, then backed away with arms crossed, taking them in.

She had to relax somehow, had to center herself. Yoga might do it. She looked around for an empty area, grabbed a towel and placed it on the floor. Although she usually went to an aerobics class these days, she'd been to enough Hatha yoga classes in New York to remember some of the postures. She pulled on her black sweatpants and a tee-shirt, and then she tied back her hair with a scarf. She stood on the edge of the towel and raised her arms to start a Sun Salutation.

Immediately, thoughts of Darla cut into her consciousness. What did she look like? Did she look like me!? Her eyes popped open. She lowered her arms and hastily reached for the hotel phone. She dialed the front desk and got the WI-FI password.

She sat cross-legged on the bed and opened her laptop. Once she was connected to the internet, she Googled "Darla Landis." Nothing. She keyed in "Improvisations Darla." The screen refreshed and five of the top listings had the information she was looking for.

"Improvisations. A Novel by Darla Seig."

Blinking fast, Alice clicked and waited, impatiently. The thumbnail book cover appeared with a short review of the book directly underneath. Alice clicked on the cover to enlarge the larger view. She focused on an illustration of a rusty western landscape, with tall jagged mountains against an expansive blue sky. The blurry image was of a blond woman in the midst of a long stride, moving toward a distant, winding, dusty road that was apparently beckoning her up into the azure mountains.

The reviews were mostly favorable. Alice skimmed them, landing on words like "original voice, but wandering", "haunting", "honest", "promising."

Alice scrolled down until she saw what she was looking for: Darla's color headshot photo on the Author's Page. She enlarged it and nosed toward the screen. Darla looked back at her with steady, penetrating blue eyes and the alluring mouth of someone caught between mirth and puzzlement. The face was nearly that of Kristie: thin, with smooth, creamy skin. There was a remarkable resemblance, but Darla's cheekbones were higher, and her lips not as full or as sensuous as her daughter's. Darla's blond hair was short and stylishly careless, but it didn't suit her somehow. It deepened the lines, blunted her glamor, strained to project the image of the "serious artist," not just another good-looking, blond babe writer. But there was no doubt that Darla had that "something"—that indefinable fascination of a woman who kept secrets and would never let you in on them.

Alice messaged the back of her neck. What was certain was that Alice did not look like Darla. Not at all, and that was a great relief. What was disturbing, though, was that Alice didn't believe she possessed any of the alluring mystery that Darla had. With Alice, what you saw was what you got. Men liked mystery, at least that's what she'd always heard. Jack surely was attracted to Darla's mystery. According to her photo, she was a mysterious moody beauty. Alice decided she'd have to work on that.

The hotel telephone rang. Alice, lost in thought, was startled. She reached for it.

"It's Nora, Alice. You got your flowers, I presume."

Alice adjusted herself on the bed. "Yes..."

"They smelled like roses," Nora said, with a girlish lilt.

"Yes, roses."

"Alice... I know you think I'm probably just an old gossip and I know you're in a very awkward position, but I want you to know that whatever happens, I wish you the best. I truly want you to be happy."

Alice glanced at the clock. It was 6:25! "Thank you, Nora."

Alice began dressing in slow, measured movements, wearing an outfit she'd recently bought in New York and intended to wear at the rehearsal dinner. She winced at the thought, then willed it away with a couple of quick blinks and an inadvertent wiggle of her nose, immediately reminding herself of Samantha on the old TV show *Bewitched*.

She stepped into snug but comfortable black wool pants that made her feel confident. Next, she pulled on a black silk turtleneck, and then finished her outfit with a form-fitting houndstooth jacket that set off the chestnut highlights of her hair and deepened the brown in her eyes.

At ten minutes to seven she slipped into her shoes: black Italian leather 2-inch heels. They would make her 5'10". Jack was about 6'2", so that would bring her up to about his chin. Snow or no snow, the shoes made her feel good, and, anyway, they'd be mostly inside. She shook out her hair, applied some mousse and added the final touches. Perfume was last. Chanel Coco Mademoiselle, a gift from Roland. He said that whenever she sprayed it on, she "was one of the most powerful women in New York." An overstatement, no doubt, but she was easily flattered.

At the first quiet knock, Alice flinched. She faced the door. That would be Jack. She looked at the diary that was lying on the bed and passed a warm glance toward the flowers. At dinner she'd tell him—tell him everything. And then she'd give him back his diary.

"I hope you know what you're doing," she muttered, as she slid the diary into her purse.

At the second knock, she straightened her shoulders, lifted her head and went to answer the door.

CHAPTER 16

Their eyes met. For one spontaneous moment, there was no hiding simple truth; none of the usual filtering of expectation or fear. Their hearts were not eclipsed by judgments or insecurities. The power of love surged.

The moment passed swiftly, in a blink of an eye. In its place came friendly but awkward words and clumsy gestures. Alice thanked Jack for the roses and complimented his tan corduroy jacket and chocolate brown turtleneck sweater. He said Kristie had helped him with the outfit and he hoped the roses would open.

"The guy at the florist promised me they would," he said.

He didn't compliment Alice: he was simply made mute by her beauty and entrancing perfume.

As they started down the stairs, they saw Nora, who seemed to be purring with satisfaction, even as they both struggled for composure.

"What a handsome couple!" she exclaimed.

Alice found a smile somewhere, but Jack expressed himself in embarrassed silence and a sharp nod of his head.

Outside, the air was crisp; the wind threw some punches as if spoiling for a fight. Flecks of snow whizzed by. Alice didn't wear a hat because of her hairdo, but during the short walk to the parking lot, the wind scattered and whipped it. All she could do was try to salvage what she could when she got into the car.

They drove for a while without speaking. Jack had things on his mind: things he wanted to discuss with Alice, and Alice's mind was spinning. She had buried the diary deep in her purse, which she held tightly on her lap. It seemed to be radiating, pulsing wildly, like her heart.

"I've never eaten at this restaurant," Jack finally said, "but I've done some work for the owner and Mike and Nancy gave it a good recommendation."

"You seem to have worked at a lot of places around town."

"Yeah, I suppose so. I've been lucky. I do some work for a guy and he recommends me to others and so on. I never have to advertise or put my business on the internet. I have so much work I can't keep up with it all. Not a bad problem to have... especially in this economy." He glanced over. "What do you do?"

"I have a candle and gift shop in New York."

"Really?"

"Yes. You'd imagined something else?"

"I guess I did."

"What?"

"I don't know, maybe a lawyer or something."

"Oh, God no! I mean there's nothing wrong with that but... no."

"Is it doing well?"

"Actually, no. I'll probably have to close it after the holidays."

"I'm sorry to hear it."

Alice tilted her head reflectively. "Yes. I really liked having my own business."

Jack paused, turning left down a main road where a heavy truck was slinging salt. He swerved around it. "Something like that would do well in Meadow Green. Tourism stays pretty steady all year. I know some people who could help you out."

Alice didn't look over. But the thought excited her.

Moments later, they parked in The Hillcrest Restaurant's lot, emerging anxiously from the car. The Hillcrest was a formidable red-brick building that had once been a bank. A Christmas wreath adorned the left of the double mahogany doors and white electric candles glowed from the windows. The lot was nearly full, and a dog's bark echoed, but there was a hushed winter serenity about the place that helped Alice relax.

Inside, Jack checked their coats, and they were led to their table by a blond, willowy young woman, who seemed to glide and gesture as if in a dance. The main dining room was spacious and elegant, with a generous fireplace, cream-colored walls and white linen tablecloths. They were seated near a window, with a clear view of a rock garden and a duck pond. Christmas carols were filtered through quiet speakers, and servers in black and white meandered through the tables attentively.

The menus arrived and their water glasses were filled.

"What did Mike recommend from the menu?" Alice asked, studying it.

"He said the Roasted Long Island Duck was good and the Chesapeake Crab Cakes."

Alice read the description of the duck: "Gingered raspberry-Amaretto glaze and almond couscous. Wow! Doesn't that sound wonderful!"

Alice glowed in the soft candlelight. Jack stared, feeling a peace he hadn't felt in years.

"And the crab cakes come with cottage fries and cabbage slaw in a remoulade sauce," she added.

"You've sold me," Jack said.

Alice looked up. "On which one?"

"Both."

Alice laughed.

"And I'll have a double order of the remoulade sauce, whatever that is."

"Ah, well actually," Alice said, "I know what that is because I made it once. A little mayonnaise, sour cream, some garlic, lemon juice and, I think some mustard, Dijon of course..."

"... Of course," Jack said, grinning.

"... And some pepper and... let me see, I think some dill weed."

Jack ordered the crab cakes and Alice the duck. Jack didn't know much about wine, so he'd called Mike, who gave him a few suggestions.

"Would a Cabernet Sauvignon be okay with you?" he asked Alice, after studying the wine list.

"Perfect," she said.

After the bread was served and wine poured in elegant crystal glasses, Alice and Jack toasted to the holidays. Then Jack asked Alice about her childhood, her parents, how she liked New York and how she usually celebrated Christmas. Alice talked continuously, enjoying the glint of pleasure in Jack's dark eyes, the way his right eyebrow occasionally arched; the way he laughed, easily, but not loudly; the way his broad shoulders enhanced the style of the jacket; the strength of his sharp jaw-line; the subtle expressions of his full sensitive mouth.

When the food arrived, they ate with an aggressiveness that surprised them. They were being driven by mild nerves and a mounting sense of urgency, both aware that serious conversation was to come. The wine gently intoxicated and then gradually eased the pace. The music entranced and helped to balance desire and trepidation.

As the table was being cleared, Alice leaned forward on her elbows, folded her hands and rested her chin on them. "So tell me, Jack, what are the latest fads for... let's say kitchens? I love nice kitchens."

"Are you serious?"

"Yes. Very."

"Okay, well, let's see. A wealthy couple who just built a home up near Laurel Lake wanted concrete countertops."

"Concrete!? I've never renovated a kitchen so I've never heard of such a thing. Granite, yes."

"Believe it or not concrete is lighter than granite."

"No way!" Alice said more loudly, feeling a little buzz from the wine.

"Yes, ma'am. Those countertops look fantastic. If I had the time, I'd put some in at the house. Concrete can be smoothed and polished like stone and you can color and texture it just like tile. It's great stuff. You can also inlay it with fossils or semiprecious stones. That's what the couple in Laurel Canyon did."

"Unbelievable!"

"But the high-end stuff is expensive."

"How expensive?" Alice asked.

Jack shook his head. "I can't believe you want to hear about this."

"I do! How much?"

"Oh, say $200 per square foot—or even more. That's about $6,000 and up for a typical kitchen. I just recently drew up an estimate for a newly retired couple."

"How much for granite?"

Jack laughed.

"What? Why are you laughing?" Alice said, with wide eyes.

"I don't know, I just never thought we'd be talking about concrete countertops over dinner."

"Don't change the subject, Jack. How much for granite?"

"It all depends. I can get deals. I always get deals. That's part of the fun."

She struck the table with her fist, more forcefully than she'd intended. A couple nearby glanced over. Alice lowered her voice. "Sold! I want you to install a concrete countertop in my apartment!"

Jack scratched his nose and looked away, amused. "Yeah, sure... Okay."

Over coffee, Jack talked more about his kids. "They teach you so much about yourself. I don't think I would have made it without them. And when you look back on things, you remember certain things as being the most special; the moments you wouldn't trade for anything."

"For instance?"

"Like Saturday breakfasts at the pancake house. We always caught up on the week: school, movies, books. We laughed a lot. We also did a whitewater rafting trip about two years ago on the Lehigh River in 40 degree temperatures. That was great fun! The rains that week were real heavy, so naturally the rapids were a little more challenging. But the kids loved it—especially Kristie. She wanted to do it again the next day. They looked so proud in their little wet suits. It really cracked me up!

Andrew fell overboard once, but the water was 58 degrees—warmer than the air—so it wasn't any big deal. When we got back to our cabin, we had hotdogs and hot chocolate. Talk about heartburn that night. Whoa! But what a great time. Such a terrific weekend. The kids still talk about it."

"You're lucky," Alice said.

"Yes, I am," Jack said, reflectively. "I'm very lucky." He quietly, politely studied her. "Did you ever want kids?"

"I didn't think about it much in my twenties. I was more interested in my career. Then I got the shop and… well, that's more than a full-time job. But I woke up one morning a few months ago and suddenly, just like magic, I wanted a baby, although I haven't told anybody else that except you." The wine made Alice bold; she held his eyes. "Probably just nature finally catching up with me."

Jack sat up a little straighter, seeing the invitation in her eyes—seeing that her face and candle-drenched hair were gleaming with life. He reached for his glass of water. Alice kept her eyes glued on him.

Jack had been working on the shape and sound of words and sentences all day, refining his approach, testing dialogue and phrases. Now, as he took another drink of coffee and held it briefly in his mouth before swallowing, he corralled his thoughts further. He stared down into the tablecloth and mustered courage. "Alice…"

She gazed at him from over the rim of her coffee cup, that she held in both hands.

"I know we've just met. I know you don't know anything much about me. But… I want to know you better and I want you to know me better. I also know there's not much time for that because there's someone else."

He looked at her, searching for any encouragement. "Is there a chance that we could have more time?"

She turned toward the blazing fireplace, silent.

Jack continued. "I wouldn't ask but... If I don't ask, you might leave tomorrow and I'd never see you again. I'd always regret not asking."

"Jack..." Her voice was low and breathy.

He waited while she gathered her thoughts.

"Jack, I shouldn't be here—for so many reasons."

"But, you are here. And the fact that you are here means something. Doesn't it?"

Alice set her cup down. "Jack... I'm supposed to be getting married on Christmas Day."

Jack slowly lowered his eyes. "Yes, you said that earlier today."

"That's where I was going when..." She stopped, glancing down at her purse. "Jack, I need to tell you the truth... the truth about everything. About why I came here. The truth about how and why I came here." Alice searched for words, then finally gave up and reached into her purse for the diary. She hesitated, frightened, her stomach a fluttery whirlwind. There was so much riding on what she was about to do. She grasped the diary, held it tightly and then, with a shaky hand, she laid it down on the table. It lay there like a live, pulsating thing. The room fell into an icy pool of silence.

Jack slumped deeply into the chair. Alice saw a wrenching anxiety wash over him.

It took a minute for Alice to find her voice. "I found it in Meadow Green. At Hattie's Bed and Breakfast in a bookshelf. It was sort of stuck behind some other books." Alice looked at him soberly. "Jack... I read it. I didn't know what it was at first. I just thought it was some old book."

Jack sat still in a dark silence.

Alice picked up her napkin and wiped her lips. "I read it and I kept on reading... I read all of it."

Jack was suddenly trapped in a fever-dream of the past. Old emotions crashed in on him like towering, smothering waves. A searing pain burned in his chest. Memories and guilt bludgeoned him. He couldn't pull his eyes from the diary.

"I'm sorry, Jack. I didn't know you then... I'm sorry I read it. I know that everything you wrote was very personal and private. I had no right to read it. I know that now."

Jack finally found his voice. "I don't understand."

Alice stumbled over words. "I don't know why I did it, Jack. I don't know why I came looking for you."

His eyes crinkled with wounded confusion. "You came looking for me?"

"I was... I was moved by it—by your words. I was moved by what happened to you and your family. I was curious. No, I was so touched by it. It was so... tender and honest."

Jack stared, blankly.

Alice continued. "I was on my way to Holbrook." Then more forcefully. "I don't know why I came, Jack! I wasn't going to. Then things just happened. Strange things and then I saw you and..."

He slowly reached for the diary, but stopped abruptly, his fingers just inches away. He stared, frozen, as if it could harm him, cut him. He withdrew his hand. "So you were curious," he said, flatly.

"At first, yes. But then I asked around, and I learned more about you and..."

"What do you mean, you asked around?" he said, crossly.

Alice saw it was going badly, but she couldn't find the right words. In a hushed desperation she leaned toward him, pleading with her eyes. "Jack... I want us to have more time. I want to stay. I want us to get to know each other."

Jack refused to look at her. He looked at nothing. He was lost in regret and confusion. The ground was suddenly loose and moving, the earth spinning out of control. He couldn't speak. He felt something inside pricking him, like a sharp knife, and it took his breath. He traveled backwards and saw faces: Darla's, his father's, his kids crying for their mother; their little eyes wet and accusing. Jack closed his eyes, trying to erase them. Erase the faces, the sounds, the smells, the shattered dreams!

"I was going to throw the diary away, Jack. Yesterday, when I left, I was going to throw it out the window. Dammit! Now I wish I had!"

Jack waved for the check. The waitress delivered it and Jack tossed down his credit card without looking at the bill. They waited in a tense silence until the waitress returned and he signed the slip.

"We should go," he said, besieged with anguish.

Alice drooped.

He grabbed the diary and pushed to his feet. He held her chair as she stood, but refused to look at her.

They stepped outside into a slinging icy rain. Alice's hair and feet were drenched by the time they got into the car. Jack threw the diary into the backseat. It bounced off the seat and landed on the floor.

As they traveled, Alice shivered. Jack had withdrawn into some remote place, fighting to hold himself together. But he drove watchfully, navigating the icy road with care, not letting his emotions affect his judgment. Alice felt some relief. Philip often drove like a maniac when he was upset, always successful at being as dramatic as possible.

Alice looked over. "Jack, I'm sorry."

"Accepted."

"I don't think so."

"It's over and done with."

"You have a right to be upset," Alice said.

His voice was low, strained. "You don't understand."

"Understand what, Jack?"

"I can't get away from it! I can never get the hell away from it! I thought I could, but it's always there: it goes away for a while and then it always comes back. The faces. The damned faces! I let her down. I let the kids down! I just didn't see!"

"Jack, it wasn't your fault."

"She knew!" Jack said, his emotions gathering force. "When Darla gave that diary to me, she knew, somehow, that it would handcuff me to her forever!"

Sleet struck the windows. The wipers slapped and fought.

Alice crossed her arms tightly against herself. "Jack... she's the one who made the decision to leave. It was her decision. Not yours. You stayed with the kids."

He shook his head. "No, you don't understand, Alice. No... I didn't write everything in that diary. I didn't write about how on one cold November morning I burst into her bedroom and shouted at her to leave! To get out! I didn't write about how I pulled her suitcase from the closet and slung it onto the floor and screamed at her to leave and to never come back! No, I had better sense than to write that! But I might as well have written it, because it's written up here," he said, pointing to his head. "It's branded up here!"

Alice was startled and puzzled. "But why, Jack?"

"It doesn't matter why."

"It does matter. Why did you ask her to leave?"

"It doesn't matter, okay!? It's none of your business! It's nobody's business. That diary was private! You shouldn't have read it!"

"I know, Jack. I'm sorry, I am, but I know you had a damned good reason for telling her to leave! I know you well enough, Jack. I know you had a damned good reason!"

He turned sharply, his face tight with anger. "Because she was hurting them! She was hurting our kids! She was beating them! They were bruised and scared and... Okay!?"

He faced the road, lost in the old nightmare. "God! She was sick! Bad sick! She needed help, but she wouldn't listen! Wouldn't go get the help! She just kept at it, drinking and yelling, wild and cruel. I couldn't stand it anymore! I couldn't stand it for the kids! No way they were going to grow up hurt and scared! No way!"

He pounded the steering wheel, turning to her. "Is that what you wanted to hear!? Is that what you've been waiting for!?"

Alice lowered her head, silent.

He jerked away staring at the road, but seeing only Darla's stormy features, twisted and wretched. He absently put weight on the gas pedal. "In the diary, when I wrote about her leaving us... Well... all that happened about two weeks after I told her to leave. She'd stopped drinking. She said she'd do better. She said she'd get some help and soon things would be like they were. We'd all be happy again, just like the old days. But I knew better. She knew better. But I still hoped. I hoped right up until I went downstairs that December morning and found her note. Then... well..."

Suddenly the SUV fishtailed. Jack was snapped back to the present. Alice grabbed the seat, seeing the frightening glare of approaching headlights. Jack reacted quickly, turning the front wheels right, dropping speed and adroitly whipping the vehicle back into the right lane. Alice slowly released her hands, tense, her head throbbing.

They didn't talk again until Jack turned into The Broadmoore parking lot and edged into a parking space. He switched off the engine and they sat quietly, staring ahead as ice battered the windshield, shattering into shards and meandering streams, creating a melting impressionistic view of The Broadmoore.

Jack rested both hands on the steering wheel.

Alice slowly faced him. "Jack..."

"Don't say it, Alice... Don't say you're sorry. It's got nothing to do with you. I thought I could forget, but I can't. I really thought I was free of her, but I was just kidding myself. As soon as I saw that diary it all came back." He wiped his eyes. "But how did it happen? I don't know. It all started with love. I loved her so much... but it just wasn't enough. When I sent her away, I killed myself and I killed her and there's no way back."

Jack looked at her. Alice saw that the fire for her was gone. It had been replaced by a weary indifference and sorrow. The energy seemed drained from him.

Alice said, "I wish we could have had more time, Jack."

He didn't speak.

She waited for a response that never came. "... Goodbye."

He reached for his door latch, but Alice's voice stopped him. "Don't walk me inside. I'll go alone. Thanks for dinner."

Alice shoved the door open and stepped out into the pelting night. She hunched her shoulders and slanted into the wind, pushing toward The Broadmoore.

Jack waited until she was inside, then drove away.

CHAPTER 17

Alice entered her room disarmed and disoriented. She found the light switch, dropped her purse on the bed and wandered the floor aimlessly. Finally, she slumped down in the nearest chair and let the events of the night sink in. She was wet and cold; the wind and freezing rain had completely flattened her hair. She stayed in her coat and wiped away the occasional trickle of water that slid from a strand of hair and ran down her face. The clock said it was after 10 o'clock on Sunday night, but it seemed as if weeks had passed since she'd first found the diary and read it. Since then, the rupture of her life had left her feeling marooned and confused. She didn't know who she was or what she wanted. What would she say to Philip when he arrived in the morning?

The howling, swift-storm wind rattled the windows. Alice closed her eyes tightly and leaned her head back. She licked her upper lip with the tip of her tongue and, amazingly, she could still taste the wine from dinner. Jack's low laughter was still rich and strong in her ears. She heard it in the gaps of surging wind. How could it happen so fast? How does one know when they're really in love? Is it the sense of peace and completeness; the

feeling of coming home after a long journey? Is it the joy
of observing and feeling the simplest things: the turn of
the head, the voice that sooths, that mystical feeling of
connection and hope? Is it the warming peace; the blazing desire to make love with bodies entwined like vines?
Is it the inebriating joy that compels laugher and praise?

Alice arose swiftly, eyes probing the walls for answers.

She forced herself to think of Philip. He had always
been good and kind, hadn't he? He'd lavished expensive
gifts on her, defended her in front of his sneering and
disapproving mother. He was handsome.

Alice felt a stinging, relentless guilt. She had difficulty
remembering Philip's face. She wiggled out of her coat
and draped it over the back of the chair, feeling weary and
depressed.

She was on the way to call him when her cell phone
rang, startling her. She reached for her purse and dug for
her phone, finally answering it on the fourth ring. "Hello."

A hissing sound.

"Hello? Hello?"

"… I need help," a feeble voice said.

"Hello? Who is this?"

"Help me… please. I've been beat up. He beat me
up. He left me… I'm so cold."

Alice suddenly recognized the voice. A bolt of heat
shot up her spine. "Kristie!?"

Her voice broke into choking sobs. "Yes… I'm so
cold. Please come. Please…"

Alice struggled to keep the alarm out of her voice.
"Kristie, where are you?"

"So cold… Please come."

"Kristie… I need you to tell me where you are. I'll call
your father."

"No! Don't get off the phone. Don't leave me alone. Please. Come... hurry. I'm freezing."

Alice glanced over at the hotel phone, wishing she had Jack's number. "Okay, Okay. I'll come. Are you outside?"

"Yes."

"Where?"

"I don't know exactly. He drove off... Route 54... I don't know." She screamed. "He beat me up. My boyfriend beat me up!"

Alice lowered her voice. "Okay, Kristie. It's going to be okay. I'm leaving right now. I'll find Route 54. I'm leaving now," she repeated, struggling back into her coat. "Kristie, give me your cell phone number, in case we get cut off."

Kristie stammered through it, her voice filled with terror, and Alice wrote it on a piece of paper she found on the nightstand.

"Hurry," Kristie said. "I'm... I'm so scared!"

"I'm on my way, Kristie. You'll be okay."

Alice seized her wool cap and kicked off her heels, keeping the conversation going. She darted over to her boots, pulled them on and laced them.

She hurried down the stairs. Nora wasn't around. She needed to contact Jack, but how? She couldn't hang up and she had to keep Kristie calm. Time was of the essence! She didn't know how bad Kristie was hurt or if she was freezing to death. Her mind raced, thoughts scrambled. She decided to leave.

As Alice stepped gingerly across the parking lot toward her car, the sleet began changing to heavy snow. She kept prodding Kristie for directions and landmarks that might help locate her, as she chopped and raked ice and snow from her front and back windshields.

Kristie sounded more desperate. "I'm near some trees... we passed a pond somewhere. I don't know! I don't know! I'm so cold... Please hurry. I'm hurt..."

Alice slid behind the wheel, winded, fastened her seatbelt and started the car. "Kristie, listen to me. I need to call your father... It will only take a minute."

Kristie yelled. "No. Don't!"

Alice slowly backed out of the parking space. "Kristie... he knows this area. He can help me find you. He can call for more help."

Alice heard a convulsive gasp. "Don't leave me. Stay on the phone! Please hurry."

Alice turned onto the highway, feeling the steady hot pulse of anxiety. The glazed road was perilous and seemingly endless. Alice tested the traction of her tires by lightly tapping her brakes. Twice the rear end made a slow sweep to the right. She had to keep correcting and righting the car as she progressed, driving only 25 miles per hour.

"Keep talking to me, Kristie. Stay with me."

"My stomach... hur... hurts. I'm col... cold."

"Are you sitting?"

"Yes..."

"Can you get up?"

"I tried, but I fell. My foot hurts. It's sprained, I think. He punched me in the face." She burst into angry tears. "That... asshole... Jerk! He just kept punching me!"

"Okay, Kristie. It's okay. I'll be there soon. Slap yourself on the arms and legs. Try to move some to keep warm. Can you do that?"

"... Yes..."

Alice was keenly aware of hypothermia. Jacinta had worked as a nurse in Maine before the twins were born.

She'd told Alice stories about nearly frozen hikers and boaters lost or trapped. Alice could already hear Kristie's garbled speech. She could also be on the verge of shock, depending on the extent of her injuries. "Kristie, I'm on the main road into town. How do I find Route 54?"

She heard Kristie struggling to speak. "Keep... going... straight. You'll see a sign... Holiday Inn sign on... on... on... right. On your right. It's near that... Turn left. That's... that's... Route 54."

Alice breathed in frustration. If she could only call Jack! Could she take the chance? What if Kristie passed out? What if she couldn't be reached after the call, because of the storm or a weak signal? She would freeze to death. But it was late. Surely Jack had arrived home, saw his daughter wasn't there and was trying to reach her on her cell phone!

Alice's windshield was fogging up. She dropped her window about an inch for fresh air and applied the windshield washer fluid. The streams shot high and splashed against the frantic wipers, clearing a hazy view into the infinite stormy night. There were few cars on the highway and they were crawling along, like wounded things. One had slid sideways onto the shoulder, his taillights flashing out a warning.

"Kristie, have you called anyone else?"

"No..."

Alice wanted to ask her why in the world, of all people, she'd called her, but she didn't. "Has anyone else tried to call you?"

"Yes, but... but... I'm afraid to answer, in case we get disconnected. I'm so col... cold. I don't want to die! I don't want to die alone!"

"You're not going to die, Kristie, do you hear me! Do you?!"

"Yes…"

"It's not gonna happen. Okay, Kristy, now try to think where you were when you got out of the car."

"Okay… I… I… we… were. We'd passed that pond…"

"Okay… I'll look for the pond. How far from the pond?"

"I don't… know…"

"Think, Kristie. Think!"

"Maybe 5 or 10 minutes."

Alice shook her head in despair. In this weather it could take her twice as along. "That's good. Very good! Then what?"

"There was a picnic table… off… off the road… some. Not far…"

"Okay. Great, Kristie! That's great! Anything else?"

"He… he tried to…" she stopped, the emotion rising. "I can't! I don't know."

"It's okay… Okay. I'll find you, don't worry. Let's talk about movies or books. Tell me about the last book you read."

"I can't remember."

"Yes, you can, Kristie! Think! Tell me!"

"I'm so cold… so cold. I'm wha… wet. Cold. Wind is so strong. I can't get under that… tree… that fallen tree."

"Try to crawl over there, Kristie. Try."

"I'm too tired."

"Okay. Tell me about the book."

"Don't know… about a woman who got lost some-where like me."

Alice fought the dangerous highway, squinting, peering into the haze of falling snow, frantically looking for the Holiday Inn sign. Kristie stumbled through conversation, as her voice grew weaker, but Alice kept firing questions at her.

An eternity later, Alice finally saw the sign. "I see it! I see the sign! I'm turning onto Route 54, Kristie! I'll be there soon!"

Kristie's voice lifted in weak enthusiasm. "Thank, God.... Hurry!"

Alice squeezed the brake petal, trying not to stab at it, though her foot had gone into spasm from tightness and nerves. She prepared for the turn, smoothly, in an effort to build the turn—to finesse the acceleration and brakes—to feel the edge of the traction. She did not want to slide out of control. She gripped the steering wheel gently with her free hand and turned left, clenching her teeth. To her relief, the car handled the turn easily. She nudged the car forward and breathed. She was on Route 54.

This road was dark and foreboding. No streetlights and few signs. Wind and snow lashed out at the lone car. Alice told Kristie to think of past summers, when it was hot. Kristie talked aimlessly about her childhood; a summer playing with her mother in a field of daisies; her father spraying her and Andrew with the garden hose, and how they leapt and ran and screamed.

"Poor Daddy," Kristie said. "He'll be so mad at me. He'll hate me. I'm supposed... I'm grou... He grounded me. I couldn't call him. He'll hate me..."

"No, he won't Kristie. He loves you."

"How do you know? You don't know."

"I do know. I've met your father, Kristie, and I know he loves you very much. He told me."

Dead silence.

"Kristie? Kristie!! Are you there? Kristie!!"

Kristie's voice was faint. "Are you close... I'm so cold... I'm just... I'm freezing."

Alice's shoulder muscles tightened, as she lightly pressed the accelerator with the toe of her boot. The car gathered speed until the speedometer said 45mph. She was taking a big risk, but she had to get to Kristie as soon as possible.

"I'm real close now, Kristie. I should be seeing the pond soon. Tell me more about summer."

Kristie stuttered. "I can't. I'm too cold. I'm numb face stinging."

Alice shouted. "Kristie. Stay with me. Kristie!"

Silence.

"Kristie!"

Silence.

"Oh, God. Kristie."

"So... cold..."

"I know, honey. Try to move. Shake your arms and your legs."

"Just... freezing. Stomach... hurts."

"Kristie, is the picnic table on the left or right?"

"Can't..."

"Kristie! Left or right?!"

"Don't... remember. Left... I think."

Alice strained her eyes looking for the pond. She had to be close. Had to! Then she saw a break in the quaking trees. That was it! Fortunately, a dimly lit sign, swinging violently, read

Poe's Pond
Ice Skating and Sleigh Rides
Christmas Trees

Alice hollered into the phone. "I'm passing the pond, Kristie! I'm only minutes away. Almost there!"

223

"… Coo… I… was go-going to say… say coo-cool… forget… that."

Alice laughed loudly, releasing pressure. "That's good, Kristie. You still have a sense of humor. Good! Think of funny things."

"My father was outside on a lad-ladder, pulling leaves fro-from the gut-gutters. Andrew was lit-little and a real terror. He grabbed the ladder and star-started shaking it. Daddy like free-freaked out and yelled at Andrew to st-stop. Andrew just sho-shook it more until the ladder started moving…"

It happened fast—only a heartbeat. Time stopped. Alice's car lurched left, losing its grip. In sudden horror, she dropped the cell phone, clamped both hands onto the steering wheel and fought desperately for power, feeling the pit-of-the-stomach feeling of raw panic as the car whirled helplessly in the flexed muscle of the storm. Seeing it was hopeless, she released the steering wheel and braced for impact. The car shot off the road past a broad and towering oak tree, and then it plunged down a shallow gully, slamming broadside into a 3-foot snowdrift.

The impact punched the air from Alice's lungs. Her brain labored to accept the violence and tragedy. She heard the raucous music of the storm, whistling, snarling and hurling fists of snow against the car. She heaved in staggered breaths, her chest tight with cold terror. Realty returned with an urgency and a scream.

"Kristie!"

CHAPTER 18

She was engulfed in darkness. The headlights were buried in the snow. The engine sputtered. Alice examined herself. Was she all right? Nothing hurt. Lucky. She released her seatbelt and made a frantic search for her cell phone. Couldn't find it. She felt for the car keys, found them and turned off the engine. She needed light. The glove compartment! She'd placed a flashlight there the day before she'd left New York for just such an emergency. Her hand snaked, reached and felt. She found the latch. She released it and all the contents spilled out onto the floor. The cold cylinder was easy to feel and she grabbed it, immediately flicking the ON switch. A strong beam of light swept the car, and she clearly saw that her side of the car was buried in snow. She'd have to climb out the opposite side. But first, the cell phone! She aimed the shaft of light to the floor, to the seat. Nothing. She arched and contorted her body forward and down, darting the beam under the seat. There it was. She snatched it up, righted herself and held the phone to her ear. "Kristie!"

Silence. Alice turned off the phone, then quickly switched it back on. The dial tone came in strong. She

225

dialed 911 and stammered though the events and relayed all the information to the calm male voice on the other end.

"Please hurry," Alice said. "If somebody doesn't get there fast, she could die."

"I'll forward that, ma'am, but it's a hectic night. We're flooded with calls and emergencies. Will you be standing by?"

Alice repeated her cell number and hung up. She didn't have Jack's number! What about The Broadmoore? Nora could call him. No, the switchboard closed at 10 o'clock! Should she take the time to call information and get Jack's number? No. She'd call once she was outside. Once she got to the road, maybe she'd see a car and flag it down.

Holding the flashlight in her left hand, she grasped the steering wheel with her free right hand and pulled and pushed herself up, wiggling and struggling until she slid into the passenger seat. A grabbing pain in her left leg made her flinch. After flexing and massaging it, she determined she'd have an award winning bruise, but nothing more. It wasn't serious. She took hold of the door latch and repeatedly slammed her body against the door until it opened wide. A bitterly cold wind rushed in, shocking her to full alertness. She pulled on her hat, her wool gloves, adjusted the collar of her coat and prepared to exit.

She slipped the flashlight into her coat pocket and, with both hands on the doorframe, heaved herself up into the doorway. Fat flecks of snow slammed into her face, feeling like stinging little pinpricks. After a final gulp of air, she slid to the edge of the seat, extended her feet and stepped down, gingerly, into a one-and-a-half-foot snow drift. Her toes and legs immediately felt the shock of it.

She leaned into the hard driving wind, swinging the flashlight beam before her, probing the best route to the road. She slogged away from the great swirling drifts to snow depths that were easier to navigate, around the trunks of dark moving trees, scrub pine and protruding rocks, trudging upwards, scrabbling and clawing toward the road.

At the crest, she slapped the snow from her coat and gloves, looked up and down the road, but saw no signs of life. She marched forward on the shoulder of the road, where there was some traction, then broke into a jog, fighting a towering dread that, in this arctic cold, Kristie could freeze to death before Alice found her.

Moments later, Alice stopped, pulled her cell phone and called Kristie. Four rings later she heard her small shuddering voice. "Hel... hel... hello..."

Alice lit up. "Kristie! It's Alice. I'm almost there!"

"Ple-please..."

"I called 911! They're on their way! I'm going to call your father!"

"He-he called... He's coming..."

"Thank God!"

"You hun-hung up."

"I'm sorry, Kristie. I dropped the phone. Stay on with me, I'm almost there!"

Then Alice lost the signal. The phone went dead. "Kristie!? Kristie!!?

Alice pressed redial. It rang repeatedly, but there was no answer. Alice dashed off into the brutal night, in a desperate search for the picnic table. Her leg hurt, her lungs burned from the cold air and there wasn't a car in sight.

Suddenly, just ahead, she saw what looked to be a single blue headlight coming toward her. She was about to wave it down, but stopped when she saw it rise into the air in erratic flight, then sweep in toward her. She watched in amazement as it grew in size, hovered briefly, then drifted in. The wind ceased, the snow stopped. The world gathered into a hush.

As it approached, something or someone began to emerge, and as it did, the shape wobbled and the light changed to the color of a bruise: orange, purple and red. A vague, dark shadow struggled to break out from the center, like a birth. A distorted human form worked in a misery, in a series of twists, contortions and moans to break free, wringing the hands, bellowing like tapped evil, punching and ripping holes through the dying scrim of crimson light. First an arm, then a leg, then a writhing black head. When it finally broke free, with a cry of low discontent, the light faded, dispersed and vanished, as if sucked away by a vacuum.

Alice backed away. Standing before her was Dr. Landis! He stood stooped, pale and grave, staring wildly from his inner world as if struggling to understand the reality. He seemed to have aged 10 years since the last time Alice had seen him. He spoke in a slow heavy voice, laboring over each word as if it could be his last.

"Kristie was wrong. If you go left, you'll miss her and she'll die. The picnic table is on the right side of the road, your right, about 20 feet in. There are two paths. Take the left path. The right leads to nowhere. Kristie is about sixty feet from there, lying near a fallen sycamore tree. Hurry... She's hurt and freezing to death."

Alice tried to move but felt glued to the ground.

Dr. Landis crept forward, contrite, his eyes beseeching. "I will watch over them. Please tell my son. Please tell my son that I will always watch over and protect them! I owe him that! Tell him I will never rest! Go to Kristie now! Hurry! Please!"

The agonized form slowly dissolved into a misty fog. It drifted up and away. Then, in a violent gust, it shredded into icy shards and was flung, violently, into the tops of writhing trees and disappeared. The wind came in a sudden burst, whipping up snow and stinging Alice's eyes.

The snow made a shocking return, driven sideways by the wind. Alice crossed the road, shading her eyes, and lumbered ahead in the direction where the doctor had indicated. When she saw the picnic table, blanketed with snow, she got an adrenaline rush. With the flashlight, she searched the area and saw the path Dr. Landis had described. She saw old footprints, nearly covered by new snow. She hiked forward, leveling the light beam on a cluster of bare trees. As she progressed, she shouted Kristie's name, hearing her voice fall flat at her feet, swallowed by the thrashing blizzard. She kept yelling, praying that Jack was close behind.

Then, finally, the thin yellow shaft of light revealed a shadowy shape, cowering next to a dark mass of a tree. Alice screamed out Kristie's name. She closed on her, stumbling and reaching. When the light illuminated Kristie's face, Kristie broke into mad tears of relief. Alice dropped to the ground, grabbed Kristie's shoulders and pulled her close, smothering her, feeling the stiff ice of her body. Kristie's body convulsed, her teeth chattered as Alice rubbed and patted her arms aggressively. Her white ski hat covered most of her forehead, and she looked back at Alice through swollen slits. Her lips were ice pale, her coat glazed with snow. She'd made herself a small, constricted ball in an area that gave some protection from the battle.

"It's okay, honey. It's going to be okay.

She strangled out words. "Help me!"

Kristie stuttered out Jack's cell number. Alice called him, hugging Kristie tightly against her. "Jack! It's Alice. I'm with Kristie!"

Jack let out a deep sigh. "Thank God! How is she?"

"She's going to be okay, but hurry! How far away are you?"

"No more than five minutes."

Alice gave him exact directions and hung up. She wrapped her body around Kristie's and waited, whispering encouragement and offering silent prayers.

Alice saw the narrow beam of light sweeping the area. She called out. "Jack! Over here! Jack!"

Jack's flashlight beam framed them. A huddled mass. He scampered over and sank to his knees, panting. "Are you okay?"

Alice nodded, releasing Kristie.

His body tightened as he looked down at her, heartbroken. "Kristie?"

Kristie pushed up, reaching, sobbing for him. He grabbed and embraced her, kissing her head and face, making grateful moans. "Kristie... Kristie girl... It's okay. You're okay now."

"I'm sorry, Daddy... so sorry."

"Don't worry about that," he said, pulling her deep into his broad chest, clasping her tightly in his arms and rocking her. "Okay... it's all okay, Kristie girl. My Kristie girl. We're going to get up, now. We're getting out of here. You'll be all right."

"My fo-foot, right foot, is hurt, sprained... maybe broken. I can't walk on it."

"I'll help you, no problem. Put your arm around my shoulder now. Swing it up… Easy… easy now. I'll lift you. I'll carry you. Let's go."

While Jack swung her up into his arms and trudged back down the path toward the car, Alice found Kristie's purse and cell phone partially buried in the snow. She took them. As she started back to the road, she dialed 911 and canceled the call, with an explanation.

Jack opened the SUV passenger door, lowered Kristie down into the seat, then covered her, up to the neck, with a brown heavy woolen blanket he'd brought along. He caught a shocking glimpse of her face in the dim light, but didn't react. Her eyes were puffy and red; her lower lip swelled, with a jagged line of brown dried blood; her face fat and colorless. She was shivering, fiercely. Jack fought a pounding rage. He wanted to kill the boy who did this. Kristie turned from him so he wouldn't see the shame in her eyes and leaned toward the vents that blasted high heat. She burst into tears again, thankful and ashamed.

Alice climbed in back, leaned forward and took Kristie's hand, as Jack jumped behind the wheel, slammed his door and shifted into gear.

It was an agonizingly slow ride to the medical center. Alice quietly explained what had happened to her on the way over and why it took longer than she'd hoped. She dared not mention the vision of Dr. Landis. It had helped her find Kristie, but she still wasn't sure if it was just an hallucination, even if a benevolent one. Kristie kept squeezing her hand, staring ahead, quivering. When they passed the spot where Alice's car had jumped off the road, she pointed toward it, lifting her chin, barely able to see the gray ghost of the nearly snow-buried car.

Jack applied his one-pointed furious concentration on solutions to every potential threat, shutting out all unnecessary thoughts, though anger, frustration and bewilderment sat perched on the edge of his mind, just waiting for the right moment to attack. Snow blew across the hazardous roads in waves, burying the land. They passed a fat yellow truck snowplowing the opposite lane, the chains on its wheels sounding like maracas. Twice they passed cars that had slid off the road, but Jack didn't seem to see their pink flares or notice their waving arms. He continued on, solemn and focused.

On the way over, Jack had called a doctor friend he'd done some work for and asked him for help. The doctor agreed to call the medical center and have a doctor and nurse standing by. A few miles away, Jack followed-up to insure they'd be waiting, and he was told they were.

Jack drove into the Emergency Room entrance, boiled out and hurried inside. Moments later, a stern-looking woman, wearing a heavy coat and a Russian fur cap, appeared with him, pushing a wheelchair. Jack lifted Kristie into it, as Alice stepped around the car and followed them all inside.

Jack went to Triage and filled out admission forms, while Kristie was whisked off by the nurse down a short broad corridor to an examination room. Alice waited nervously, finally strolling into the crowded waiting lounge. She found an empty green plastic chair near the soda machine and eased down with a deep sigh, completely drained. She closed her eyes and immediately fell into a light sleep, hearing murmurs and scratching footsteps on the tile floor, the dull ring of the intercom and the call of a doctor or nurse. She awoke only minutes later, feeling vaguely disconnected and lost. It took a half hour, with her coat on, before she shook off the cold and felt the life return to her toes and curled fingers. Then she paced, sipped a paper cup of coffee, gazed down the corridor and prayed that Kristie would be all right.

At three in the morning, Alice saw Jack striding wearily along the corridor, his head down, his heavy winter jacket swung over his shoulder. She trashed her coffee cup and went to him, meeting him at the entrance to the lounge, noticing the dark shadow of his beard and his bloodshot eyes.

"How is she?" she asked.

"She's asleep. They're treating her for exposure, frostbite and some injuries." His voice dragged with exhaustion. "She has a broken bone in her right foot—not serious, but broken, and she'll have to have a cast. She's also got some cuts and bruises. But... something's wrong with her stomach. She keeps saying it's sore and tender. She can't stand up straight... has spasms. She said... she said... he kicked her there after she fell."

Alice felt sick with disgust. "What do they think it is?"

Jack's eyes held misery. "Don't know. They're going to do another x-ray and some other thing... I don't remember what they called it." He met Alice's eyes and his gaze sharpened. "It's good you found her when you did... thank you."

"... She told you... everything?"

He wiped his forehead and stared into the tan tiled floor. "Yeah, we talked. He beat her up because she wouldn't... you know..." He couldn't go on. "I guess he stole the car from the lot where he works. He was drunk." Jack turned away, brushed by her, and made his way to the soda machine. He punched his selection and retrieved it. The lounge had nearly emptied. There were only two drowsy people watching TV. Alice overhead a meteorologist say that the worst of the storm had passed. As Jack popped the tab and took a generous drink, Alice wandered over. She knew she looked a mess: her eyes were also bloodshot, her hair tangled and her face blotchy, but she didn't care.

"I can drive you back to The Broadmoore when you're ready," he said.

"… I want to stay, Jack."

He looked at her carefully. "Are you all right?"

"Yes, I'm fine, just tired. A little shaken up, but I'm okay."

"You sure? Maybe you should have a doctor examine you."

"No, really. I'm fine. Have you talked to your son?"

Jack was surprised and pleased that she asked. "I called him a while ago. He's upset. Wanted to come over on his bike, but I told him not to. I told him you were here with me. He seemed happy about that."

"Jack, I need to explain some things."

He ignored her. "I'll call this guy I know. He'll pull your car out first thing in the morning. Won't cost you anything."

"Jack… I…"

He looked past her. "He owes me a favor."

"Jack…"

"The police will want to talk to you about all this," Jack continued. "Al Bledso's the Sheriff. He's a nice guy. I've done some work for him. Anyway, I told him you'd be leaving tomorrow, so…"

"Jack… I need to talk to you about…" she stopped, wishing she didn't have to say it.

Jack held himself in, his jaw tight.

"Jack… before I met you at the ski shop, I was on my way to Holbrook. Kristie was hitchhiking. I picked her up because she looked so vulnerable. I was scared for her. That's how we met. I didn't know she was your daughter. Not until after I drove her to Tylerville so she could meet... her friends."

Jack bristled. He glared from beneath his eyebrows.

"Jack... I know you have questions. I was so concerned and frightened for her, that I gave her my cell number and told her to call me later that night, last night. I told her I'd pick her up and bring her home. So, she called and I did. That's the truth. I know it sounds... I don't know how it sounds, but that's what happened. When she told me her name, of course, I was shocked. Frankly, I couldn't believe it. The diary... your diary was in my purse. Coincidence? I don't know."

He lifted his shoulders slightly. He put an edge on his voice. "You should have told me about it. You should have."

Her face darkened with guilt. "Yes, I should have. I wish I had. I'd give anything if I had. I should have done a lot of things and I shouldn't have done a lot of others. I just..." her voice trailed off and fell silent.

Jack didn't respond. He went to one of the chairs and sat, clutching the soda so tightly it made a crinkling sound. Through wounded eyes, he began seeing a sequence of images: Kristie at birth, a little helpless thing, so beautiful to behold. He saw her pink room that he and Darla had painted so happily together. In that room, he heard his own words echo back, as he held Kristie to his chest and rocked her. The oath he'd whispered low, so only they could hear. "I'll always take care of you, little one. Your daddy will always love and protect you." She'd looked at him with her brand new blue eyes and reached for his lips. His eyes filled with burning tears.

He saw her stumbling in the summer grass, under the full flood of sunlight, her fat arms flailing, mouth puckered in irritation at her own clumsy progress. He saw her chubby body miraculously be transformed into a lithe charmer with long golden hair; saw when she danced around the house with her ballerina attitude of pride, tossing her hair for effect. He saw her in the dark, creeping toward his bed, felt the gentle give of the mattress as she slipped under the sheets and drew close, because she'd had another nightmare. He saw her ecstatic face when he'd opened the Christmas present from her: a new power drill she'd bought with her own money, money she'd earned by working as a lifeguard at the town swimming pool. Before he'd opened it, she'd jumped up from her cross-legged position, wrapped his neck with her arms, and kissed him on both cheeks.

"Merry Christmas, Daddy."

He'd memorized the poem she'd attached:

> *A drill for Daddy who likes to fix,*
> *All those things that get broken.*
> *Everyone says he's the best around,*
> *And all those folks can't be jokin'.*

He felt a piercing in his chest, a stabbing cut, and then a sudden spilling out of guilt and rage. It stunned and weakened him. It was the slicing of a hot boil, oozing out old heartbreak, loneliness and sorrow; draining years of poisonous loss, disappointment and despair. Jack slumped over, his face bent toward his knees, and he silently wept, convulsing with grief.

Alice looked on, helpless. She wanted to go to him— to touch and comfort him—but she knew it was his private moment. She knew there was nothing she could offer, so she walked away into the hallway, drifted aimlessly for a time, then stopped at the hospital entrance and looked out the two double glass doors. She buttoned her coat, pulled on her cap and gloves and went out.

The snow had nearly stopped; the wind was calm and the streets quilted white and glistening. Cars were snow-coned. The leaning snow-heavy trees would be perfect postcard photos in the morning light. Alice roamed through a peaceful and innocent loveliness, where only a few hours before, Mother Nature's violence had destroyed and terrified.

The world was a fairyland—sugary, enchanting and ready for Santa. It was a playground for every kid who would awaken in the morning yelping with glee, knowing that school was closed and Monday was free of the usual schedules and demands. It would be a day of snowmen, sledding and ice skating.

Alice kicked at the snow and gazed into the empty streets, feeling an invigorating chill on her face. She hurt for Kristie, Jack and Andrew. She felt close to them—connected to them—and it had happened in only a few days.

She grew discontented. It was a feeling she couldn't put a finger on at first. So she strolled, probing her life history, carefully uncovering heavy, psychological rocks that, in the past, she'd side-stepped, not taking the time or having the courage to lift and explore beneath them. How had she arrived at this place? "Examine your life, Alice. Examine your intentions," her mother had often said.

Abruptly, the air softened, like a night breeze in spring. The scent of lilacs assailed her nose and, though Alice was keenly aware of the impossibility of this, she turned, instinctively, seeking the source. Alice thought of her mother and then presented her face to the sky, remembering that lilacs were her mother's favorite flower. In spring, bouquets of lilacs overflowed their vases and intoxicated the family with their scent.

Alice walked in a wide circle and for a brief moment, in the stillness, she had the hair- standing-up-on-the-back-of-the-neck prickly feeling that her mother was near. She sensed her presence. Alice gently lifted her hand, letting it rise skyward. It was a curious and clandestine moment, when their exploring fingers seemed to touch. "Mom!" she whispered, her eyes tearing. With that tremendous sensation came swift, vivid images flowing quickly like a movie. Alice watched in astonishment.

She saw Philip's mother, slouched in loneliness, her dull gray eyes blank, yet filled with a kind of shock, as if her very soul were constantly being assaulted by the burning ache of a life that had lost its way long ago; by an emptiness with no bottom; by a lack of a vital connection to love. She was nearly "soul killed," and alcohol was speeding along her death.

Alice saw Philip's father, with his sharp blue eyes and Hollywood handsome looks. It was a face ripe with practiced confidence, made a little harsh by too much success and too little time for family or self-reflection; too little time to remember love or, perhaps, to remember that love heals, expands the heart and makes life worth living.

"Who am I to judge?" Alice thought. "Who am I to presume anything about anyone?" Her own life stood starkly before her: images flickering on a screen. She witnessed her own hectic and fearful ambition; saw the expressions of impatience and anger at her customers and at Philip. She remembered her tense body inclined forward, rushing off down the street through bustling crowds, her eyes hypnotically fixed on attacking the next breathless goal. There was no time to pause, to enjoy the moment, to think or examine any motive. "Living" was much too demanding and serious for that! Love was something that existed on the periphery of life—an unexplored territory—a secondary thought, just like her relationship with Philip had been.

Alice saw Philip and herself, much older, with graying hair and subtle wrinkles around the eyes and mouth. They were sitting on opposite sides of a wide, spacious room surrounded by every luxury, but lost in a quiet melancholy. Alice felt her loneliness, like a betrayal, like an ironic twist in the search for happiness. She and Philip smiled at each other, but there was no joy in it. It was an acknowledgement of two people who had settled for a comfortable alienation. They were living on separate islands, and neither had an inkling how to navigate the sea between them. They stared like statues, hollow, with bored eyes.

The night chill returned with a burst of whistling wind and Alice faced away from it, just as her mother's presence faded and her fingers seemed to slip away into a night fog. Disturbed and gloomy, Alice lowered her hand and peered into the black restless sky. She turned strangely defiant. She almost resented this mystical intrusion, or whatever it was, that had bullied her with visions. She pivoted toward the medical center, seeking some answer, some additional insight into the riddle of the night, but she only felt emptiness.

Alice was shaken. "The dead should stay dead... and buried," she thought.

When Alice went back inside, Jack was gone. She took off her coat, hat and gloves and sat down, feeling an overwhelming exhaustion. Had she ever been this tired? Ever felt so lost?

In an isolated corner of the room, she dropped down in a chair, leaned her head back against the wall and shut her eyes. In the twilight between sleep and wakefulness, she knew but one thing: something inside had been awakened. She'd never be the same.

CHAPTER 19

Voices stirred her. There was the sharp smell of ammonia, then the scent of peppermint and Alfred Dunhill Cologne. She heard the clatter of metal carts. Alice's eyes would not open; her dead head was too heavy to move, her body was a wet concrete sack. When she heard her name, she finally managed to pry open a glassy eye and focus on the shadowy person standing above her: Philip!?

"Good morning, Alice. Don't you look incredibly chic," he said, in his usual cultured voice.

Alice had fallen asleep in the waiting lounge, and at some point during the night, a nurse had brought a pillow and blanket. Alice had wrapped herself up completely, with only her right foot exposed. Saliva was thick in her throat; her neck was stiff and her leg sore from the accident. She tried to speak but only the sound "Wha... ter" escaped, in a scratchy contralto.

"Water?"

Alice nodded, forcing the other eye open, squinting as if trying to peer through the fog and find reality.

"I'm a very good water boy," he said. "Did you know I was the water boy for a minor league baseball team when I was a kid?"

Alice shook her head. "Wha... ter."

"All right."

Philip went on his errand and Alice peeled back the blanket, sat up, stretched, yawned and blinked around the room. It was standing room only for the anxious and bored. Some watched the TV that flicked through snowy images of the storm, cutting away to personal accounts of disasters and survivors. In the waiting lounge, children whined or played with toys, ate snacks or had faces pressed against the windows, noses distorted, staring longingly out at the snow. The clock on the wall read 8:30. The thought of Kristie and Jack jarred her back to full consciousness, just as Philip returned with a white paper cup filled with water. He handed it to her and she drained it, still feeling groggy.

Philip stood with his hands on his hips, in a slightly irritated manner. He wore dark blue slacks (he never wore jeans), a white shirt with a crisp collar and a blue cashmere sweater. His dark hair was combed back tightly, revealing his smooth forehead and refined features. "So, I went to The Broadmoore, and a woman named Nora sent me here. She's not the friendliest of women, but I was finally able to win her over, somewhat, by complimenting her hair. Women love it when you compliment their hair. I learned that from you. By the way, Nora's around here somewhere."

"She is?" Alice asked, looking about.

"Oh, and it seems that the police want to talk to you, too."

Alice messaged her tired eyes. "Yes, they would."

"They would," he repeated, offhandedly.

Alice pushed to her feet. "I need to find out how Kristie is. She's…"

"I know all about Kristie and you, and your car accident and many other things. I spoke to Nora, and to your friend, Jack."

Alice swallowed hard. "Jack?"

"Oh, yes. I'm very good at asking questions and learning the truth. Jack said you saved his daughter's life."

"Her father would have found her."

"That's not what he says, or what many others in this room say."

"What others?" Alice asked, darting nervous glances.

Philip gestured. "Most of the people in this room are here because they're Jack's friends. They heard about Kristie. Heart-warming, isn't it? I've talked to many of them and they're all singing your praises. They might even make you a saint."

"That's not funny, Philip." She swung her hesitant stare toward them. Some looked back, curious. "So how is Kristie?"

Philip's mouth firmed up. Alice saw the shrewd light of perception in his eyes. "Your friend, Jack, is in the hallway talking to a Sheriff Bledso. Why don't you go ask him?"

Alice didn't speak or look at him. She found the women's room, entered and immediately splashed several handfuls of cold water onto her face. She did the best she could with her hair, brushing it thoroughly, shaking, patting and placing wild strands, but it didn't improve her weary expression. She stretched wide her mouth, thrust out her tongue and pinched up her face, hoping to erase some of the signs of sleep, but only met with small success. She stepped back and stared at herself in the mirror and saw melancholy. She looked washed out, her eyes small. Last night's intense images seemed a distant blur—a string of improbable events and hazy revelations that left her feeling dull and irritable. She applied light makeup and some lipstick and dodged the cruel artificial light that aged her.

In the hallway, she saw Jack surrounded by concerned people. She hesitated, but he waved her over. She did not feel sociable, but she approached, presenting her best possible face.

Jack stepped away from the group and met her half way. She saw that sorrow had changed the shape of his sensual mouth to a disillusioned frown. It was obvious he was fighting a great inner battle. She lifted her head and looked at him with appeal.

"How is she? Kristie?"

He pocketed his hands. "They did a full abdominal examination early this morning and found a rupture. A small one. A 0.5 centimeter rupture. That's all. Thankfully no other abdominal injuries. They're going to wait until tomorrow morning to do surgery. They want to make sure her strength is back."

Alice nodded. "That sounds positive. Have you talked to her?"

"Yes. Some..." His grin was tired. "She was pretty shocked when she found out you were the woman I went on the date with."

Alice looked away, sheepishly. "Yeah... I'm sure." Alice saw Andrew out of the corner of her eye, leaning back against the hallway wall, looking dejected. He caught her eye and smiled demurely. It was a smile that brightened her mood. She waved and he nodded back, then hid his face.

Jack hesitated before reaching into his pocket for some keys. He handed them to Alice. "So your car is right out front in the parking lot. It's running and it's been cleaned, inside and out."

Alice took the keys. "Thank you, Jack."

"I talked to the police earlier. Told them everything, but they'll still need to ask you a few questions, for the record." Jack pointed to a tall, thin policeman standing by the door, looking back at them. "That's Sheriff Bledso. He's easy enough."

"Of course. What about the boy?"

"They have him. They found him at home. They booked him for auto theft, driving without a license, drunk driving and aggravated assault. Kristie will have to testify when the time comes. I'll help her with that."

Alice was aware that Philip was watching her, stalking back and forth. "Jack, Kristie will need counseling."

"No, I don't think so. I'll make sure she's okay."

She softened her voice. "You might just think about it. Maybe talk to a professional."

He shrugged. "She'll be okay. I'll make sure of it. Andrew and I will take care of her." He quickly changed the subject, lifting the tone of his voice. "So I met your fiancé, Philip. He seems nice. He certainly speaks highly of you. But then, I guess that stands to reason if he's going to marry you." He pocketed his hands. "So you'll be leaving this morning?"

"No, not until the surgery—until I know Kristie is okay."

"Oh, she'll be fine. The doctor said it's not a difficult surgery."

Alice's face was set in determination. "I'm not going until I know for certain that she's okay."

Jack looked at her, admiringly. "She'll be happy to hear that."

Alice indicated to the crowds of people. "You have a lot of friends."

His eyes shifted down and away. "I've done work for most of them."

Alice started a smile, then stopped. Tears glistened. "Jack Landis, your work obviously weaves magic."

They held each other's eyes for a moment, before they disengaged.

"Things got kind of complicated," Jack said.

"Yes, they did."

"Well, anyway, must be for the best. You'll be getting married."

Her hand that held the keys tightened into a fist. "It wasn't calculated, Jack. None of it. I know it all seems like it but..." Alice dwindled into sadness. "It wasn't. Not really."

Jack stood a little off-balance. "I don't know what to think anymore, Alice. I can't get a hold of anything or understand anything anymore. It's like I'm lost. I mean, my daughter is lying in that room, beaten up by some punk, and she didn't even call me. Why didn't she call me? I'm her father. Why didn't she?"

"I don't know, Jack."

"She said she thought of you. She said that she heard a voice telling her to call you. She said she knew you'd come. What do you think about that?"

Alice shrugged. Just when she opened her mouth to speak, Philip stepped up and interrupted, his expression stern. "Ready to go, Alice?"

"... Yes, Philip. I'm ready. Goodbye, Jack."

Jack nodded.

Alice answered all of Sheriff Bledso's questions, while Philip waited, stalking a back-and-forth path, with his hands locked behind him.

Alice took her car and followed Philip back to The Broadmoore. They parked next to each other in the plowed and salted lot and emerged without a glance, walked purposefully across the shoveled walk, up the stairs inside.

In the room, Alice shed her coat and started for the bathroom. "I can't wait to get into that shower."

"Do you want to eat here or grab something on the road?"

She stopped at the bathroom entrance. She didn't face him. "I'm not going back today, Philip."

There was a long, painful silence.

Philip finally spoke. "I see. When are you going back? On Christmas Day? On our wedding day?"

Alice cocked her head. "No... I don't think so."

"Okay, now I don't see."

Alice turned. "Philip... I really do need some time. I'm not ready for this marriage. I know this is a helluva time to realize it, but... Maybe I'll be ready in a few days or a few months, I don't know, but I'm not ready now."

Philip's face reddened. "I don't know who the hell you are anymore. I mean, it's like you've become a stranger. I really don't know you!"

Alice took a step toward him. "And that's the problem, Philip. Neither do I. I didn't want this to happen."

Philip moved toward her. "You're not being fair to me, Alice."

"I know that, Philip. I don't think I've been fair to you for a long time! You deserve better than that. I don't know any more what I feel about us... about you. That's why I'm asking for more time."

Philip gave her a long, sober look. She saw his absolute rigidity, saw a flurry of thought wrinkle his forehead and focus his searing eyes, as he searched for the precise words to mount an attack that would stir, inspire and surely lead to a rousing triumph. Then he turned and saw the roses—the roses Jack had sent. Philip's body loosened. His shoulders dropped, and his expression melted into a combination of disbelief and resigned sadness. When he spoke, his voice was soft, but filled with force. "No, Alice. No. If you don't know now about us, after all the time we've had together, after all we've been through together, after all we've meant to each other, and let me tell you, you mean the world to me, but..." his voice trailed away. "But, you know what? As the song goes, I don't see me in your eyes anymore. You've gone away someplace... You've changed."

Alice fought tears. "I just need time, Philip. Don't give up on us."

He shook his head. "It's not me who gave up, Alice. I'm still here. You left. I don't know, maybe you left a long time ago, and I just didn't see it or want to believe it." He looked toward the window. "Well... I'm leaving for Holbrook, and I'm leaving right now. If you want us... want us to get married and share our lives together, then you'll follow me. If you don't, then..." he spread out his hands. "Have a good life."

Alice began to cry, reaching and fumbling a tissue out of the box near the bed. "Philip..."

He turned and left the room.

"Philip." Alice trembled, weeping. She moved unsteadily to the bay window and watched Philip's easy stride across the parking lot. She'd always loved his walk. Such self-assuredness, so revealing of a man who always knew what he wanted; had never second-guessed himself about anything. There was such comfort and security in that.

She waited until his car disappeared around the trees before she turned toward the bed, tears streaming down her cheeks. She went to it in a rush and buried her body into it, pressing her face deep into the pillows, sobbing.

CHAPTER 20

After Philip left, Alice slept deep into the afternoon, finally pulling herself out of bed and dragging her punished and hungry body into the shower.

When she called downstairs for something to eat, Nora got on the phone and rapidly told her how proud she was of what she'd done. Alice didn't want to talk. She thanked her and then asked for any kind of omelet.

Fifteen minutes later, a mushroom and Cheddar cheese omelet appeared, with toasted whole grain bread, strawberry jam, a slice of cantaloupe and hot coffee. Food had never tasted so good.

After eating, Alice began making calls to family, friends and the wedding vendors. She didn't call Philip's parents or siblings; she'd leave that for him and write them later. Making the calls was depressing and agonizing, and as much as she'd wanted to postpone them to a better day, time was running out and people needed to make other Christmas plans. Everyone was, of course, stunned, and wanted details. Alice gave few, even to her close friends. As the calls progressed, she gave even fewer. Her stock explanation finally became "We decided that it just wasn't working and it was best to end it now, before we were married. I'm sorry if we've caused any inconvenience."

Roland was ecstatic and nearly made her cry again. "Now you can hit the streets again, baby, a free woman wearing the badge of 'You done him wrong.'"

Sometime after 8pm, Alice lay stretched out on the bed, dressed in a powder blue flannel nightgown. She dreaded the last call the most. It was to her father. After she dialed the number, she closed her eyes.

"Well what in the hell happened?" he asked.

"I told you, Dad, I needed more time and Philip... look, the truth is, I realized I wasn't in love with Philip. That's it. It's that simple."

"Nothing is that simple."

"Well, this is."

"What about all the people who were flying in from all over the place? Some from California, for Pete's sake! I mean, they were coming to spend Christmas with you. This is a helluva thing, Alice!"

"I've called every one. I've told everyone!"

"What did they say?"

Alice mustered patience. "Some were okay and some were not. One person hung up on me."

"Well, I don't understand it. All the plans were made. You've been with him for two years! What the hell happened?"

"I just told you!"

"That guy was goin' places, Alice. He was bright; he came from a helluva wealthy family! I mean, I just don't..."

Alice cut him off. "Dad, can I come for Christmas?"

"What?"

"Can I come home for Christmas?"

Silence.

"Dad?"

"Well, sure, Alice. I'm just a little shocked, that's all. All of this is just a helluva shock. I'll tell you one thing, I wasn't looking forward to that trip, especially around Christmas with all the maniacs traveling. Hey! The airlines aren't going to give me a refund on that ticket, are they?"

"I don't know. I'll have to call them."

"They probably won't, those rascals!"

"If they don't, I'll pay you for the ticket."

"Ah, forget it. It cost a fortune though!"

"I'll pay you."

"No way! I wish you'd told me sooner though."

"Dad, what about the woman you're seeing?"

"What about her?"

"Will she be over?"

"Sure. We'll all have a helluva time. You'll like her. Oh hell!"

"What now, Dad?"

"I paid for her, too! I won't get reimbursed for that ticket either! Son of a bitch!"

"Dad, calm down! I'll fix it! I'll pay for both. Okay? Now drop the airline ticket thing, please!"

"I hope your business is doin' good, with you throwing money away like that."

She ignored him. "I'll probably get there sometime late tomorrow."

"All right, honey. Did you call Jacinta about all this?"

"Yes… I did. She was disappointed. She really liked Philip."

"I did too. It's a helluva thing."

"So it's all right if I come?"

"Yes! You come on. I'll cook something for us. Bake a chicken or something, with rosemary potatoes. I still

have your mother's recipe. She had so many good reci-
pes."

"Yes, she did."

"This woman I'm with can't cook a lick. Can't fry an
egg. She's a vegetarian. It's a helluva thing."

"Yes, Dad. See you, Dad."

"Safe trip, Alice."

Alice slept fitfully, tormented by bad, guilty dreams of
Philip and good dreams of Jack and the kids. She was up
at the first gray light. She lay with her hands laced behind
her head, thinking about Kristie. She took a long, hot
shower and packed, fighting depression. She decided to
skip breakfast, despite feeling hungry, but she wanted to
avoid a long conversation with Nora or any other curious
guest. She dressed in jeans, a blue denim blouse and a
white V-neck sweater. Her white sneakers felt good after
an infinite day in boots and they'd do, despite the weather, since she'd be in the car traveling and not sloshing
through snow.

After she called the front desk for help with her bags,
she dialed the hospital and asked about Kristie. She told
the nurse who she was and then, somewhat reluctantly,
the nurse gave her an update: Kristie had had surgery early that morning and was already back in her room. The
surgery had been a complete success, and she was in good
condition.

Ozzie appeared, and with a variation of wide and narrow yawns and slow, sluggish maneuvers, he carried the
bags out of the room and parked them at the foot of the
stairs.

Alice looked back at the roses once more before she
left the room and strolled glumly through the hallway and
down the stairs.

Nora was in the office, sipping coffee and flipping pages of a Christmas catalog. When she saw Alice, she went to her.

"How are you feeling?" Nora asked, taking Alice's cold hand.

"I'm fine, Nora."

"Your hands are so cold. Have you eaten breakfast?"

"No, I have to get on the road. My father's waiting." That had slipped out, and Alice quickly saw the mistake register on Nora's observant face.

Nora's forehead lifted. "Father?"

"Yes. Is my bill ready?"

"Where is your father?"

"Cincinnati."

"Not going to Holbrook?"

"No... Is the bill ready?"

"I had a cousin in Cincinnati. What part of Cincinnati does your father live in?"

Alice hesitated. "Mt. Adams. He has a condo there. I really do need to go, Nora."

Nora slowly retracted her hand. "Your bill's been taken care of. Paid in full."

Alice straightened in surprise. "Paid by who?"

"Anonymous, Alice. Anonymous. But, between you and me, Jack Landis has a lot of friends."

Alice could feel the tears return, but she fought them away. "Well... please thank whoever it was. Thanks." Alice reached for Nora's hand and looked deeply into her beaming eyes. "Thank you, Nora. You've been very kind."

Nora smiled. "I have so enjoyed your company, Alice. Wherever you go, know that you are always welcome at The Broadmoore."

Alice drove away under a clear blue sky, with an uncontrollable feeling of loss. The roads were clear, traffic light and wind calm. She looked up at birds swimming the sky and wondered what species of birds stayed through the winter. She wondered how they survived the storms and the cold. What were their techniques?

In town, she found a little red brick flower shop that had just opened for the day. She bought white carnations, roses and pine. The Medical Center was only ten minutes away. Alice parked near the entrance, shut off the engine and waited before getting out. Would Jack be there? She hoped not.

It was quiet inside, such a different atmosphere from the night before. She saw things she hadn't noticed: a Christmas tree, decorated with silver ornaments and red lights; snowflakes, snowmen and little sleighs stenciled on the windows and entrance doors; children's artwork depicting winter scenes and Santa posted on a bulletin board near admittance.

At the nurses' station, a nurse told Alice that Kristie was still asleep and probably wouldn't awake for some time. Alice explained that she had to leave town and that she just wanted to visit her for a moment and deliver the flowers. Just as she was approaching Kristie's room, she met Dr. Ballard, a trim, slight, African-American man. His speech was quiet, reserved, almost clipped, but his smile was generous and warm. He explained the operation and recovery process. "Just a few days. She'll be fine. Probably go home tomorrow. The foot will be in the cast for about 6 weeks."

"How is she emotionally?"

"I've discussed some options with her father. You just missed him. He and Andrew left about fifteen minutes

ago. I'm sure they'll be back soon. Of course you can go
in. Stay as long as you like."

Alice entered quietly. Kristie lay on her back, her
beautiful mane of hair falling gently around her face. Alice's breath caught; her chest jerked with sudden emotion;
tears flooded her eyes. Thank God she was safe! She was
such a beauty!

Alice wiped her eyes and studied Kristie's pale face.
Her lip was still slightly swollen, but her breath was gentle, her sleep peaceful. Her foot was elevated and in a
cast.

Alice quietly unwrapped the vase of flowers and laid
them on the table next to the window. After arranging
them, she leaned over and took a little whiff. She found a
pen in her purse and, stepping to the window for light,
she wrote on the card.

> *Dear Kristie:*
>
> *I'm so happy and thankful that
> you're safe and recovering. Know that
> you'll always have a friend and confi-
> dant, and more: a person who loves you
> and wishes you great success and hap-
> piness in all things.*
>
> *Love,*
> *Alice Ferrell*

Alice slipped the card into the envelope, gave Kristie a
final look and left the room.

The five-hour drive to Cincinnati went smoothly and
without incident. Time passed swiftly, probably because
she finally began to scrutinize her unexamined life. The

miles of road and the drone of the engine allowed her to escape time, focus, and begin to contemplate what it was she really wanted out of life. Was it just to be busy? To make money? To be a successful businesswoman? To work mega hours so that the fatigue at the end of the day anesthetized her into a satisfied emptiness? To settle for a marriage that didn't strike her heart with the force of startling love and certainty? Did she really want kids? Why? What would she do with Kristie if she was her step-daughter? Could she have handled the heartbreak that Jack felt, seeing his rebellious daughter beaten up and abused? What would she have done or said to her? Could Alice have possibly raised Kristie and Andrew as well and, apparently, as lovingly as Jack did? She did not know. But she did know that she felt a lightness—a kind of inner peace—that she had never felt before.

Her candle shop, and all its business problems, seemed light years away now. And with that distance, she realized that she *did* want more out of life than the elusive goal of success and the endless hours of work that went along with it. Success was, of course, a good thing, but she also wanted to be in love, and she wanted to share that love. Jack Landis and his family had shown her that, and she was grateful.

Mt. Adams is an historic neighborhood that overlooks Cincinnati, the Ohio River and the Kentucky hills. Alice drove up the steep winding streets past renovated nineteenth and early twentieth century homes, as well as fashionable and trendy stores, chic bars and restaurants. She parked in her father's designated visitor condo parking space. She swung her laptop case over her shoulder, tugged her suitcase and valise from the trunk and started for the entrance, noticing that the snow on the ground was barely two inches deep.

Inside, she took the elevator to the sixth floor, got out and strolled down the slate blue carpet until she arrived at 6D. She pressed the doorbell.

John Ferrell was 62. He was broad and compact, with salt and pepper hair, bushy eyebrows and a square jaw. His gray/blue eyes held a playful fire; his expression was often one of dubious evaluation, as if he were sizing up a new opponent in a boxing ring. His voice was deep and loud; his hands nearly always in motion, expressing some grand emotion. He'd been in the offset print business most of his life, owned a business for 15 years and sold it when his wife was diagnosed with lung cancer, so he could care for her full time.

"Hey! Look at you!" John exclaimed, grinning, showing his Teddy Roosevelt teeth. She dropped her bags and he bear-hugged her.

"Hello Big Dad."

He pushed her back at arms' length. "Watch the Big Dad, here! That woman's made me lose eight pounds."

"And what's *that* woman's name?"

John gathered up Alice's bags as she closed the door behind them. "Marla West, attorney at law. She's a vegetarian and she's got me eating tofu and sprouts. Unbelievable the power women have over men."

"And you love it."

He snorted, waving a meaty hand. "What the hell. I'll eat anything. But I have some frankfurters in the fridge. Want one?"

Alice and her father spent the rest of the afternoon catching up, while snacking on hotdogs, potato chips and soda at the kitchen's island bar. Alice showed him her bruise; it had grown to the size of a hamburger patty and was the color of an eggplant. Several times, he mentioned how lucky she'd been that her injuries weren't more severe, and that she'd done an incredible thing by saving Kristie.

"I'm proud of you, Alice. That was a helluva thing! Your mother would be too."

After eating, they moved into the living room, a spacious room with contemporary furnishings and a white and cream color scheme. They talked well into early evening about their favorite subject: her mom. They reminisced about past Christmases, and suddenly John shot up and went to his brass music stand. He selected a book of music, sat down behind his Lowrey organ, like a big bear, and pounded out Christmas carols. They sang loudly, laughing at themselves.

Marla arrived about seven o'clock and they went to dinner at one of the local restaurants. She ate veggies and cheese. John had chicken, Alice ordered salmon. Marla was in her late 40s, feisty, verbal and voluptuous. She loved to talk and boss. Alice was amused to see that her father was love-struck; she was happy for him.

When they parted, Marla insisted that they go to her brother's for Christmas day. "The whole family will be there. They'll love you, Alice. You've got to see how the kids love your dad. And my divorced sister (three times) keeps trying to figure out how she can steal John away from me, the little bitch!" she said, seizing John's arm and jerking him close. "You should see how she flirts! No way, Jose!"

Her father grinned merrily, like a high school kid on a first date.

Alice stayed in the second bedroom, a combination guest room and den. The trundle bed had a blue-white-

and maroon striped bedspread and ruffle, her mother's favorite color scheme. Next to it was a chest of drawers with a TV, and on the other end, a little night table, with a photo of her mother at 30, in Florida, wearing a two-piece bathing suit. She looked back squinting, waving, thick red hair blowing. Next to the window was a contemporary recliner upholstered in a blue-and-maroon tweed stripe and, on the wall behind it, hung a poster from the Baltimore Museum of Art. Alice remembered her mother had purchased it ten years before. When her father married Marla, as he probably would, all these would go. She would miss them.

Perhaps it was the fact that she was "home," but Alice slept well that night. She dreamed that she and Jack were cross-country skiing in the hills of Mt. Adams.

She spent Tuesday and Wednesday sleeping late, Christmas shopping, and talking on the phone with Roland about the shop. Unfortunately, despite strong sales, the numbers were still down from last year. She tried to push that out of her mind; she'd be back in New York soon enough, probably forcing herself to leave the day after Christmas. She'd have to go to her and Philip's apartment, pack her things and move in with Roland until she closed the shop and made the decision whether to leave New York or start looking for a job. She was not looking forward to any of it.

Wednesday night she couldn't sleep. Finally, she threw back the covers, got up and rambled through the house in her pink fuzzy slippers and a flannel housecoat. She paused in the living room to see a walnut-framed family tree with photos of her ancestors in Ireland, great grandparents whose children (her grandparents) had made the trip to the U.S. It comforted her to think of family continuity, love and support. Of being there for each other. "Mom, please help me through this phase of my life," she whispered.

On Thursday morning, Christmas Eve Day, John came into her room carrying a FedEx package.

"Well, Alice in wonderland," he said, in his usual booming voice that startled her up to her elbows, "You have received a package from someone in Pennsylvania named Jack Landis! Oh, and Philip's on the phone and wants to talk to you. He says it's important. Rise and shine!"

CHAPTER 21

On Wednesday morning, the day before Christmas Eve, Jack sat behind his antique oak desk, scratching out the draft of a letter on a yellow legal pad. The blank flat screen monitor looked back at him, but he ignored it, with disdain and suspicion. He still didn't feel comfortable with the thing despite the many tutorials Andrew had given him. He didn't trust it, and because he didn't trust it, he was sure it wouldn't perform properly for him. This letter was too important and personal for that, anyway! This had to be in good old longhand; black ink, precise, well-formed letters, in thoughtful script.

Jack began, but the words resisted, the phrases seemed clumsy. He drummed his hands nervously on the desk and stared distractedly at the high ceiling, and then at the bay window, where ample morning light streamed in. Every sentence seemed flat, silly or arrogant, but he struggled on, having put Andrew in charge of looking after Kristie and the house until the job was done. He had shut off his cell phone. His face was frozen in concentration and effort. He first tried for a casual style, then a kind of swinging nonchalance and finally, after numerous drafts, crumpled pages and missed basket hoops, he got up and paced, feeling like a lion in a cage, glancing frequently at his watch. Time was rushing by. He'd have to finish in the next hour if he was going to make FedEx Next AM! A sense of urgency burned. He had to write it now! He had to take the risk.

He began writing again with renewed determination, trying not to think so much; he should just feel and write, like he had when he wrote in his diary. He began.

Dear Alice:

I heard from Nora that you did not go to Holbrook after all, but to Cincinnati, to see your father. Please do not be angry that I found your address. Andrew is somewhat of a wizard at finding things and people on his computer. He said finding your father was easy (despite a lot of Johns) once he knew he lived in Mt. Adams. I had suggested that we just call information, but he gave me a look of death. Obviously, he was in charge.

Anyway, I know I'm being forward, but I thought maybe things had not worked out for you and Philip. I thought that, when I heard you hadn't gone to Holbrook, I'd been foolish to let you leave. That was my fault and my mistake. I was confused. I was grieving for Kristie and when I saw Philip, I was jealous.

Alice, I have since realized that because you read my diary, you probably know me better than anyone else. You know things I have barely even admitted to myself, let alone to another person. But are they really that important? My little revelations and ramblings? No, except that I've learned something. I was angry at you for reading it because I was embarrassed by my failures in marriage and in raising my kids. I thought people would think less of me for what happened to Kristie. I thought everyone still blamed me for Darla's leaving and her death. But no. People have been kind, helpful and supportive. I never knew I had so many friends, or maybe, until I met you, I was just closed off.

Well, finally, I am taking the bold step of asking you to a Christmas party. It's Nora's annual Christmas Eve party at The Broadmoore. She's invited me for years but I've never gone. This year, I would like to go with you, Alice. I know this is sudden and forward of me and maybe I'm presuming a lot here, but here it is. It starts at 5:30. There will be carolers, food, presents... I've always heard it's one of the best parties in town.

Kristie is home and improving a lot. She said she "misses you a lot." She was very disappointed when she woke up and learned you'd left. She has your flowers and card by her bedside and wants me or Andrew to change the water every day. Andrew grinned when I asked him if it would be all right if I asked you to come. He has been bugging me to call you ever since. I thought this letter was more appropriate. I don't want you to feel pressured in any way.

But the truth is, Alice, I miss you. I was lost when I heard you left town. I still feel lost. You once said "I want to stay. I want us to get to know each other." I didn't answer you then because I was a fool. I was still trapped in the past—still guilty and self-pitying.

Alice, I burned the diary last night. It took all my strength, but I finally let it go. It was deep in the night and quiet in the house. The kids were asleep. Kristie was safe. Andrew had dropped off downstairs in the Rec. Room. I built a roaring fire and stepped close to it, feeling the heat on my clothes and face, feeling a heaviness that pulled on me. But I didn't hesitate. I tossed it in. I watched it curl and shrivel into a black thing, an old worn out and dead thing. And as it fell into ashes, I began feeling lighter. At dawn, I took the ashes outside and slung them up into the fading stars. At that moment, I felt free. For the first time in so many years, I felt a lightness and a kind of rebirth, and I thought of you. I want to move on with my life now, and I am moving on.

Alice, I thought maybe we could get to know each other better over the holidays. You can stay with us. (We have a large private back bedroom with a private bath.) On Christmas morning, Kristie usually makes great apple pancakes. (This year, she can tell us how to make them.) Andrew cooks a mean sausage and I make coffee. For dinner, I'm in charge of the turkey, although I could sure use some help. Anyway, after the holidays, we can see where it goes from there.

If you can't come because of family or if you decide it isn't right, we will all understand. I just had to say it. I had to offer.

I've enclosed Nora's invitation and menu. But again, no pressure! I'll be there from 5:30 until ten. Whatever you decide, I just want you to know that you have changed my life—or more accurately—you've help me to come back to life, and it feels so good to be back. I'll never forget what you did for Kristie and I will always admire and care for you.

With warm regards,

Jack

Jack read the letter twice, made a few changes, and then copied it on two pages of creamy bond. He glanced at the 5x7 invitation Nora had given him, and he re-read the menu.

Victorian Christmas at The Broadmoore!

*Cocktails and hor d'oeuvres at five-thirty o'clock
With live carolers and sing-a-longs!
Dinner at seven o'clock.
Immediately following dinner, excerpts from
"A Christmas Carol" and
"'Twas the Night before Christmas"
Performed by Local Children in
Victorian period costumes!
Dress: Christmas Attire
Menu: Mulled Wine
Creamy Carrot-and Leek Soup
Crown Roast of Pork with Savory Fruit Stuffing
(Chicken and Vegetarian Available)
Winter Vegetables
Wild Rice with Mushrooms
Christmas Chopped Salad
Apple-Onion Chutney
Christmas Pudding*

Jack paper-clipped the invitation and menu to the letter, shot up and ran downstairs. He was out of the house in minutes, driving to the nearest FedEx office.

CHAPTER 22

Nora had gone all out, as she always did. Her Christmas Eve party was her passion, "her madness" her husband used to say. She'd spent thousands on indoor and outdoor decorations and this year was no exception. She'd hired extra help to place wreaths in every window, and to wrap white Christmas lights around the trunks and limbs of trees along the tree-lined driveway. Live greenery was planted near the hotel entrance that included boxwood, magnolia, nandina and holly. She'd used 500 yards of ribbon for the red velvet bows that accented the gazebo, the wraparound porches, the trees near the pond, the inside staircases and, of course, there was one for the broad neck of Mr. Dog. He'd scratched at it and fought Nora at every turn, but, in the end, he lost. Nora was a combat general when it came to everyone getting into the Christmas spirit and Mr. Dog would be no exception!

She'd added four Christmas trees to the two she'd bought on the first of December and placed them in the sitting room, the dining room, the gold-and-white parlor and the fireside room. All were decorated with bright tin candle holders with white candles and a collection of authentic Victorian ornaments. Piled underneath were surprise gifts containing candy, cookies, homemade breads or fudge, all wrapped in white tissue paper and tied with red and green silk ribbons.

Bowls of Christmas ornaments were on mantels and broad windowsills; and she'd hung pomanders and tied mistletoe above the doorways.

Nora had planned a Christmas Stocking Hunt for the children, many of whom would be performing after dinner. Various green and red small stockings were filled with a variety of candies, nuts, crayons and gum and then the children would be sent on a Christmas version of an Easter Egg Hunt, with stockings hidden in various out-of-the-way spots around the house. It was always a big hit.

Guests began arriving at 5:15. The waiters, dressed in Victorian attire, had just finished polishing the chandelier (Ozzie had forgotten to do it that morning) and setting the table with ribbon streamers attached to wrapped holiday favors. The china glistened, the fireplace crackled. A huge Christmas pudding was carried in by two rather large waiters, who played football at the local high school. They eased it down on the center of the table, while a nervous Nora arranged evergreens and holly around it.

Jack arrived at 5:29, dressed in a blue suit, white shirt and burgundy tie. His clothes were brand new, including his black leather shoes and silk socks. Kristie had chosen everything, going the more conservative route, since she didn't really know what Alice liked and wasn't about to take a clothes risk and be blamed for failure by Andrew. Using his phone, Andrew had filmed his and his father's trip to the mall, where they had made some selections. Kristie carefully reviewed the film on her laptop at home, lying on the couch making careful notes. Andrew picked the tie, although Kristie nixed his three previous choices. And yes, they had fought about it, and continued fighting about, even after Jack had left for the party.

Jack felt the gnawing agony of the unknown ever since he'd FedExed Alice the letter. She hadn't called. What did that mean? Had she received the package? Yes! Andrew had the confirmation number and was able to go online and see that it was signed for by John Ferrell. But maybe she'd gone somewhere else and not gone to Cincinnati. Maybe she'd changed her mind and gone to New York. Had she and Philip made up? Maybe she'd been insulted? Angry?

Nora spotted him, came over with a cheerful smile, took his arm, wrapped it in hers and led him into the sitting room. The entire house smelled of Christmas: fresh pine and sweet cinnamon. Jack was soon sipping a cup of eggnog and found himself the center of conversation, about everything from Kristie's condition, to questions about kitchen cabinets, floor tiles, new home design and masonry fireplaces. While people talked and he mostly listened, Jack's eyes wandered anxiously, searching for Alice. As soon as he'd drained one cup of eggnog another appeared. A bank president, Harvey Delb, asked if Jack wanted to be part of a group of contractors and architects who were bidding on constructing his new house. Jack said he would and took Mr. Delb's card. There were other offers and cards and questions, and more eggnog. Carolers wandered in and sang *"Deck the Halls with Boughs of Holly"* and *"We Wish You a Merry Christmas."* Waitresses offered hors d'oeuvres of stuffed mushrooms and garlic bread with melted cheese. Jack abstained. The eggnog was creamy and delicious.

At a quarter to seven, Jack had wilted in a chair near the fireplace in the sitting room. Children dashed about looking for stockings, while glowing guests sipped their nog and belted out *"Frosty the Snowman"* in various anguished keys. Meanwhile Shannon, Nora's niece, played the beautifully carved, mahogany Franklin upright piano.

Mr. Dog sauntered in, dispirited, despite the holiday bow still around his neck, and he nuzzled his cold nose into Jack's dangling free hand. Jack padded his head. "Merry Christmas, Mr. Dog," he said, feeling the mellow buzz of the eggnog. He looked down at his watch continuously, while checking his cell phone for any messages. He gradually became disconnected from the gaiety. She's not coming, he thought. Alice is not coming.

He got up and went to the window, parting the creamy drapes, staring out into the blaze of Christmas lights and the little gazebo decorated with garlands, red bows and holly. Sobered by disappointment, he wondered what he'd tell the kids. "What can I say? Old Dad blew it." Something like that.

Suddenly, Jack saw a figure emerge from around the right side of the gazebo, lingering for a time in a shadow, away from the white glow of the lights. It appeared to be a man, large, a bit stooped, head down, hands clasped at the waist, as if he had to make a decision. Jack watched, curious, calculating the distance at 60 feet. There was an uncomfortable familiarity in the form, the stance. There was also a slow creep of dread in Jack's gut—an old savage memory.

The man took a few steps forward and then halted, abruptly, as if ordered to do so. He hid from the light artfully; he seemed to reflect the shadows; light couldn't touch him. He waited in a rigid posture, repentant. A hand slowly lifted; then he worked at a feeble, hopeful attempt at a wave. Jack struggled against understanding, giving a little shake of his head and leaning back from the window. What he was thinking was impossible!

Suddenly, Jack's mind was flooded by a sharp memory. He shut his eyes, pinching the bridge of his nose. He saw, with excellent clarity, a Christmas when he was 11 years old. Images and emotions swept in as he relived every detail, clearly, as if he were standing there in his old bedroom.

He saw himself waking up on Christmas morning. He threw back the covers and sprang out of bed, rushing to the window. He gazed out in wide-eyed wonder at a blurring white world with drifts and mounds of blanketing snow. Snow glistened the trees. Snow fell in swirls. A noisy wind shuddered the windows. Turning, Little Jack dashed out of his bedroom in bare feet, his face alive with joy and anticipation.

He scrambled down the stairs, leapt over the last three steps and hit the floor running, edging and sliding left toward the broad living room. When he saw it, he skidded to a stop on the polished hardwood floor. In his drowsy excitement, he let out a gleeful yelp, clapping his hands as he gazed up at the shining, towering 15-foot tree. Beneath it were colorfully wrapped boxes, with bows and ribbon and steamers. In the corner, an electric train tooted and circled the formidable-looking solid oak armchair recliner. His father's chair. The sparkling tree lights were reflected in Jack's eager eyes and he studied the festival of light and color, beaming. He couldn't wait to dive under the tree to dig and explore.

When he heard his father's deep, craggy voice, he froze.

"Wait, Jack! Don't move! Do not take another step!"

Jack was rigid with fright and dread. His father scared him. He was a hard man. A strict man.

"Jack... I want you to close your eyes now. Close them tightly."

Jack obeyed.

"Now turn around."

Jack did so, but slowly, wishing that his father had not spoiled his Christmas joy.

"Now, open your eyes, Jack."

Jack's eyelids fluttered. He was afraid. Very afraid that he'd done something wrong. His running down the stairs must have awakened his father. And his father seldom slept well anyway. He was always getting calls in the middle of the night.

"Open your eyes, Jack."

Jack's eyes opened.

Dr. Landis loomed large above him, his granite chiseled face watching his son with stern eyes. He was dressed in his olive green housecoat and black slippers.

Jack shrank a little. Then he noticed that his father was holding a large box, carefully wrapped in red and white paper, with a lavish red bow.

"Jack, I have something for you, son."

Jack swallowed.

Dr. Landis squatted down and presented the boy with the gift. "It's a little heavy, son. Be careful."

Jack hesitated. He looked at the gift with an awakened curiosity. His father had never personally given him a gift. His Christmas gifts had always been under the tree and Jack knew it was his mother who bought and wrapped the gifts.

"Go ahead, son. Take it."

Jack did, surprised by the gift's weight. He lightly set it down on the floor, kneeling, gazing in expectation.

"Open it, Jack. What are you waiting for? Go ahead, now."

Jack went to work, one eye on the gift and one wary eye on his father, who was looking on impatiently.

Jack unfastened the bow, peeled back the layers and, like an archeologist exploring an artifact, Jack peered down at the gift revealed. His eyes blinked fast in cautious excitement. He lifted his nervous gaze to his father. "Yes, Jack. Yes." He was smiling. Grinning. Jack had never seen that before. "Open the latch."

It was a large red box. A toolbox! Jack flipped down the metal latch and opened the lid. Inside were wrenches and screwdrivers and a hammer! He lifted the tote tray and peered inside. There were boxes of nails and screws, a woodworking plane, duct tape and a drill. Overcome, Jack reached for the cordless drill. He held it up, like a trophy. "Wow!"

"Now you'll have to be careful with that, Jack. Your mother said you're too young for all this, but I said, 'No. Jack loves to build things, so let's get him a toolbox. A real professional toolbox!' So, now you have one. Take care of it, son."

Jack stared at his father, quivering in contradiction.

"Well, do you like it, Jack? Do you, son?"

Jack could only nod. He wanted to say something, but he couldn't speak. He only nodded.

"Okay, Jack. Good then. You go and find your other gifts now."

Jack sat back cross-legged, staring at his toolbox, not wanting to leave the prized moment. It was the greatest Christmas gift he'd ever received.

Jack opened his eyes, blinked a couple of times and reoriented himself. He'd forgotten all about that Christmas. He'd forgotten his father's thoughtful and generous gift. He'd forgotten his father's uneasy smile.

Jack faced the window and peered out, searching. He saw the man stand in dim shadow, then slowly drift away from the gazebo, melting into oily shadows, away from the haze of light, back into darkness.

Jack stood, straining to understand. He struggled with emotion. He struggled with his past. Finally, he closed the drapes and turned from the window, inhaling a deep breath. He recalled now, with some tender nostalgia, that he still had the toolbox, stored away in the attic.

Minutes later, as he found a seat near the fireplace, he allowed himself to rerun that special Christmas. This time he smiled a little, grateful for that good and true memory of his father. Jack reran it once more, as if to anchor it in his memory. From now on, he would re-member it easily and hold on to it like a secret code whenever he thought of his hard and gruff old man.

Nora worked the rooms with her bright face and gra-cious magic, connecting all the threads of personalities, food, music and play. When she saw Jack alone on a couch by the fire, brooding and slack, with Mr. Dog at his feet, also downcast and low, she went over.

"Come on, Jack, have a little faith. She'll be here. I know it."

Jack stood, and Mr. Dog got up and shook his sandy-colored body. When he did so, the Christmas ribbon noose went flying. He seized the moment of freedom and scampered off. Nora frowned.

"I feel like I'm made of metal, Nora," Jack said. "I'm all tensed up."

"What you need is some more eggnog."

"No, no, I've already had..." he scratched his head. "Well, now that can't be good. I don't know how many

I've had, and it's playing weird tricks on my vision. I'm seeing strange things."

"You're just hungry, Jack. Come on in the dining room. It's time for dinner, and some food will do you good."

"In a minute, Nora. You go ahead."

She folded her hands with a look of reluctance and went to greet a young couple standing in the corner of the room. She led them toward the dining room, as other guests began filing out of assorted rooms. Jack lingered, gazing into the flames, hearing their "Ooos and Ahhs" at the lavish spread of food and decorations. He drained the last of his eggnog and was about to leave when he saw her in the circular glass of the gilded framed mirror that hung over the fireplace. It was Alice! For a fleeting moment, he thought it was another apparition or a dream. He turned sharply.

She wore a long red silk gown with spaghetti straps that accented every striking curve and angle of her body. She was tall and statuesque in three-inch black satin heels. Pearl and diamond chandelier earrings glittered and played in the candlelight. When Jack saw her parted crimson lips and rich long auburn hair, he became mute with admiration and joy.

She smiled into Jack's eyes, speaking in a smoky alto. "Hello, Jack Landis. You look very handsome in that suit."

Jack felt like someone was knocking hard inside his chest. "Hello, Alice."

"I would have been here sooner, but, well, frankly, I wanted to make a grand entrance, be mysterious and leave a lasting impression. Have I... been mysterious? Have I made a lasting impression?"

Jack swallowed away the lump in his throat, but another appeared. "Yes, Alice, you have."

"I guess that says something about me, doesn't it?"

"Yes, I suppose it does."

"Still want me to stay for the holidays?"

He took easy steps toward her and reached for her hand. She moved in close, and when they touched, it was electric. Their eyes met in an exciting intimacy.

"Oh, yes," Jack said, "I still want you to stay. If I go home without you, the kids won't let me in."

Alice took a quicker breath. "Then I'll stay."

Jack did a little rocking on his heels. "Good."

"And where are the kids?"

"Home... We're opening gifts at 10:30. My New Year's resolution to them is to be home for dinner every night. And not to be so busy."

"I'm working on that 'not to be so busy' one, too," Alice said.

"Maybe we can work on it together."

Alice smiled, as she explored his face and eyes. "I like the sound of that."

Jack noticed she was holding something behind her back. "Is that for me?"

She presented it and nodded. "Yes." It was the shape of a book, extravagantly wrapped in red and white paper, topped with a big, glossy green bow.

"I bet I can guess what it is."

"I loved your letter. That's what made me think of it."

"As long as you promise not to read it."

Alice grinned, mischievously. "I can't promise that."

Jack leaned in toward her. Their lips brushed.

"I suspect, Alice, that you and I will never have to keep secrets from each other."

Alice lifted a shoulder and slowly moved into him, parting her lips, holding him in her eyes. "Well… I *do* have a few secrets to tell you about… but they can wait."

They kissed, gently, longingly, hungrily.

When Nora found them sometime later, they were sitting in the loveseat by the fireplace, laughing and touching like two newlyweds, each with a pen in hand, writing something in—what looked to be—a diary.

Thank You!

Thank you for taking the time to read *The Christmas Diary*. If you enjoyed it, please consider telling your friends or posting a short review. Word of mouth is an author's best friend, and it is much appreciated.

Thank you,
Elyse Douglas

Other Novels You Might Enjoy

Christmas for Juliet
The Christmas Bridge
The Date Before Christmas
The Christmas Women
Christmas Ever After
The Summer Diary
The Summer Letters
The Other Side of Summer
Wanting Rita

Time Travel Novels
The Christmas Eve Letter (A Time Travel Novel) Book 1
The Christmas Eve Daughter (A Time Travel Novel) Book 2
The Christmas Eve Secret (A Time Travel Novel) Book 3
Time Shutter (A Time Travel Romance)
The Lost Mata Hari Ring (A Time Travel Novel)
The Christmas Town (A Time Travel Novel)
Time Change (A Time Travel Novel)
Time Sensitive (A Time Travel Novel)

Romantic Suspense Novels
Daring Summer
Frantic
Betrayed

www.elysedouglas.com

Editorial Reviews

THE LOST MATA HARI RING – A Time Travel Novel by Elyse Douglas

"This book is hard to put down! It is pitch-perfect and hits all the right notes. It is the best book I have read in a while!" 5 Stars!
--Bound4Escape Blog and Reviews

"The characters are well defined, and the scenes easily visualized. It is a poignant, bitter-sweet emotionally charged read."
5-Stars!
--Rockin' Book Reviews

"This book captivated me to the end!"
--StoryBook Reviews

"A captivating adventure..."
--Community Bookstop

"...Putting *The Lost Mata Hari Ring* down for any length of time proved to be impossible."
--Lisa's Writopia

"I found myself drawn into the story and holding my breath to see what would happen next..."
--Blog: A Room Without Books is Empty

Editorial Reviews

THE CHRISTMAS TOWN – A Time Travel Novel
by Elyse Douglas

The Christmas Town is a beautifully written story. It draws you in from the first page, and fully engages you up until the very last. The story is funny, happy, and magical. The characters are all likable and very well-rounded. This is a great book to read during the holiday season, and a delightful read during any time of the year."
--Bauman Book Reviews

"I would love to see this book become another one of those beloved Christmas film traditions, to be treasured over the years! The characters are loveable; the settings vivid. Peri-

od details are believable. A delightful read at any time of year! Don't miss this novel!"
--A Night's Dream of Books

THE SUMMER LETTERS – A Novel
by Elyse Douglas

"A perfect summer read!"
--Fiction Addiction

"In Elyse Douglas' novel THE SUMMER LETTERS, the characters' emotions, their drives, passions and memories are all so expertly woven; we get a taste of what life was like for veterans, women, small town folk, and all those people we think have lived too long to remember (but they never really forget, do they?).
I couldn't stop reading, not for a moment. Such an amazing read. Flawless."
5 Stars!
--Anteria Writes Blog - To Dream, To Write, To Live

"A wonderful, beautiful love story that I absolutely enjoyed reading."
5 Stars!
--Books, Dreams, Life - Blog

The Summer Letters is a fabulous choice for the beach or cottage this year, so you can live and breathe the same feelings and smells as the characters in this wonderful story."
--Reads & Reels Blog